MONKEY AND THE CASTLE BY THE SEA

MICHAEL J. SUTTON

ISBN: 978-0-6455671-6-8

Published by Hidden Road Publishing

DEDICATION

To my mother for her encouragement, support, and love.

MICHAEL J. SUTTON

1.

This is the story of how the world was in the beginning before humans shaped it in their image. It was a time when animals lived freely and safely in forests and glens, hills and mountains, swamps and rivers, fields, and grasslands. This ancient, primeval happiness was destroyed forever by the arrival of a race of beings the animal kingdoms fearfully called 'giants.' This book is one small chapter in the history of the world, or rather the history of the world before the present age, when animals and humans have little to do with each other.

This story is about one creature, a small creature, by the name of Monkey. This story is about how Monkey in a world threatened by giants, discovered true friendship, and with his friends, Rabbit, and Fox stopped the giants of their day from destroying the world they loved, at least for a brief time. That is all anyone can be expected to do, make a difference in their own lives, and pass that responsibility onto the next generation. The freedom and safety that came as a result of freeing their world from the giants were only possible after Monkey, Rabbit, and Fox met the tall, strange creature who Monkey called 'Mr. Big Nose.' Who he was, who he claimed to be, and what happened to him, are not really questions this book addresses, though I am sure people will read this book and try to find out. All that mattered to Monkey was that Mr. Big Nose was his friend, and that was that. In this world, having one or two good friends is all we can ask for, and if that is how you see the world, then you are already beginning to see the world from Monkey's point of view.

Giants did not always live on the land where our story takes place. They came from far away, across the vast blue ocean, from distant lands, now forgotten. They left because, from all accounts, they burned their world with fire. Giants were always at war with each other, and their lust for war saw them destroy what must have been a pristine, and peaceful land. Where they came from, whom they destroyed, and what they did there don't really matter. All that does matter is that they destroyed what they touched and did not understand what they did.

Before the giants came, the animals on the island lived in peace with each other, and in harmony with the world around them. The forests were full of life. The rivers teemed with fish. The trees grew tall and strong. Birds made their homes in their branches. Monkeys frolicked and played in the canopy. Life was abundant. Before the giants came, all the animal tribes lived according to an ancient order. Each tribe had its own customs, leaders, and ways of doing things. Everyone showed respect and got on with life. Animals spoke to each other with courtesy, and nobody upset what is now called the Ancient Order of Things, or the world before giants. There was balance and harmony.

The arrival of the giants changed everything. The giants were not people as we would understand them today, but larger, taller, and stronger. In some ways, they were weaker. A tall person by today's standards would seem small to them, perhaps reaching the chest or shoulders of a giant. People today are agile, and some can be athletic, but giants were heavy and slow by nature. They lived like humans, married, bore children, tilled the soil, built, crafted, and hewed. The giants built their homes from wood and stone, crafted temples and shrines, and designed castles. The animals did well to name them giants, for they made their presence felt across all the island. Nothing was ever the same again.

The story of Monkey begins not on the mainland where the giants and the animal kingdoms lived, but on a tiny island, about ten miles off the east coast, surrounded by whirlpools and fast-moving currents. On this tiny island lived a small tribe of monkeys. They arrived one day from the mainland, but for reasons that shall become clear, quickly decided to forget how or why they came. As soon as they arrived, the monkeys did not climb into trees to rummage around for berries and nuts, nor did they huddle next to each other picking out fleas. They might have done that if they had lived during the Ancient Order of Things. These monkeys had lost their primeval innocence and had been stained by the world of the giants. The old order of balance and harmony had been tossed away for the new.

Few remembered the old days or the old ways, and the Ancient Order of Things had become more of a legend or a myth. Monkeys and all other animal tribes had, for reasons of survival, copied the giants, their customs, ways, and values.

So, when the monkeys arrived on this tiny, forgotten island, a few miles from the mainland, they decided to live in the remains of a village that was already there. It had forts and roads, walls and buildings, farms and shrines, with an old bell on top of the highest hill, overlooking the cliffs and the ocean below. When they arrived on the island, these monkeys decided to assume temporary residence, at least until the real occupants returned, an event which they assumed would eventually occur. The village was long deserted but had been built by giants.

The monkeys brought their tribal customs to the island and adapted them to their new surroundings. Their leader was a religious and political figure who called himself the 'high priest.' He was a warrior, feared by all in the monkey kingdom. He had led his followers in battle on the mainland against the emperor of the monkeys, and he fought against other animal tribes. He offered prayers to the ancestors and performed rituals and ceremonies. Like all monkeys, he had a fierce belief in a creation myth held only by them, a version of the broader cosmology held by all the animals. The monkey's version of their creation myth, not surprisingly, had them at the center.

The common creation myth was a relatively simple one, and eminently fair to everyone. It was commonly held during the Ancient Order of Things. It was simply that all life sprung from what everyone called the Great Mountain, at the center of the mainland. It was a paradise, a place of untouched beauty and wonder. At the Great Mountain, a powerful spirit gave all the animals their name and purpose. There was some confusion as to whether this spirit was from the ocean, the sky, or the mountain, whether he flew, or walked, whether he had wings or not, or whether he spoke or gestured.

Nonetheless, everyone agreed that it was on this Great Mountain all the animals received their names and purpose from this spirit, who breathed life into the world. The naming ceremony and the one who did the naming were always spoken of with the deepest reverence. No one knew the name of the one who named them. They never asked him, nor did they think it was important at the time. Since the inception of that era, most of the animals left the great mountain and kept away from it. Even to this day, it is still there, with its treacherous summit and mist shrouding it from view.

As the monkeys and other animals left the Great Mountain, the Ancient Order began, and life spread out to all four corners of the land. The tribes developed their own pantheon of gods, spirits, and monsters, most of whom occupied a principal place in their songs, poetry, and oral tradition, for no animal could write during that age. In those days, monkeys lived in trees, rabbits in tunnels, raccoon-dogs in holes, and foxes in the depths of the forest. Animals were, as they are today, doing their own thing. Every tribe had its high priest, and every tribe had its version of how the world began.

The high priest of the monkeys, living in exile on the tiny island, a few miles from the mainland, had descended from an extensive line of priests they claimed could be traced back to the early generation of those who left the Great Mountain. This high priest had no room for any other animals in his view of the world and believed that the spirit of the ocean, or the sky, or wherever he came from, belonged only to them. The departure of this high priest brought great relief to the emperor of the monkeys, and he was not replaced. The position and title of the high priest were also abolished.

The high priest, however, along with his predecessors, knew what happened when the giants arrived. It could have been called the Great Temptation, but this would have been a lie. The giants did not prompt change or ask for support, they just did what they did, and the animals quickly overturned the Ancient Order of Things for something new. Through their actions and lifestyle, the giants lured the monkeys out of the trees, the rabbits out of their tunnels, the raccoon-dogs out of their holes, and the foxes out of their glens. The tribes learned to write and speak a common language but most important of all, they discovered how to fight. There was nothing about the giants they did not copy, and within one generation, the Ancient Order of Things vanished from view like the mist in the morning sun.

In this new age, it seems strange that the animals would remember anything about the past, but two pieces of tradition survived. These were brief fragments from the Ancient Order of Things and lingered on in the minds of raccoon-dogs, rabbits, foxes, and monkeys. The first fragment was the idea that the ancient spirit could walk from his world to the world of the forest. Some said that this path came from out of the earth, others, across the mountains, and some claimed he came from the ocean. No one could agree, and because they were deeply superstitious, shrines were built across the land in case this ancient spirit should ever make an appearance. What he would say when he appeared, or what he would do, was a mystery to all of them. The animals just simply believed that his appearance would make all the difference and he would make everything clear.

The second fragment was that the appearance of this spirit was known to hold a red face and an incredibly long nose. Why they remembered the nose was pondered by many, including Monkey. The high priest of the monkeys believed that this spirit with the long nose loved the monkeys, but he had not given them his name as he had chosen not to reveal it, and so the monkeys, being polite creatures, accepted this.

After the giants came and the traditions were all lost except for the two fragments, the monkeys decided to return to the question of who named them. After much argument, they decided upon a name, but it was not a very satisfactory one. Eventually, they settled on an awfully long name to accommodate all the different perspectives, factions, and schools of thought. The name was: 'The One Who Named the Monkeys and Who Lives on the Great Mountain.' From the very beginning, this name provoked debate, division, and eventually civil war. When they settled upon a name for this ancient spirit, monkeys were already trying to copy the ways, principles, and values of the giants. They were able to use swords, bows, and fire more effectively than arguments and reasoning and so the monkeys turned on each other and did so regularly as disputes multiplied.

The first wave of giants, the ones who changed the world of the animal tribes forever, built a great civilization, but it was eventually destroyed during an extremely dry summer in the form of a huge forest fire. Few survived the calamity. After the smoke cleared, the monkeys, for a time, entertained the idea of reviving the Ancient Order of Things. Some wanted, of course, to maintain the way of the giants, a set of values they had come to love, admire, and copy. A few revived the Ancient Order, a few foresaw the calamity, and a few it is said lit the kindling that brought disaster. The prophets and traditionalists were exiled or killed for the legacy of the giants was too strong for most. In any event, the decision was made for them, for a new wave of giants soon arrived on the mainland from across the deep, blue emptiness. These giants were seafaring people and loved boats and so they set about building a giant castle by the sea.

The monkeys ignored the new giants and continued to argue among themselves and disputed over the appropriate name for the tall, red-nosed being who named them. Most of the other tribes lived in fear of the monkeys at this time and simply waited to find out what they would do. Many generals and warriors from across the animal tribes would regret their silence at this time. Had they all banded together, they might have been able to push the new wave of giants back into the sea, but they waited too long. Had they known about the growing madness in the monkey kingdom, they would have rushed forward and won the day, but nobody could believe what would come next, nor the difference one monkey could make, for good or ill.

There was already traditional racism in the monkey kingdom as there was in other tribes, but one young monkey proposed the view that the one who named the monkeys, named only the monkeys and no one else. The spirit of the ocean belonged to them, and no one else because the ancient spirit, in his opinion, was the first monkey. He didn't have a long nose, nor did he walk like a giant, but he was in fact one of them. He proposed the idea that anyone who entertained accommodation with other creatures needed to die.

Their leader, whom we have met before, the high priest, was factitious, charismatic, and xenophobic. He believed he was the only one who possessed the truth about the world and wanted nothing to do with their closest kin, the rabbits, foxes, and raccoon-dogs. He also wanted nothing to do with the giants and fought against them in a place the giants named 'The Valley of Tears.' He was the first to take up arms against the giants. His actions astonished everyone, especially when he was victorious in battle. His actions struck fear into the hearts of the giants and terror in everyone else. He stirred antagonism between the giants and the many animal kingdoms. Some rabbits, foxes, and raccoon-dogs, inspired by this high priest, took up the fight against the giants, hoping to use their weapons against them such as spears, swords, and bows.

What terrified the giants about the high priest was that he thought like them in battle and in many ways, was even more cunning. He had an extensive network of spies and even recruited some giants who were critical of the actions of their emperor who lived in the Castle by the Sea. This resentment eventually would lead to a rebellion we will read about later in our story. Soon, the monkeys stole swords and spears during raiding parties, but soon they began to manufacture their own crude weapons. Even the corrupt emperor of the monkeys knew a line had been crossed when rumors of a rudimentary sword-making forge and experiments with explosives began to surface.

The emperor of the monkeys was not alone. Most monkeys were shocked by the attitudes of this high priest and were weary of war. When the giants proposed a truce after years of bitter fighting, they decided to take it. The emperor of the monkeys signed a peace treaty with the emperor of the giants at a place the monkeys would call 'The Day of Regret.' The first condition of the treaty was that the terrorist known as the high priest be banished to a faraway island where he would no longer cause trouble. It was the giants who sought clemency for the family of the high priest as they didn't want them all to suffer, so they wanted them to be banished to an island they saw as cursed, a relic of the past, an ideal place for self-reflection. The emperor of the monkeys however, wanted them dead, for he knew that eventually, the high priest or one of his descendants would make it back to the mainland and start a war all over again. Nonetheless, he too was weary of conflict and accepted the proposal of exile. The high priest, his family, and his followers were dutifully dumped on the island by boats captained by the giants and left to fend for themselves.

Their new home had suffered years of weather, rot, and decline. The sea air was harsh and there were many storms. Most of the structures had long since collapsed. There was an old shrine at the top of the tallest hill on the island, behind which were precipitous cliffs to the ocean below. Teetering on the edge of the cliff, was an old bell tower. There were the remains of a fort near the beach and a few houses on stilts near the shrine. There were buildings with artifacts, paintings, and tools.

The shrine was connected to a building that became known as the Hall of Masks. This was a long wooden hall with a veranda around it. Inside was a polished floor and on the wall was an assortment of beautiful masks. The monkeys assumed that all the masks were of giants, but the Hall of Masks contained a secret, known only to the high priest. When the high priest saw it, he hid it away in a secret chamber known only to him. He called it a 'relic of special significance,' too holy for the eyes of others. Sometimes, the high priest would secretly go to his hidden chamber, find the mysterious object, look at it, and wonder if he had lived his entire life in vain. It was too late for him to change and so he would always hide it away again. He never told his followers the truth. He only showed the mask to one other.

With his secret safely buried, the high priest encouraged the other monkeys to focus on the future. The seasons came and went, with their obligations, festivals, and rites of passage. In no time at all, most of the monkeys forgot their past and found that they enjoyed living on the island that they came to call home. They studied and experimented with agriculture, and soon were growing crops and other food for daily life, as well as learning crafts and trades.

The castaways were to get their first rude shock in the form of an earthquake. They had experienced them before on the mainland, but this island was tiny and so the effects seemed to be far more violent. Monkeys were superstitious and saw major seismic shifts as proof of the displeasure of their ancestors. The first significant earthquake occurred during the celebration of a moon festival. During the festival, a baby monkey was born to the eldest son of the high priest who lived in the Hall of Masks at the top of the hill near the village bell. The fact that he was born the night of the earthquake was enough to convince everyone that he brought bad luck.

Early the next morning, following a much stronger earthquake, an ocean wave swept onto the beaches of the island, roaring inland, swallowing entire families in its fury. When the wave struck, the high priest spent the time, pleading that the tsunami would also destroy the Castle by the Sea and even his nemesis, the emperor of the monkey kingdom.

While he was thinking of revenge, news came to him that his eldest son had tried to rescue some monkeys in danger, but he was swept out to sea and drowned. When his wife heard the news, she gave up the will to live, for the birth of the baby had not been easy and she had not been strong. She kissed the baby monkey on the forehead, whispered into his ear some words of love, and died.

The little baby monkey was adopted by the high priest and his wife. They resisted naming him because everyone felt that the baby had brought bad luck. The community insisted the baby be tossed into the ocean to appease the ocean spirit, the one who was never named, but the high priest rebuked them for their cruelty. But he could not even come up with a name because the circumstances of his birth brought sadness to his heart. Any name he decided upon brought tears to his eyes. Therefore, he felt that it was much simpler to postpone the naming ceremony until the monkey was of such an age to make the decision himself.

The baby monkey was simply called 'Monkey.' During the evening of the next moon festival, he was formally adopted by his grandparents. Monkey came to live near the Hall of Masks at the top of the hill, near the village bell, the grandson of the high priest.

2.

During the early years of his life, Monkey grew up in peace and tranquility. He quickly accepted the realities of life and lived with his grandparents as if they were his own parents. He and his older brother (his uncle) became good friends. His grandfather, the high priest of the clan, was a kind and gentle monkey, large for his age, but with a broad grin that seemed to extend from one side of his face to the other. In the evening, he would often sit Monkey on his knee, and tell him exciting tales about the distant past that would make Monkey's head spin. He told him of the origin of the clan, the one who named the monkeys at the Great Mountain, and tales of war with the rabbits, foxes, and raccoon-dogs.

His grandfather hobbled around with a walking stick, an injury in his youth preventing him from catching up with Monkey as he ran and bounced across the meadows at the bottom of the hill, in the open fields, and across the streams. These meadows were covered in seasonal flowers, often knee-deep, and only the top of Monkey's little head could be seen clearly as he ran. He would often collect flowers, bring them back home and give them to his grandmother and she would put them in a vase by the wall. Monkey would wait until she arranged them neatly and then he would smile and look at the flowers for a while before he went off into the meadows to explore some more.

His adopted mother was a large but gentle monkey who often made delicious cakes and other delicacies. She, like other monkeys, had learned the craft of cooking from their time on the mainland and she utilized what she could in the new homes they had made on the island. Monkey's earliest memory was the smell of the pantry and cakes baking. He loved cakes, all kinds of cakes, regardless of size, color, or ingredients. He didn't mind healthy food, the staple of green vegetables, nuts, and bugs and he ate them diligently, but he consumed them silently and joylessly, never speaking. His eyes were only on the pile of pastries and cakes on the table that were made fresh every day. Everyone was surprised by how quickly he could eat and how much he could eat without affecting his size. Monkey himself thought it must have been because of his constant exercise, walking around the island, exploring new paths, finding new fishing spots and places to sit and ponder.

Monkey loved to fish, almost as much as he loved to eat cakes. At the time of his birth, the tsunami destroyed all the buildings by the ocean, including the wharf, fort, and port. The sea had its revenge. It was a beautiful inlet. The beach was covered with thousands of round stones that had been worn smooth by centuries of waves crashing upon them and these stones would chatter amongst themselves as the waves struck them and retreated to the ocean.

Monkey would sit on the edge of the beach and watch the sun rise across the horizon. In the distance, he could see a vast blue, as far as the eye could see. The inlet was in fact on the far side of the island. That part of the island which faced the mainland was full of high cliffs and treacherous waters. Monkey at this stage knew nothing of the world his parents and grandparents had left behind. Instead, he watched the sunrise by the ocean many times and watched the rays of light shimmering across the waters, resting upon the thousands of pebbles that chattered amongst themselves bringing in a new day.

As for fishing, Monkey knew all the best places on the island for catching fish. Nobody taught him. He was a natural. He knew the best places to find slender bamboo rods, their appropriate length and width, and where to find the right twine from the trees. His grandfather told him about bait, but it was Monkey who would go to the river and find all kinds of small things to attach to the wooden hooks. He developed his own style of fishing, going out to the furthest rock outcrop on the beach at low tide with a prepared lunch of his favorite cakes. He would wait until the tide came in. He had no fear of the waves and loved to see them roar and crash onto the beach and it was there on the rock he would catch his fish. Once he had caught enough fish for everyone at home and all the cakes were gone, he would dive into the waves that would carry him to shore.

Within a short while he overcame some of the moral dilemmas

regarding fishing. He felt conscience stricken the first time he caught a fish because it occurred to him that it was as alive as he was, though they could not speak the same language. When he first began, he tried to speak the language of the fish but ended up swallowing too much water.

His grandmother often worried about Monkey and tried her best to shield him from any possible dangers that came along. Monkey viewed her as stricter than his grandfather. His grandfather was just as strict, but his rules did not cover important issues for a young monkey such as eating too many cakes or wrestling with his brother, whom he called 'brother monkey.' Brother monkey of course had his own name, but since Monkey was simply called 'Monkey' he thought it only fair to extend the same privilege to his only brother. Monkey and his brother developed mutual interests, especially discovering the life of the forest, and shared a common love for beetles.

Monkey did not think it important to retain trivialities such as names or titles. He treated everyone the same, with the same respect, both high and low, including creatures outside the monkey kingdom. In that sense, he was an unusual monkey. By this time, monkeys tended to place immense pride in their name, where they came from, and their clan of origin. Monkeys rarely befriended creatures outside their clan as it was frowned upon as a sign of rebelliousness.

Monkey was about the usual size for monkeys his age. He was small, a little chubby, with a round head, ears, and a tail and a disposition for tea and cake at any time of the day. He, like all monkeys, had a tail, but since he did not like climbing, he often wondered why monkeys were given them. In those days, monkeys no longer lived in trees. The giants had lured them out of the trees, and they walked on their hind legs like people do today. Walking on all fours was considered incredibly crude and impolite, a sign of uncivilized behavior.

In the life cycle of the monkey, he was not a baby, nor was he an adult. He lived somewhere in the middle, between youth and tribal initiation when he would assume a title, position, and peer respect. In fact, Monkey, unknown to Monkey himself, continued to be the subject of discussion. The high priest tried to discourage such gossip. The main cause for contention was the original moon festival that occurred on the day of his birth. Those who believed that Monkey was an omen of bad luck revised their original position and came to the realization that while he was not bad luck personified, he was somehow connected to events beyond the control of anyone.

This meant that his birth was not an accident. It had a purpose, and this was significant. Monkey, despite losing his parents was still royalty in the clan even though he would never become high priest. Deep in his heart, the high priest knew that the giants had been benevolent in allowing them to live on the island, but at any point in the future, this kindness might be replaced with wrath and revenge. As a result of the tribal discussion over Monkey, he decided that the clan needed to be prepared to face any future attack.

The tribal leaders saw in Monkey's advent a divine reminder of the need to be vigilant and therefore, without arousing suspicion they prevailed upon the clan the need to return discipline to the now lax warrior class. They argued persuasively that the younger ages were not as cultivated in their behavior and that in this climate of loose morals, it was time that the young spent more time looking to the community interest rather than their own. Unknown to Monkey himself, his little entrance into life motivated the elders to rebuild the forts, strengthen the island defenses and train the younger warriors into a more effective and efficient force.

This was all quite irrelevant to Monkey. He never noticed the return to discipline or the positioning of warriors in the forts or the rebuilding of the walls. It had nothing to do with him. The clan elders saw Monkey as bad luck and tended to stay away from him. In time, years later, he would only have good things to say about his time on the island even though it was shaped by sadness.

Monkey's hobbies were a little unusual. He collected smooth pebbles from the creek and loved to look at flowers in the spring. He also tried his hand at poetry, encouraged by his grandmother. He wrote poems and put them in a book he kept near the vase in his house. Most of his poems at this stage were long, descriptive, and verbose, but he was simply following the traditions of his clan. All their poems tended to be the same. He struggled with poetry and wondered why poems could not be shorter and simpler or contain one idea.

Monkey liked flowers almost as much as he liked small smooth pebbles, but good flowers were difficult to find. He preferred pebbles because they did not fade after a day or two and he could rub them in his little hands. He would often bring them home to show his grandfather. He made the study of pebbles an art form, but after his grandfather tripped on part of the collection at home, Monkey was forced to contemplate the life of pebbles from outside.

Flowers on the other hand reminded him of the brevity of life and they sometimes made him feel sad. While he could not speak with the same eloquent articulation as his peers, he seemed to understand the realities of life. His grandfather was much older than he was and hobbled around with a walking stick, trying to catch up with Monkey's brother as he ran through the field. This taught Monkey that one day, he would be like his grandfather. He could not run as fast as his brother and after walking around the hill all day, he felt weary and in need of a good sleep.

Pebbles, on the other hand, taught him about character. He would often sit by the creek that ran past the hill and watch the pebbles in the water. He noticed that rocks under the water were smoother than rocks outside the water and reasoned that it was the running water constantly pressing on the rocks that smoothed out the rough edges. He tried an experiment one day to test this theory, but the next day he forgot where he placed his pebbles, became frustrated, and gave up.

On the good days, when the sun was shining and all was good and bright in the world, Monkey's mind was preoccupied with pebbles, flowers, poetry, and fishing. But from time to time, when he could catch no fish, or gain no inspiration for his poems, he would return to the question he would normally ignore: his name. Monkey had often wondered why his name was 'Monkey' while other monkeys had names. Most days he did not think of it, but sometimes after a cup of green tea and a cake, it began to gnaw at him, and he became confused. He reasoned that it might have something to do with him, but he was afraid to broach the subject because no one mentioned his name at all, not in front of Monkey himself.

It was New Year. The monkeys of the clan who had left the mainland celebrated the occasion with song, dance, and food. Monkey was asked to help prepare the delicacies along with his brother. It was the middle of winter. Snow fell on the ground and the monkeys huddled inside their homes surrounded by hearths and warmth and good soup. Monkey had not been able to fish for a few days as it was too cold, and his mind was especially restless. He had dropped his best fishing rod in the ocean the last time he was swimming near the ruins of the old fort, and he could not seem to find the right twine to make a new one.

The question of his name returned to him at this time, but he pushed it aside in favor of the festivities and the food took his mind off what was troubling him. Aside from his grandfather, grandmother, and brother, everyone else seemed to avoid him. He had never noticed it before. It was the first time he sensed it. He thought it might have been the result of one of his many pranks or misadventures involving pebbles, flowers, fish, beetles, or a combination of all four.

On the third day of the New Year festivities, a thought came to him in the late afternoon, just before his grandmother served him tea and cake. The day had been full of laughter and frivolity but as the celebrations grew more boisterous, Monkey seemed to retreat further into himself, and the question of his name stayed with him despite the smell of the cake and the warmth of the cup. His heart felt a rising melancholy like the soup he had just enjoyed. Sadness was not an emotion he often felt but he did feel sad on this day. He looked around at his relatives, all with nice, interesting names, even though he could not really remember them at all.

So, when his grandmother came over to ask if anything was wrong, Monkey asked her simply: 'Why am I called 'Monkey?''

The question made everyone stop talking and the room fell silent. Monkey looked around and saw the smiling faces of all his relatives and friends vanish, to be replaced by faces of anxiety and fear. His grandfather was called and came into the room, sitting down beside Monkey. Monkey was silent. He had left the cake and the tea by now was cold. He did not feel like eating. One by one, his relatives got up, thanked their hosts, and left until Monkey was alone in the room with the high priest.

His grandfather explained to him the circumstances of his birth, the terrible wave from the ocean that killed his father, and his mother's death. He explained to him quite honestly the reason he wasn't given a name and why some of the monkeys were nervous around him. He did not broach the taboo subject of why the clan left the mainland – that was a subject for another day. His grandfather put his arms around him and hugged him. Monkey just looked at him.

'Sometimes even though it is difficult to understand, bad things still happen,' his grandfather advised. 'While we do not understand why, these bad experiences help to build our character and teach us valuable lessons about life.'

Monkey looked up at him and nodded, with tears in his eyes. He stood up and walked silently away into the dusk, head bowed, holding his favorite pebble in his little hand. His adopted parents looked at each other but said nothing.

Monkey returned home later that night because his grandfather heard his little feet on the wooden veranda and the sliding of the doors. He was worried about the effect his story might have had on his grandson. He tossed and turned all night. When he finally fell asleep, it was already morning, and he awoke to the sound of Monkey running through the house chasing a beetle that had come in the night before. After a few crashes and general mayhem, his grandfather was relieved to know life was back to normal.

Later, Monkey sat on the wooden veranda and gazed up into the sky. The dark expanse of the night held great fascination for him. The village was shrouded in silence, except for the restless occasional bird call. The stars stood bright in the sky above, and as he gazed, Monkey realized how the sky was full of lights, in patterns and pictures. In awe, his little hands held tightly the edge of the veranda. His grandfather noticed him sitting there. He wanted to join Monkey there and ponder the stars, but he needed to prepare for the next day. It was a particularly auspicious day with an important ritual to perform. He did not know that this ritual would change Monkey forever and that this day would be, perhaps the most important in the monkey kingdom since they left the Great Mountain. Instead, he said nothing and went into the Hall of Masks, so he could ponder the awful secret he knew lay the hidden chamber, alone.

3.

The ceremony that his grandfather was preparing for was at the heart of the religion of the monkey kingdom. It was introduced some years after the first giants had arrived in the world. The ritual did not belong to the Ancient Order of Things when everyone lived in peace and the world was in balance. The giants might have forged weapons, built castles, and fought battles, but it was the monkeys who were the first to develop what they called the Art of War. They created this form of martial etiquette by observing the way the giants fought and realized quickly that there were drawbacks to the way they conducted battles.

In short, there was little strategy or coordination, and almost no real leadership of which to speak. The giants simply charged forward with their swords and clubs, spears and fire, and hoped for the best. Monkeys are known for their curiosity. If you ever see a monkey staring into space, he is not dozing, but deep in thought. This staring at the giants from the relative safety of the trees enabled them to fully appreciate and understand how to perfect war and emulate a way of life and thinking hitherto unknown.

It was in observing the giants and their way of life which lured the monkeys out of the trees, the foxes out of the forest and, the rabbits and raccoon-dogs out of their tunnels and holes in the ground. As Monkey would often say in the future: 'One giant is enough for a world of trouble.' Monkeys may have never left the trees and that is why they stay away from people today. They understand everything people have to say and want nothing to do with us. If your pet ever looks at you strangely, know that they understand everything you have just said but thousands of years of experience have taught them to simply plead ignorance and say nothing.

Before the arrival of the giants, monkeys were peaceful and

kept to themselves. Early disputes were resolved amicably by politeness and cordiality. Eventually however, as the populations grew and geographical fondness flourished, conflict arose between monkeys and other animals in the forest, especially the raccoon-dog, a kind of small, foxlike, dog-like creature, with a strange mousey face. Rabbits were naturally the most warlike of all the animals, perhaps because there were so many of them and they quickly formed into tribes, clans, and factions. Foxes were the most aloof of all the animals, graceful and elegant, and xenophobic. They were the ones who invented the monarchy first, after watching the giants and their strange customs of deference, loyalty, and hierarchy. What started as a joke among the other animals soon became the norm and quickly all the animal groups were no longer simply families, clans, and tribes, but kingdoms, with emperors, nobility, and royalty.

The foxes dwelt with their hereditary female monarch deep in the forest glens, while the rabbits lived in the great plains beyond the forests up to the mountains, whilst the monkeys and raccoon-dogs dwelt together closer to the coast and in the forests. No one knows who was originally to blame or who threw the first punch or who violated the first courtesy but soon the raccoon-dogs and monkeys were at war. Had the giants not arrived, the monkeys and raccoon-dogs would have resolved the conflict with a bare-knuckled brawl and then a party afterward, but the giants had arrived, and so the monkeys developed instead, the Art of War.

The high priest of the banished clan who lived on the island away from the mainland was preparing to celebrate the most important ritual in the Art of War, called the Rite of Truce. It was the only ritual of war recognized outside the monkey kingdom and by the time of Monkey's arrival in the world, even the giants knew of it. It had even saved them in some battles with the high priest before he was exiled.

In theory, it was the opportunity for both sides to stop fighting for a season by suggesting an alternative to the continuation of the conflict. In practice, it was a face-saving device, so that two parties completely exhausted from war, could politely decide that it was time to go and do something more productive. There were a few popular excuses. The most common excuses for not fighting included the marriage of someone important, a certain seasonal festival to observe or attend, or the most popular one, the arrival of fish in the rivers, and the need to go fishing. Both warring parties knew that fishing, marriage, and seasonal events were codewords for 'this war is going nowhere,' and it would usually lead to a temporary truce.

The Ritual of Truce was only one of many rituals and festivals animals observed to mark rites of passage and times and seasons, for they were communal creatures. Monkey enjoyed festivals, especially eating the various kinds of cakes and delicacies that were made available during such times. There was often dancing and drinking, and these events were perfect occasions for meeting prospective future companions. Monkey had often seen and sometimes participated in these esoteric rituals of life. His mind, however, was always on the open field, the next hill, the undiscovered forests, and all that lay within. He liked being by himself and loved the silence in the forest, when all that could be heard were the songs of birds or the bubbling brook.

That morning Monkey had forgotten about the festival. The day was unusually warm, and the cold had retreated, giving the village a respite. He had spent the night thinking about his name and then later how to catch a particularly elusive beetle. He was quite exhausted. After breakfast, he decided to sit on the veranda once more and he looked up into the sky. It was an especially hot day and the sun shone brightly in the blue sky. The more Monkey looked, the more his little eyes became watery and soon he had to squint. When he opened his eyes, they were cloudy, and he could not see clearly. He was about to rub his eyes when in the corner of one of them, he noticed something rather unusual.

The ground seemed to sparkle. This was most puzzling, thought Monkey, for as long as he had lived, he had never seen the ground sparkle before. The glint in the sun seemed to come from the middle of a field of grass which stood in the distance from his home. In the middle of the field, it seemed as though a small tree shone in the sun. This, thought Monkey, was worth investigating and jumping off the veranda, he began to walk towards the light. He did not notice the activities around him, and so walked almost in a trance toward the strange object in the field.

Soon Monkey arrived at the strange sight. He rubbed his eyes and to his surprise, the light was in fact not a tree, but a long shiny object stuck in the ground. He had never seen such an object before in his entire life and this made him more curious. Upon reaching the object, he noticed that his face was reflected on its side, and seeing this, his eyes opened wide. He remembered the first time he saw his face in the river and the surprise it brought him until he realized he was looking at himself. This was different because this shiny object was still and did not move.

Monkey decided, as all monkeys do, that the best way to find out more would be to touch the strange object in front of him. He stretched out his hand and touched the edge of the object. In the flash of a moment, he felt pain in his finger, as if his skin were opened by a sharp object. Pulling his hand away, he saw blood. He was astonished.

'Monkey!' shouted a stern voice behind him.

Monkey turned around and looked up to see his grandfather standing above him. His eyes were angry, and his hands were on his hips. 'Do not touch that again Monkey,' he said firmly.

Monkey nodded. He had no intention of touching it again for it had brought him a lot of discomfort. He held up his little hand to show his grandfather. A few drops of blood fell to the grass below. His grandfather pulled a piece of cloth from his robe. He knelt and proceeded to wrap Monkey's finger with the cloth. Monkey realized that his grandfather was both kind and stern. It puzzled him as to how it was possible to show love and anger at the same time.

'What is that thing?' asked Monkey pointing to the shiny object in the ground.

His grandfather looked down at him with his large eyes. He continued to wrap Monkey's finger. 'That, Monkey, is a sword.'

'A sword?' Monkey asked. 'What is it for?'

'Well,' said his grandfather, 'it is forged in a fire for the purpose of bringing life to an end.'

Monkey looked at him confused.

'Well,' continued his grandfather. 'We use little swords or knives to cut fish and in cooking, don't we?'

Monkey nodded.

'Well, this is another kind of knife, but it is not used for cooking.'

'What is it used for grandfather?' asked Monkey.

'It is used to kill monkeys,' he said.

Monkey's face showed complete astonishment. He could not believe what his grandfather had just said. 'Do we eat other monkeys?' he asked quite innocently.

His grandfather shook his head. 'Absolutely not, of course we don't,' he said.

'So, why do we need a sword?' asked Monkey.

'Sometimes, monkeys do not agree, and this disagreement leads to a big fight and swords are used to bring the fight to an end.'

'Why would anyone want to bring life to an end?' asked Monkey looking at the sword. He was deeply disturbed and felt a fear within, wanting to be as far from the sword as possible. He looked up at his grandfather. 'This thing called a 'sword' does not belong in our village. It is such a horrible thing. One day, I will stop all monkeys using swords and we will all be friends again.'

He looked up at his grandfather. The old monkey said nothing and continued to wrap up Monkey's finger. He stood up and pulled Monkey away from the sword. They both stood in front of the sword side by side for what seemed a long time. His grandfather went on to explain the Rite of Truce.

A monkey who wished to entertain a truce with his enemies would walk out onto the field of battle and then put his sword into the ground as an act of deference to his enemies. If his enemies decided to attack, then the one without the sword would be defenseless and probably killed, so there needed to be delicate negotiations between both sides so that the Rite of Truce could function. His grandfather kept saying things like 'I know you probably will not understand this,' or 'I know this is too difficult for you to grasp this,' but Monkey was not as stupid as his grandfather and everyone else thought.

Monkey just had no interest in war, nor would he ever want to fight, nor would he ever have the desire to kill. If this made him stupid, then Monkey was quite happy for everyone to think that. But that day, as his grandfather spoke, he realized that his grandfather was talking about something that he felt passionate about and that even though he had never seen him raise a sword, fighting was in his blood. Monkey looked up at his grandfather. Sometimes, Monkey thought that his grandfather held the most intense emotions, but that he kept them hidden inside, standing resolutely against the elements. His face was still, but Monkey knew that he was deep in thought.

A small tear formed in his grandfather's right eye and began to slide slowly down his face. He looked down at Monkey. He knew that Monkey was right. Swords had no place in their lives, but it was too late for them to change their ways, far too late. Too much blood had been spilled, and he could not dislodge the desires for revenge that lay deep in his heart. He lived for revenge every day, and he could find no contentment on the island. The pebbles, the fish, the clear skies, and the peace were not enough to settle his heart of anger which yearned to take up the sword again and have his revenge. He wanted to kill the emperor of the monkeys and those who betrayed him.

Monkey did not say anything but stood still. He didn't know why his grandfather was crying. Perhaps it was because of his own selfishness in wanting to touch the sword in the first place, or maybe he was upset with his general behavior of late. Monkey felt guilt rising inside him, and he thought that there in front of the sword more than a polite apology was necessary.

He held up his bandaged finger and examined it more closely. At that moment, in front of the sword, with his bleeding finger, next to his grandfather, filled with guilt, Monkey resolved to better himself, starting from that very moment. He closed his eyes quietly and when they opened, he felt a warmth overflowing across his face as the sun seemed to emerge from its hiding place behind a cloud.

'Let us be going Monkey,' said his grandfather quietly, and hand in hand, they walked back to their house. Monkey turned and looked again at the sword deep in the grass. It was such a dreadful thing, he thought to himself. He was shocked that such a thing existed in his world, and it was such a contrast to all things beautiful and all things good. He resolved at that moment that he would do all he could to take this sword and anything like it out of the world he loved.

The next few days saw the end of the New Year's celebrations and Monkey tried to bring himself to enjoy them as much as he could. He attended the other rituals and the parties and celebrations, but it was cold, and it began to snow again. It was impossible to do anything other than huddle around the hearth during the day and stay warm under blankets at night. In the mornings, the wind came upon the island from the depths of the sea up the coast and the lowlands and through the village, blowing under the doors and through the cracks in the wall so no one was warm.

Monkeys don't need an extra layer of fur as their body is covered from head to toe and even their feet are well insulated from inclement weather. But they are not immune from the cold, and they feel it as much as anyone and so fireplaces and blankets, such as they were, made a difference. Monkey's grandmother kept a close eye on the cut to Monkey's finger where he touched the sword. It healed quickly, but the wound to his spirit didn't heal and he would carry that wound until the day of his death.

Up to that point, he had not really understood the reality of the world around him. The monkey kingdom was unlike any kingdom he had known. Unlike the beetles and bugs or fish or birds, who seemed to live together in harmony, monkeys did not, and they could not resolve their differences properly unless they fought each other.

Monkey had opened the stomach of fish after he caught them with a little knife he found in the kitchen, but only after he apologized to the fish for killing it and saying a prayer to the ancestors. He remembered seeing the blood ooze out and the eyes of the fish roll around and its tail flap until every breath of its life was spent. He washed the fish and scaled it and prepared it and ate it. Until that fateful day, it was just something he did, to live, to survive and exist. The thought of that terribly large sword cutting into the stomach of a monkey or severing a limb or causing death to someone, turned Monkey off fish for a long time, and he returned to things without blood such as vegetables and nuts.

The painful encounter with the sword changed his life. He began to see the world differently from that day. He noticed that there were monkeys walking around with armor, and swords on their waist. He began to realize that there were forts in the village and walls made of stone and wood. He began to see other weapons of death such as the bow and arrows tipped with stone and walls and banners unfurled in the wind. He wondered whether these things had always been there or whether something had changed.

He had no idea that he was at the root of all things, as many saw his birth as an ill omen, that the past might wash up on the shore again one day and then they might have to start killing again. The warriors were always polite to Monkey. After all, he was one of the family members of the high priest. They bowed deeply and Monkey always returned the gesture, but he felt uncomfortable in their presence. He felt all their eyes looking at him with a feeling of unease. All the soldiers felt that Monkey was bad luck and avoided even his shadow.

Still deeply upset by the whole experience, his mind turned to poetry and one day huddled near the hearth he saw a little beetle muddle its way across the floor towards the heat. Monkey dropped his blanket and tried to grab the beetle, but it slipped through his fingers. He tried again but fell flat on his face. The beetle leapt off the floor and landed on him and Monkey tried desperately to get rid of it. Eventually, the beetle took flight and flew off through a crack in the floor. Even though he could not capture the beetle, he thought he could 'capture' the beetle with words. Monkey was true to his little promise to himself.

That next morning at breakfast, Monkey announced that he had finished a poem and he asked permission to read it out. It was an unusual thing to do for poems were long and elaborate. Monkey had not written one for quite some time and the beetle furnished him with the right material. Monkey looked at everyone and then produced a small scrap of paper that had been folded several times.

He unfolded it and read:
'A little beetle in the house –
to and fro –
The monkey's chase –
Where can it go?
Where can it hide?
Where can it flee?
To the sliding door said me,
if only open it could be...'
Monkey bowed to the applause of his family.

'Bravo Monkey,' said his grandfather, 'it is a good poem, but it is too short. As you know poems are supposed to be much longer, but it's winter, and maybe it's too cold to write long poems.'

Monkey smiled and appreciated the compliments. Monkey spent the next month or so writing poems as it was too cold to go outside. He looked at the world go by from a distance. He noticed that he spent less and less time with his brother. In fact, he hardly ever saw him. His brother spent most of his time out in the village. He snuck out late at night by himself and would only come back in the early hours of the morning, sliding the door open slowly and closing it behind him.

It was around this time that his brother began bringing him small handfuls of ginkgo nuts and leaving them on his poetry book near the vase. Monkey loved all kinds of nuts, but he loved ginkgo nuts the most. They were small and yellow and while trapped in a hard shell, they were delicious when eaten. He only ate a few at one time because his grandmother told him that they were special nuts and were to be treasured if found. Monkey found that even eating two or three made him feel refreshed for the day ahead and the thought of more ginkgo nuts inspired him to write more poetry.

This burst of creative fervor began at the outset of spring. Everything became warmer and at night he didn't need the hearth or the blankets. Monkey was waking earlier, and the sun was shining brighter during the day. It stopped snowing and the wind became less frequent and more pleasant. Spring fell upon the village suddenly one day and Monkey was caught with a burst of inspiration to write a poem. He ate his ginkgo nuts and went down to the stream where he caught the bait for fishing. He put his feet into the water. It felt cool as the sun began to rise across the sky. He found a nice comfortable place under some overhanging branches and had a customary nap.

A little while later, his brother joined him under the tree. They sat there for a while as the rest of the village went about their daily chores. They could hear the warriors training in the distance and the farmers digging in the field, but for the two monkeys, they might have been in a different world. Monkey's brother had brought with him a large knapsack full of ginkgo nuts. Monkey could smell them.

'How is your hand these days?' he asked.

Monkey looked at his little hand. The pain had long gone, but his feelings about the sword had not changed. 'It is all healed,' he replied.

Monkey's brother stretched out on the grass, putting his arms behind his head. Monkey copied him.

'Have you written any more poems?' asked his brother.

Monkey nodded.

'We shall like to hear them one day Monkey if you would like to read them to us. Your poems are so different, full of life and energy and they always contain one single idea, instead of a string of ideas. It is not traditional. I like that. We both like that.'

'Thank you,' said Monkey. He picked up the knapsack and

took out a small ginkgo nut. His poems were like these nuts, he thought, but his mind went to what his brother had said. 'What do you mean 'we'?' asked Monkey, puzzled.

His brother smiled and took the knapsack of nuts. 'I have always enjoyed being your brother,' he said.

'I could not have asked for a better brother,' replied Monkey, his eyes on the knapsack of ginkgo nuts.

'Just before you were born, your father asked me that if anything happened to him then I was responsible for you.'

'I did not know,' replied Monkey honestly.

'Your father was my older brother. He was much wiser and stronger than I am. He fell in love much sooner and took a wife. Father knew that he would make a good high priest one day and no one assumed that he would die of anything but old age.'

He looked over at Monkey. 'You look like your father, but you have the spirit of your mother. He had the warrior's spirit in him, but I don't think you do. You are more of a peacemaker than a warrior. We all saw that during your encounter with the sword at New Year's.'

'I really hate swords,' replied Monkey. 'I don't know why they were ever invented by monkeys.'

His brother laughed loudly. 'We did not invent them at all!' he exclaimed. 'We just adopted the idea from others who came before us. You have never met them. I hope you never do.' He looked at the knapsack of nuts.

'But that is not why we are here today, and I did not answer your question,' continued his brother. 'Like your father, I am soon to take a wife and become an apprentice to my father, so one day I might take over the clan as the high priest. My son will become the high priest after me.'

'I am sure that you will make a good father one day,' said Monkey. He suddenly realized his brother was in fact his uncle. As his teeth crunched on a ginkgo nut, he knew that just as winter was ending, so too was this lifelong friendship. The divide between them had become a chasm. He had always assumed that due to the common interests they shared and the similar outlook on life they had, they were in fact the same in some way. He never viewed his brother as an uncle. It did not occur to him that his brother was from the same generation as his father.

'That explains the ginkgo nuts,' he realized. His brother opened the knapsack so Monkey could partake of the dozens of yellow nuts inside.

'Last night my father met with the father and mother of a monkey whom they wish me to marry. We have known each other since we were in our mother's arms. That is where I have been lately, at their place, chatting with her and getting to know her parents. They have a huge ginkgo tree next to their house.'

'We will still be able to play together and look for beetles and so on, won't we?' asked Monkey. His uncle looked over at him and frowned.

'I would love to Monkey, but with marriage comes responsibilities too. I will be sent on the path to the priesthood, to take my father's position one day when he is too old to work in the shrine. If I can find time to join you on some adventures, I will,' he said with a smile.

Monkey knew this meant no. He munched on ginkgo nuts and returned the smile but deep down he knew that this would be the last day they would be equals. He knew that the life of a priest was full of obligations and ceremonies and being asked to visit various monkeys at all hours of the night, to care for the sick, to mediate disputes, to lead, and to argue politics with the other elders. He knew that his grandfather would also have loved to have spent more time with him, but the business of the shrine continually pressed upon him.

'If I find a nice beetle or a smooth stone of peculiar beauty dear brother, I will be sure to show you from time to time,' said Monkey, his heart feeling sad.

His brother nodded and smiled. 'That would be wonderful Monkey. I will always make time for you. You will always be welcome in our home, no matter what the occasion.'

Monkey knew that the lovable, friendly brother was already succumbing to the strictures of politeness in offering this open invitation. As he looked at his brother, he began to see for the first time the elder monkey who was hidden by the playful times of beetle hunting and frolicking in the stream. It was always there, but his brother chose to put it aside until the day it was needed. He then realized those days were especially precious. He needed to treasure them in his heart.

He did not harbor any ill feelings toward his brother. Everyone had a role to play in the clan. He looked at his brother and for a moment he thought he had caught a glimpse of his father in his eyes, and this made his heart warm. As he was thinking this, a voice called from the other side of the stream. It was the monkey to whom his brother was engaged. She was calling him. His brother looked at Monkey. His face was frowning and already he seemed burdened with responsibility.

'I must go,' he said.

Monkey bowed to him ever so slightly and politely. 'I understand brother,' replied Monkey.

'Please enjoy the ginkgo nuts,' said his brother, and jumped to his feet, brushing off the grass. He skipped across the stream and stood in front of his bride-to-be. She looked over to Monkey sitting next to the ginkgo nuts and waved. Monkey returned the wave and then lay back on the grass looking up into the branches of the tree. From today, he thought, he would have to travel the streams and the forests alone. He sighed and continued to munch the nuts. Becoming tired of his usual position, he moved onto his side and surveyed the life of the village unfolding before him.

His brother walked up the stream with his bride-to-be and they disappeared. Two older monkeys were walking down the stream on the way to the fields. One was carrying a sack over his shoulder, the other some tools. They were both already laden with dirt, so they must have risen early to plant crops. In the distance, he heard the tapping of some tools. Monkey patted his stomach. It felt full and he felt good inside, even though in his heart he felt sad that his brother was to be more preoccupied with things other than adventures and beetles. But, thought Monkey, perhaps it was for the best. 'All things change,' he said to himself, and with that popped another ginkgo nut into his mouth. As he sat under the tree, quite content with himself, Monkey did not know how soon change would come. Already, the blossoms of spring were falling.

4.

The next day, after breakfast, Monkey left for his morning foraging around the village. His brother, or rather his uncle, had already left to prepare for the coming wedding and his grandfather had gone into the Hall of Masks as he did every day to perform rituals for the ancestors. Monkey had never been in the Hall of Masks because only the priests could cross the threshold and he had no interest in such matters. It did not occur to him that being the son of the son of the high priest he should have been trained in the art of priesthood or at least made aware of the basic principles of their collective faith, but he wasn't.

Had his father survived, Monkey would have been first in line to succeed him as the high priest, and by now he would already have been invited into the Hall of Masks for preparatory training. The reality was that even his grandfather held lingering doubts about the existence of Monkey, which were only confirmed by his heretical views at the sword ceremony. Monkey's reaction to the sword was instinctive and instead of seeking deeper knowledge or submitting to the authority of his elders, he simply overturned generations of tradition by expressing his desire to abolish the ritual entirely and extinguish the role of swords in the life of the clan. This abrupt and radical spirit his grandfather found most disturbing, a contrast to his younger son's compliant and obedient attitude.

Monkey's brother, or to be more precise his uncle, was the perfect candidate for the priesthood. He had no questions, for his mind was relatively superficial, but more importantly, he believed in the traditions and would happily maintain the rituals simply because he had inherited them. He wasn't interested in the history of the clan, nor would he ask uncomfortable questions and he would therefore readily accept the inherited wisdom on the roles and responsibilities of clan leadership. He also displayed little real compassion for anyone but was a stickler for the rules and he would make sure there was obedience without question.

A priest with ideas, compassion, and selflessness was the worst kind of priest, thought Monkey's grandfather. Such a priest would lead the clan to their ruin. The fact that the clan was stuck on the island, and that the high priest's behavior had led the clan to this exile were completely ignored by the old monkey who looked over his own faults and highlighted the weaknesses of others. As a grandfather, he was kind to Monkey, but as the leader of the clan, he had led his clan to ruin, and he saw in his son the same qualities he saw in himself.

Like in all things, a good leader often has strong followers. The high priest was no exception. The power behind the throne in his clan was in the hands of two of the priest's most trusted warriors, a tall, thin monkey with one ear, called 'One Ear,' and another with one eye, called 'One-Eye.' Both had fought alongside the high priest during all their battles. These two monkeys were held in the highest esteem within the clan. Since their banishment, there was simmering resentment in the hearts of many monkeys and some yearned to have a new leader who would take them to victory. All of this was unknown to Monkey.

Monkey was oblivious to the politics of the clan. Life was simply to be lived each day. As was his custom, Monkey wandered aimlessly around the village driven by the slightest shift in the breeze, the scent of fresh flowers, strangely formed clouds in the sky, and the sound of buzzing insects. The morning passed quickly and soon the sun was overhead. It was about this time that Monkey found a beetle of unusual size. His meanderings brought him back at last to the Hall of Masks. His house was next door and he had intended to return and see what delicacies were being cooked in the kitchen by his grandmother, but the beetle, of exceptional size and brilliant color caught his eye at the bottom of the steps.

Monkey followed it as it flew up the steps. Upon reaching the top the beetle seemed to vanish behind one of the sliding doors on the veranda. Monkey then realized that he had lost his sandals. He must have dropped them somewhere, perhaps by the creek where he found some beautiful fresh bamboo stalks.

On that day he felt an insatiable desire to pursue the beetle wherever it would take him and so he climbed up the steps until he was standing on the veranda. This was as far as he had ever been. He had never been inside the Hall of Masks, but there he stood in front of the door. He had never been forbidden to enter, but he always felt a heaviness in his heart whenever he passed by, a sense of foreboding. He felt that the Hall of Mask had questions he had no interest in asking and he was better off just staying away. The Hall of Masks seemed to be a door he had no desire to go through. It was the place for his grandfather and now his son, and Monkey had no business there.

But as he stood there that day, on the veranda, the sun shone brightly and warmed the wood. His feet began to get hot and so he moved into the shade to avoid the burning sensation on his feet, and he soon found himself on the edge of the sliding door, for that was the furthest from the rays of the approaching sun. It was as if the orb in the sky was pushing him inside.

He pressed against the sliding door, which was made of delicate wood and paper screens. Monkey was especially careful not to poke a hole through the paper because he would incur the wrath of his grandfather, but soon his position became untenable, and he had to do something. He could hear the beetle scurrying around on the floor on the other side of the sliding door and Monkey decided that, at the very least, he needed to make sure the beetle was able to find his way out again and so he slid open the door.

The Hall was silent. Monkey stood at the entrance peering in as the sun's rays lit up the ground and the room was basked in light. The beetle was nowhere to be seen. Monkey did not step into the Hall as it always seemed a place forbidden to him, a place of solemnity and ritual. Monkey surveyed the hall that stood before him. The sun shone through the cracks in the wooden walls and Monkey could see pillars of dust settling in the shadows.

Monkey thought that the name of the Hall was also unusual as he had never seen a mask before, nor had the clan used them. His grandfather had explained to him in the past, that sometimes monkeys wore another face over their existing one for some ceremony or for dancing. Monkey thought that this idea was quite absurd and dishonest, believing that one face was enough. Monkey was quite naïve and assumed that everyone was as upfront and honest as he was. The proposal that someone would play-act and put on a face made little sense to him.

The floor was made of polished wood. He looked down and could see a faint outline of himself reflected. He was pleased with this. He liked his own face and he thought that he had a nice, honest face. He hoped that others would always know him to be honest. His eyes looked up at the wall broken by cracks. He soon found that faces were looking down at him. Faces hung on the wall, all spaced evenly right above him to the end of the wall which was shrouded in darkness. The first face was not like his, nor like any other monkey he had ever seen.

On closer inspection, Monkey realized that it was probably not a monkey at all. It had a pale, whitish color, enlarged cheeks, two narrow slits for eyes, and a stare that seemed to extend right across the room. The mouth was sitting on the face as if it were pouting, or panting, due to loss of breath and Monkey wondered why anyone would have a face like that. He walked to the next mask. It was without paint or pigment, with round eyes and a cheerful face, its smile betraying a mouth without teeth. Monkey counted twelve masks in all, different faces, some solemn, some strange, and others terrifying. Monkey noticed that none of them bore the resemblance of monkeys but of creatures with large eyes and thick eyebrows, long noses, and wide mouths. Only a few of the faces had any hair. Monkey touched his face and thought it strange that any creature could live without their facial hair.

Monkey noticed in the far corner of the room was a special shelf upon which sat a vase with a flower on it. Above the vase was a long scroll with interesting writing. Monkey had learned how to read and write but even this strange calligraphy was too difficult for him. He decided to ponder its meaning more closely and stood up on the wooden shelf. He realized this poem was special as it was worthy of such a prominent position in the room. As he moved forward to stare at the words more closely, his hand touched a wooden panel in the wall and suddenly it moved. Puzzled by this, he pushed on the panel ever so lightly and he disappeared behind the wall.

A moment later, his grandfather came into the Hall with a bucket of water and some cloth, wearing work clothes. He placed the bucket of water at the edge of the room and stopped in his tracks. He looked intently at the floor and traced his eyes back to the entrance of the Hall. His eyes followed the imprint of a set of small footprints all the way across the floor to the scroll painting on the wall. His grandfather smiled to himself and walked over to the painting. He looked at the poem and read it aloud.

'In the darkness, all alone, a firefly lights my path.'

A sound of approval came from the other side of the wall. His grandfather laughed to himself and left the room. He returned with a tray of sweet dumplings and two cups of green tea. He sat down in the middle of the room, facing away from the scroll painting.

'In the middle of the day after exercise, the best thing to do is to have some nice tea and sweets,' he said and waited. 'Especially those nice sweets my wife makes for us on special occasions. It is a pity that I will have to eat them all alone!'

He took a dumpling and began to eat it. Behind him he could hear some scraping and banging, and confusion muffled by the wall. It could only be Monkey, thought his grandfather. No other monkey would get himself into such situations. His grandfather was surprised that Monkey was so quickly able to find the lever that released the panel. He ran across the polished floor and quickly sat in front of his grandfather.

'Hello,' he said out of breath.

'This is a surprise,' replied his grandfather. 'Please have some tea and sweets.' He handed Monkey a cup of tea. Monkey thanked him profusely. Together they quickly ate all the sweets and drank all the tea sitting on the floor.

'They go so quickly,' Monkey observed.

'It is one of those mysteries in life,' added his grandfather.

Monkey told him about the hidden panel and the nice poem and the beetle and apologized for being in the Hall of Masks. He also asked the reason for the hidden room. His grandfather sighed and decided it was time to tell him something about the secrets of the Hall. 'Let me explain about this room, young Monkey,' he began.

'It is a fascinating place,' replied Monkey.

His grandfather nodded slowly. 'We did not build this village. We came to this island from the mainland when I was much younger. This building we call the 'Hall of Masks' because that is all we know. We don't know anything about the twelve masks you see displayed here. Perhaps they were the faces of the creatures who lived in this village, but we don't know. We thought originally that these creatures were still living here when we arrived, but they were never found, and we only know about them by what they left behind. But we discovered, as you did today, that the Hall of Masks contains hidden doors, passages, floors, and walkways. I decided to keep these hidden places a secret. We thought that there might be a passage to the bottom of the cliffs and the beach beneath us on the other side of this building, but we could not find it. If there were such a secret passageway. it might give us more clues as to what happened here. It is clear to us now that the original inhabitants are not coming back.'

'Maybe there are clues in the forests?' asked Monkey. It seemed strange to him that anyone would want to leave such a beautiful place.

His grandfather shook his head. 'There is nothing,' he said sadly. 'It is as if they all vanished. We sent search parties to all the darkest parts of the island and found nothing. Aside from what they left behind they left no clues as to their disappearance.'

'That is a mystery,' said Monkey. 'Why would they have hidden rooms and hidden doors and these strange masks? It is as if they were not happy with who they were.'

'What do you mean?' asked his grandfather.

'We already have one face,' said Monkey. 'One face is enough for others to see us. If we have more than one, then how do they know they are seeing us as we are?'

'I guess that is what a mask is Monkey. It is designed to hide our true feelings.'

'I don't understand,' insisted Monkey. 'But maybe, that is why they vanished. Maybe, one day everyone saw each other's real faces.'

His grandfather stared at him with surprise. It was quite a profound comment for his grandson to make. 'If that is so,' he added, 'imagine a world where all emotions and thoughts were unveiled for all to see, what would happen?'

'It is better for all to know what the others are thinking,' replied Monkey.

His grandfather smiled and nodded but said nothing. He was much older. The idea that all emotions and aspirations and ambitions could be revealed would be quite catastrophic. There would be an outbreak of violence and death as the shock of what everyone thought of each other dawned on them and they would react with anger. His grandfather knew that masks were needed to save everyone from themselves. They were needed to hide, conceal, and protect.

Monkeys were very polite but beneath that politeness was deep emotion and feelings that needed to be hidden. Monkey's radical thoughts once again confirmed in his grandfather's mind his decision to keep him from the leadership of the clan. This little monkey had ideas that could unravel the entire kingdom and even the giants at the Castle by the Sea. Where did he get such radical ideas?

Monkey interrupted his train of thought with a question. 'Why did we come here? Why did you leave the mainland? How?'

His questions shocked the old monkey. His grandfather looked at Monkey frowning. Perhaps it was time for him to hear the truth or at least some of it. He thought for a while about where he could begin.

'You know Monkey, think of what happens when you play in the stream, and you place a leaf on the water. The stream carries the leaf downwards until it reaches the ocean.'

Monkey nodded.

'That is how we came to this island, on boats, pushed by the currents of the sea.'

'We cannot return?' asked Monkey.

'We have no reason to be there,' said his grandfather. 'We have everything we need right here.'

Monkey was, by this stage, quite aware of the ocean. The death of his father and the passing of his mother introduced the power and ferocity of the ocean to him. He knew the power also from experience, by the way the waves lifted him up and threw him onto the land when he was fishing. He often pondered its depth and was amazed at how many fish seemed to come from it. There was an abundance of life in the ocean that dwarfed anything he saw on land.

'But why did we leave in the first place?' asked Monkey.

His grandfather sighed. It was time that Monkey knew something of the origin of their clan. 'I will tell you what I know Monkey, you have a right to know the truth,' he replied. 'It is best to start at the beginning.'

'All life came from the Great Mountain, a huge, beautiful mountain that rose out of the earth. Long ago, during the Ancient Order of Things, there was simply life. Monkeys were created first and therefore we are considered the most significant of the kingdoms. We were brought into being at the Great Mountain. The one who created us was the 'The One who Named the Monkeys and who Lives on the Great Mountain.' We do not know his name, and no one dared ask him. He did not reveal it to us.

'He was, and is, the source of all life in our world, and he created all the animal kingdoms. For a long time, monkeys lived there on the Great Mountain alone with this being, and then much later, other creatures were brought into being such as rabbits and foxes, bears and boars, birds, and fish. It was our role to teach them about the world, lead and guide them. All the kingdoms accepted our authority until one wily and crafty group of creatures tried to usurp our position through devious trickery. They were the raccoon-dogs.'

'How did they do that?' asked Monkey.

'For whatever reason, the raccoon-dogs were endowed with a special gift, and instead of using this gift for good, they used it for evil. They can change their form, their outward appearance, into something they are not. They can change their entire body into another body simply by concentrating. It has always seemed like a curse to me but change they did, and their trickery provoked division between the families of monkeys who lived on the Great Mountain. Where there was peace, there was now discord, where there was joy, there was now suspicion and as the result of their trickery, monkeys began to fight amongst themselves.'

Monkey was deeply shocked. He was already trying to come to terms with the idea of a mask, how someone could put on a mask and hide their own identity. Now he had discovered that the racoon-dogs could change their entire appearance. 'It is horrible to think that some creatures have this power grandfather,' he complained bitterly. 'It means that you cannot know for sure to whom you are speaking.'

'Exactly!' exclaimed his grandfather. 'The raccoon-dogs used their gift to sow division among the clans and there was the first war between the monkeys on the slopes of the Great Mountain. With claw and club, the monkeys fought until they lay exhausted on the field. It was then only then that they realized they had been duped by the raccoon-dogs because they changed back into their original form and laughed at our ancestors from the trees and the forest. It was then that the monkey clans became one and they fought against the raccoon-dogs until all semblance of friendship had been extinguished and such enmity formed between the two kingdoms that it lasts even until today.

'During this war, the rabbits joined us, but the foxes stayed aloof and have always done so, never wishing to involve themselves in the affairs of any of the kingdoms. In this first war, we did not use swords like the one you cut your hand on, but we used our claws and our strength in numbers. It is really the only way to have a fair fight, with claw and club. After all, if you kill your opponent, you cannot fight them again and so all monkeys prefer to fight with our bare claws.'

'Who won the war grandfather?' asked Monkey.

'No one. Just before the triumph of the monkeys, word came from the coast that a new creature had landed. This creature declared war not only on monkeys and raccoon-dogs, but on all living things. These new arrivals to our land were creatures no one had ever seen before. Their first action was to burn down the forest. They cut down ancient trees and killed raccoon-dogs, rabbits, and bears for their skin so they could keep themselves warm in winter. No one knows where they came from or what kingdom they belonged to, but they were giant in stature, standing tall even above some of the trees in the forest.

'They were better organized than the monkeys or other kingdoms at the Great Mountain. They had come to destroy everything we knew. It was only later that we discovered through the birds, their real intentions. They wanted everything. They wanted the wood of the forest for their houses, the water for their baths, and the fish for themselves. They consumed everything. The Great Mountain had a huge waterfall that gave life to all the rivers and the rivers flowed into an immense lake, a beautiful lake, with clear water, full of fish and abundant with life.

'Despite the war between the monkeys and raccoon-dogs, all the kingdoms appreciated the beauty of the lake and did not bring their disputes there. For the sake of the beauty of the lake, it is said that there even monkeys and racoon-dogs could enjoy ancient fellowship. The raccoon-dogs, even though they were our enemies called it 'The Lake of a Thousand Blessings.' They were right. But alas, it came to our attention that the giants were planning to build a huge castle at the lake.'

'What's a castle?' asked Monkey.

'Of course, Monkey, you have never seen one. I have only seen one castle in my lifetime, and I hope I never see another. A castle is a sign that something is wrong with the world. It is a signal to the world of the reality of power, real power over all created things, and a desire to rule over others. It is built in fear, fear of the outside, fear of the unknown, and fear of others. It is built with large stones from the hills and brought together with great difficulty, on top of each other, until a huge wall is constructed.

'The only way this can be done is with the whip and the threat of death. Many died while building the castle. These giants brought other giants with them to build the castle, slaves, and old enemies long vanquished. Our ancestors said that they never wept as much as they did when they saw it: chains around their necks, chains around their arms, and chains around their ankles. 'Build, build, build they were told, build the castle wall.' These were some of the words of a poem I heard in my own lifetime when I saw another castle being built, but I can only assume that others sang a similar song long ago. The castle tower and walls prevent anyone from getting in, but they also act as a prison for those inside.

'It soon became clear to my ancestors that the castle was just the beginning. If the giants spread out and farmed the land and lived in peace with our ancestors, then all might have been well. We have this inbuilt desire to travel you see Monkey, this desire to move. I see this in you, your love of beetles and fishing and exploring. I cannot imagine there would be any place on this island you will not visit one day. I can only imagine how far you would travel if you were back home in the deep forests, or my birthplace, Three Rivers, a place of exceptional beauty. It is the same with the racoon-dogs, the rabbits, and the foxes, indeed all the kingdoms. We all have the urge to move forward. We don't know where this urge comes from, but we are thankful for it. Never stay still Monkey, always move on, always move forward.

'But it was not so with the giants. They wanted to stay still and build their castle. It seemed strange to us. There were no enemies to fight. They all seemed united in their purpose and there was no division among them. Maybe they feared the forest, or us, or others who might come across the seas. In any event, the giants began to build their castle on the side of our beautiful lake deep in the forest. They dug into the slope of a nearby hill to place their boulders. It gave them complete control of the region. They were able to keep their eye on the entire coastline of the lake and see everything that was happening. They had stolen from us what belonged to all the kingdoms. It was their strategic advantage. But it was just the beginning.

'As soon as their castle by the lake was constructed, the giants cut down the trees in the forest to build their homes and their town and their forts everywhere. With their forts, they dug agricultural land, diverted rivers, planted strange crops, and poisoned the water. The giants also had an appetite for flesh and hunted the lesser creatures such as rabbits, bears, wild boars, and foxes. There were many other creatures too, beings of power, majesty, and beauty. Our ancestors called them friends, but the giants killed them all and they are now just memories. Eventually, the rabbits and foxes were hunted to near extinction, surprising as that may seem, such was the malice of the giants.

'Our ancestors tried to work together with the raccoon-dogs but there was too much bad blood between us, and they did not trust us. We regretted our long enmity for our true enemy had appeared. So, one day, the monkey clans massed our army and called out to the giants hiding in their fortress.'

'They went to war against the giants at their castle?' asked Monkey.

His grandfather nodded. 'They announced our intentions with the conch shells.'

'What are they?' asked Monkey.

'They are large shells that we often find on the beach or in the ocean. You put the shell up to your mouth and blow with all your energy. The sound the shell makes is haunting and yet powerful, and the sound can travel a long distance. All the tribes blew their conch shells, and we went out to meet the giants. We had clubs and claws against swords and spears and fire. The giants easily repelled us and in one day most of our warriors lay dead.

'Seeing our sacrifice, the raccoon-dogs relented and joined us on the field of battle as dusk fell but it was too late. They too suffered heavy losses. By dusk the giants had pursued us to the foot of the Giant Mountain routing what was left of our combined armies. It was a day of terrible slaughter. It was only the dark mist of the waterfalls that held them back from killing all the clans.

'It seemed that all was lost. The remnant of our ancestors gathered in the mountain crevices and watched the forests burn into the night. We put aside our long-held differences with the raccoon-dogs and in the end, when all hope was lost, we held them as dearly as brothers. There was great despair and fear that once the mist cleared, the giants would return and finish their work at wiping out the last of the kingdoms. They huddled in terror.

'Unknown to our ancestors, one monkey, a rabbit, and a fox left their tribes, formed a pledge of friendship, and went to the Giant Mountain in search of the one who had brought them into being. As you know, monkeys, rabbits, and foxes are rarely friends. If we form a pledge of friendship, then the world is so bad that we need any friend we can get. We don't know the names of these three creatures. Their real names are lost to us. These three creatures found the one for whom they searched and woke him from his slumber. They asked him why he had ignored their cries for help and told him that the forest was dying.'

'What did he do?' asked Monkey.

'The One who named the monkeys went to meet the giants. He told them to repair the forest and stop their actions that were causing so much harm to the kingdoms. They just laughed. He warned them that if they did not stop their actions, then he would act against them. They refused. So, the one who named the monkeys, with the monkey, fox, and rabbit stood alone against them on the field of battle. The giants in their armor and terrible weapons massed on the field to face one solitary, lonely figure with his little band of friends. Once more he pleaded with them. At that time, a few giants relented. They retreated, leaving their families and clans to contemplate their actions in the dark places of the forest, confronting their shame. There they still tend to the forests they once destroyed. They live far away from everyone, where the three rivers meet the sea.

'The rest of the giants fought on the field of battle. The one who came from the Great Mountain and who had no name fought them all the way to the castle and he burned it to the ground. It was there, in the fire, that he was last seen, with all his enemies surrounding him. The monkey, fox, and rabbit perished with him in the fire. The giants rejoiced and our ancestors thought all was lost, but then something remarkable happened. Even today, we do not know what truly happened. The giants suddenly began attacking each other with unspeakable violence. By the time the embers turned black in the ruins of the castle, every giant lay dead.'

'All of them?' asked Monkey disbelieving. His grandfather nodded.

'Why did they kill each other?' asked Monkey.

'Nobody knows,' answered his grandfather. 'There are many different views about it, but no one knows for sure.'

His grandfather paused. He had not told this story for years. No one had ever really asked about it, and sitting there, with Monkey, his blood stirred for the first time since he had arrived on the island. He loved the clan, and he loved the old ways of the monkeys, but deep inside, he knew that something was wrong with the world. He knew it had to do with the way he lived, the way they all lived, and he knew that it had something to do with the way they had all copied the giants. He was the high priest. He knew the old stories. He knew about the Ancient Order of Things, before the coming of the giants and he knew how much the world had changed. He knew how the monkeys compromised on so many things to the point where they began to believe that the swords and the spears and the fire and the new ways of thinking meant they could change the world and become giants themselves.

Back on the mainland, he remembered how he refused to obey the emperor of the monkeys and accept their treaty with the giants from the Castle by the Sea. He remembered the rebellion and how he started it, how his blood flowed through his veins, and how excited he was when the clans and tribes rallied around him in the forest. He remembered how he denounced the giants and promised his people that he would rid the forests of all the giants they could find. He wanted to drive the giants back into the sea and longed for the day when giants no longer walked in the forest. He remembered how they burnt the little houses and villages all along the ancient roads and paths of the deep forests and killed all the giants who lived there, from the edge of the forest to the plains at the foot of the Great Mountain. How terrified they were when they heard the shrieks of the monkeys and the conch shells and the rattling of spears and swords. He looked at Monkey. Monkey had assumed the pause in the story was because his grandfather needed a break from talking and was just sitting there, not saying a word.

'Maybe the giants saw into the hearts of each other,' said Monkey suddenly, his eyes widening as he recalled what his grandfather had said about the masks.

His grandfather was dumbfounded. He had never thought Monkey was capable of such a deep insight. He nodded slowly and looked at the masks on the wall. He continued his tale to his grandson.

'After the battle, there was a great storm at the Great Mountain and there was so much rain, more than anyone could remember. As a result, the land grew rich with abundance and within a brief time, the forest returned to life and the castle by the lake virtually disappeared into memory and was consumed by the forest. The remains are still there, but only birds sing there now.'

'What did the one who could not be named look like?' asked Monkey quickly, as he had been thinking about it as soon as it was mentioned.

'Was he a monkey?'

His grandfather shook his head.

'No Monkey, he was no monkey, but he was the one who brought our clans into existence and was with us in the beginning. The first the giants knew or saw of him was the day he appeared to them to tell them to stop destroying the forests. For my whole life, it was my deep belief that the giants worship no one and that they have no respect for anyone except themselves. This belief is common to all animals, even raccoon-dogs. But I made a terrible discovery when I first arrived on this island Monkey, a terrible discovery.'

'What are you talking about grandfather? What terrible discovery?' inquired Monkey, his mouth open.

His grandfather sighed. He stood up and went to the wall that Monkey was hiding behind. He pressed a plank of wood and the wall opened. He stepped inside and was gone for a few minutes. He emerged with something wrapped in a purple cloth. He sat back down with Monkey. He looked at his grandson. He was surprised that he had mentioned his terrible secret to Monkey, for he had not told anyone else. He dared not. But for some reason, he knew that

Monkey would keep his secret like he kept his word. He had never shown this object to anyone in the clan, not even to his wife. It was a secret he thought to carry to his grave, but as he looked at this young monkey sitting next to him, he saw in Monkey something of his younger self, before he fell to the lure of the sword, power, and lust for control. The old monkey unwrapped what he held in his hands and Monkey could see it was a mask. He held it up and showed Monkey.

'The One who named us at the Great Mountain, who brought us life and who died fighting the giants, well, he looked like him.'

His grandfather held up the object in front of Monkey. It was a mask. The face was red, and a long, red nose came out of the face below two large, piercing eyes. As soon as Monkey saw the red face with the long red nose, he laughed. He laughed so loudly that he began to cough and needed to drink some tea. His grandfather was upset and rebuked him harshly.

'Monkey!' he said sternly. 'He is the one who named our clans, who deserves our absolute devotion and respect. He is the one who brought everything into being. Monkey, I am deeply disappointed.'

'But he has such a long nose, and it is really funny looking,' replied Monkey.

This seemed to infuriate his grandfather even more. 'Don't ever say anything like that Monkey. Even if you feel this way Monkey, you must resist the feeling. Everyone deserves the respect of others, no matter who they are or what they look like.'

Monkey tried to take away his smile. 'I'm sorry grandfather, I should not have laughed out loud.'

'Please never speak of this mask to anyone Monkey, this is a secret I have never spoken of with anyone.'

Monkey stared at his grandfather. 'I promise grandfather, 'he said. 'I will never speak of it.'

There was a long pause in their conversation. Monkey was the first to speak. 'Why would the giants have the mask of the one who named the monkeys in their hall? Did they worship him as well?'

'It is impossible. He comes from the Great Mountain, and he belongs to the monkeys and the other animal kingdoms. The giants come from a faraway land, across the sea. They believe in nothing but themselves.'

'And yet,' said Monkey, 'here he is.'

His grandfather looked at Monkey. He was right. Here he was, on the wall, next to the other masks. Why did the giants have his face? When did they meet him? Why would they worship him? These were the questions that had haunted him the day he saw the mask next to the others in the Hall of Masks. The answer was out there, somewhere, on the mainland and if he were to find it, he needed to go there, but he knew it was impossible. So, he pondered in the dark, holding the mask and looking at it under the dim light of a candle. He decided to leave the question with Monkey and return to the subject at some opportune time in the future. He had also said nothing about the Castle by the Sea, but his heart was already too full of sadness to broach that subject.

Monkey stared at the mask. He wondered why any creature would have a nose the size of this one and thought that it must have been the most inconvenient, especially when eating. But the more he looked at the mask there was something mysterious about the face, something familiar yet also foreboding. Monkey tried to hold all these new thoughts in his head.

He had woken up in the morning chasing beetles and finished the day learning more about his history than all other days combined. But then he had a deep thought. It was the kind of thought that comes from deep inside, near the stomach and rises into the head so fast that it produces an unusual kind of clarity. He realized that there was more to life than beetles and poems and eating ginkgo nuts. His grandfather had introduced him to a world he never knew existed. His grandfather noticed this, but he also realized that Monkey had listened patiently and quietly to what was an incredible tale and he felt that it was time for some relaxation.

'Why don't we go outside for a walk and continue our discussion there?' he said. Monkey nodded.

'And, on the way, we can have some more sweets.'

He pointed to a bag he kept by his side, away from the prying eyes of Monkey. Monkey was elated. He jumped up and ran out onto the balcony. His grandfather followed him. As they walked onto the grass, Monkey remembered that he had in his pocket a nice pebble to give his grandfather. He realized that he must have found the pebble when he forgot his sandals and as they left the Hall of Masks, he had completely forgotten about the beetle.

5.

The day of the wedding of Monkey's brother to his bride was also the day Monkey got himself lost in the hidden rooms of the Hall of Masks. As a result, he missed the wedding party though he was not noticed during the proceedings as the eyes of all present were unaware of the misadventure of the young monkey. It was not until nightfall when the first alarm was raised but by then Monkey had already by accident helped to answer one of the clan's deepest fears about the island's past.

The morning sun rose as it usually did, and Monkey was especially excited about the wedding party not so much because of the significance to the happy couple but because it was an occasion for much food. His grandmother and a few others had already spent the previous day preparing many different dishes, some with fruit and berries from the forest and some choice delicacies from the river, vegetables from the gardens and finally, on this morning, baked cakes. Monkey could already smell the aroma seeping out of the kitchen into his room. He squealed with delight. Today would be a wonderful day, he thought, a day to remember.

The wedding party was set for noon, and so Monkey had the morning free to do as he pleased. This was normally the case anyway, but he decided not to venture too far just in case he came back too late for the wedding feast, so he sat on the edge of the balcony and pondered what he should do. It occurred to him that he should make another visit to the Hall of Masks and the hidden room. His grandfather had arrived before he had the chance to fully explore this strange compartment. Monkey thought it might be a clever way to spend a few hours before returning next door to the wedding.

Monkey jumped off the balcony and walked down the path to the main road of the village, took a left and then a right, and walked up the steps to the Hall of Masks. At the top of the steps, he removed his sandals and placed them neatly side by side. He stepped onto the cool floor of the Hall and walked towards the hidden room. He did not glance at the masks this time, careful to avoid his gaze in their direction. The wall was easy to manipulate and as it slid forward, Monkey stepped into the room and the door closed behind him.

Monkey felt around the room with his hands. The wood was smooth to touch but also covered with cobwebs. This did not deter Monkey for spiders had never caused him trouble in the past and there was no reason for this to change in the dark room. Eventually, after feeling the length and breadth of the entire room, Monkey's hands found a side to one of the walls and pushed gently. A panel opened and suddenly a rush of wind blew past his face, stinking of old age and a strange smell he had not encountered before. This surprised him, but it added to the feeling of adventure. Monkey stepped forward and found himself at the top of some stairs. Behind him, the door closed suddenly. Monkey tried to open the door again, but it was to no avail. It would not move, nor could he find a panel that shifted. Monkey realized that he may not be able to return the same way and he began to worry. This was not such a clever idea after all, he thought.

Monkey walked slowly down the stairs. They were made of stone, but also seemed to be part of the ground so someone crafted them. The contours they made and the feeling to his feet made him realize that he was in a cavern. The smell was damp, like the aroma after rain and everything felt musty. Monkey realized that no one had ventured there for an awfully long time. Soon he found himself at the bottom of the steps and he stood in what seemed to be a large amphitheater.

Looking behind him, he could see the path he took to the bottom. The walls seemed to rise out of the ground revealing a large room. The dirt was beneath his feet and aside from the beating of his own heart he could hear nothing. Monkey sat down on the ground and listened to the sounds of the cave. He closed his eyes and felt the coolness and the solitude. He could not live in a cave he thought as he sat there because even though the cave brought a degree of quietness, there was something special about noise and tumult that made him feel alive. Monkeys dreaded caves for they stank and were dark, but Monkey did not mind either of these things, as they were just part of life.

His eyes quickly adjusted to the darkness and when they could see clearly, he saw something he did not expect to see. He saw many white sticks all over the place, like someone had scattered them. He went up to them and noticed that these sticks were large, much larger than he was. He found one which was about his own height, thick and strong and decided to use it as a walking stick.

He then followed his nose. For a monkey he had a remarkable sense of direction for monkeys are easily distracted by even the slightest smell or sound, but young Monkey had always been quite determined when he set his mind to something whether it was catching beetles or gathering food, though he never really did much of that. Rather, he would expect others to do that for him so he could benefit from all their hard work.

Monkey had walked a fair distance down the cavern and as he walked, he noticed the air had become quite stale and that it was becoming increasingly difficult to breathe easily. He decided that this was probably not a place where the original inhabitants dwelt. It was more likely to have been a passageway to some other place. His curiosity aroused, he walked faster but, in his haste, he slipped and fell down some stairs. When his tumbling stopped, he realized he was still holding the stick. He had fallen into another cavern. In this cavern the air was cleaner and fresher and seemed to be replenished by a wind which gushed past.

It was then that Monkey saw them. He had never seen them before, but they were made from wood, long vessels, many times his length, capable of carrying lots of monkeys at any given time. They were wide and made of thick wooden beams and sat on stone platforms that themselves had been chiseled and worn by many days labor and effort. Monkey saw tools on the wall and piled up at the edge, many sharp and interesting implements. Monkey thought of telling his grandfather when he saw something else quite remarkable at the end of the cavern.

He walked until the light outside burst in and blinded him. The air was clean and fresh, and he could look out across the trees, but they were not ordinary trees for they were mangroves and marshes. Monkey had found the river, which flowed past the bottom of this secret cavern, out to the ocean itself.

The river was not difficult to reach, but the mangroves and the swamp were so thick and the roots of the trees so precarious that his grandfather and those who arrived on the island would not have passed this way before. It would have been impossible for them to locate this place for the sharp and jagged rocks of the bottom of the cliffs would have hidden this tiny inlet. The air was also thick with mosquitos and gnats, bugs that easily torment even the most robust monkey.

Monkey surmised that those wooden items he saw in the cavern were meant to float on the water, but he also realized that it would take a great many monkeys to lift them up and drag them to the river's edge. Monkey stood near the edge of what might have been once the place where such endeavors took place, but the wooden beams and platform there had been much eroded. Monkey went to take a closer look at this most interesting platform, but the wood underneath his feet creaked and croaked and cracked and Monkey fell straight through into the water below.

It wasn't the water that caused concern for Monkey as he fell, but rather his appearance for he knew that he could not possibly go to the wedding covered in mud or smelling like the river, not least because there would be too many questions asked and too much concern made over his little adventure or to be more accurate, his misadventure. He had fallen into the water with a great splash and went right under, still grasping his stick.

It was about this time that the wedding party of his brother had been proceeding rather nicely. There were the speeches and the songs. Monkeys, it should be known, loved to sing, though whether it constituted singing or not was a matter for much dispute among most creatures of the forest. Birds sing because it is their nature, and so do a few other creatures for that matter, but monkeys do not naturally sing. Rather their singing is more of a kind of chaotic groaning cacophony of various kinds of sounds all jumbled together. It would be melodic if birds copied such sounds, but it was customary practice for birds to vacate the general area any time that monkeys began to sing. But on days like this, the monkeys were joyous for the son of the high priest of the clan was married and succession was secure.

The only one to be missing was Monkey and at this time, his mouth was full of water, and his fur was covered in slime and mud. For the next little while he conversed with a few frogs and even a green snake before climbing out of the water and onto the rocks. Monkey was to retrace his steps through the cavern and hopefully back to the Hall of Masks, or at least that was his intention. It took him longer than he expected.

His grandfather was the first to notice his absence. He organized a search party, breaking off the celebrations when all the usual haunts were found to contain no sight of his grandson. He started to become worried when the tracks led back to the Hall of Masks, for it should also be known that monkeys have a very keen sense of smell and can track anything in the forest. They do not emphasize this skill because monkeys feel that it distracts others from their more important contribution to the life of the forest, such as poetry and song.

But his grandfather put all that aside on this day and searched frantically for any sign of little Monkey. He had arrived at the steps to the Hall of Masks with a few warriors and some priests when a wet, grumpy Monkey appeared at the top of the steps, completely covered in mud with some pieces of reed clinging to him. He was still holding his white walking stick which was almost as tall as he was. When his grandfather saw him, his mouth opened in surprise until he saw the stick Monkey had by his side. All the others noticed it as well and knew it for what it was. Monkey, for his part felt quite embarrassed but pretended not to notice his dreadful circumstances and asked simply, 'Did you save any of the cakes for me?'

While Monkey was being scrubbed by his grandmother, his grandfather and some of the warriors of the clan went through the hidden passage, and down the steps, finding the cavern and the boats and the river, all as Monkey had said they would. They also found the pile of sticks as Monkey called them, where he said they would be, but no one spoke to him about their true name or where they probably came from, for this would have been too shocking for him to hear.

The stick was in fact a bone, probably a bone of one of the original inhabitants of the island, and the scattered sticks he found were the remains of skeletons that had been there for quite some time. The fact that the boats were still there suggested that the original inhabitants never left the island or the village and were not to return to reclaim their homes. The high priest and his two trusted generals carefully sifted through the remains of the bones until they came to a startling discovery. They arrived at this discovery by a careful examination of where the bones lay and what the figures seemed to be doing at the time of their deaths. It seemed quite apparent that all the giants died around the same time, perhaps at the same hour. They had, in fact, killed each other.

When the high priest was told this by his generals, he knew for the first time that at least a little piece of the historical record was true. He did not know for certain what else was true, but what he could plainly see was that the giants, in a moment of terror, turned on each other and murdered each other until they were all dead. But it was quite impossible.

These giants must have been a group that had broken away from the ones who built the Castle by the Lake. They had no way of knowing what happened that fateful day on the mainland, but maybe they sensed something was wrong, or maybe they saw the smoke from the fires going into the heavens. Whatever they saw, they decided to take the long climb down to the boats to get away from the island, but they never made it. Whatever madness overcame them killed them before they had a chance to leave, and they turned on each other in the caves until there was nothing left but the wind.

6.

Monkey rested for the next few days. His experience in the cave of bones kept him awake during the nights and so he was exhausted during the daytime. He was disappointed that he missed out eating all the cakes and delicacies of the wedding feast. This really gnawed at him as did his own personal disappointment that he ended up attracting a lot of unwelcome attention. He had just enough energy to wake up and eat breakfast but he found he no longer had any appetite for exploration or seeking beetles or small round stones and so he went each day and lay under the tree near the river.

He followed this habit for several days. On the third day, he found himself under the tree near the river once more. He tried to sleep but it was too difficult and so he lay there with his eyes closed as the sun rose and set out across the sky. His eyelids closed and he fell into a deep sleep, so deep that he thought that he was awake and sitting in the cave once more. The light bathed the cave and stretched out into the darkness.

It was then he heard the crunching of feet in the dark, the soft pressing of feet into the stones and the steps came closer. Monkey looked up and saw a dark figure standing there in front of him, covered from head to toe in a dark robe. The figure had no face. It was hidden under the hood. It stood silently in front of him as if it did not notice Monkey's presence. The figure turned to leave and so Monkey sighed in relief. At that moment, the figure turned back suddenly and looked at Monkey, tilting its head slowly to one side and back again as if it was trying to see who or what was there.

The hooded figure then reached out its hands towards him, and Monkey looked and saw that the hands were not hands, but bones, skeletal and without flesh. Monkey froze in terror as the skeletal hand stretched slowly towards him until its long fingers reached his fur. Monkey woke up in a fright and looked around. He was still on the side of the river. He could hear monkeys chatting nearby and the sound of birds in the trees. He quickly ran home.

That night, Monkey dared not sleep in case he had the same dream. He sat in bed, looking outside onto the veranda and the courtyard beyond. The night was still. The house was a lot quieter since his brother was married, so there would be no late-night rendezvous with his future wife. Even his grandfather seemed to spend less time in the Hall of Masks since their awful discovery of the cave of bones. Monkey found out about the bones by overhearing hushed conversation at home the day before. The moon was full, and the night was clear. Monkey thought of the strange, red-faced creature on the wall, the one with the extraordinarily long nose. Monkey wondered if he would ever see that creature in his lifetime, but he dismissed the thought as his grandfather had told him that this creature died in the fire at the Castle by the Lake. But his death certainly brought new life to the entire world, thought Monkey: the giants died, the land returned to abundance and the monkeys and racoon-dogs lived in peace.

It was at that point that Monkey realized that his grandfather never finished the story and never told him why they had come to the island and why they were not, in fact, on the mainland. If all was well, why hide on the island away from the other monkeys and far away from the Great Mountain?

The next day, Monkey awoke as usual and went for a morning walk around the hill, deciding to look for some unusual things to add to a new collection. It was a bright and sunny day, as spring was already in full swing and cherry blossoms were beginning to bloom around the Hall of Masks and along the river. The sun was especially bright, and the sky was a rich light blue. It was beautiful Monkey thought and looked up for an instant.

His eye caught something in the sky. It looked like a flower. Funny place for a flower, he thought, so he dismissed it from his mind. But he looked up again and sure enough, it was a flower. It was pink and had several petals and was being blown in the wind. As soon as he saw it, Monkey knew that this was his flower, it had come to him, and he would devote all his energy to obtaining it. He kept his eye on the flower and tried to jump up and catch it but alas it was always just out of reach.

After a while, Monkey realized that he was running further and further away from familiar sights and sounds. Eventually, he would have to stop, or he would not be able to go any further due to the scrub and the trees. He had passed the river by simply jumping over it and he ran quickly through the farmland and down the trails towards the beach where he went fishing. His trek took him past the fort by the edge of the forest that had recently been rebuilt and he saw some warriors training.

He reckoned that he had at least one or two more good jumps left. Monkey was getting tired, and his eyes were getting blurry because of the sun's glare. One last jump he thought and with all his energy, he jumped up high, and grabbed the flower and then fell back down to earth, but the earth had vanished from under his feet, and he found himself tumbling. He tumbled and he tumbled through the undergrowth and suddenly, he was at the bottom of the hill, past the fort and in the scrub.

He was disorientated. He looked around trying to find some familiar sight. He realized he was near the beach. Monkey stood up. His head hurt, as did the rest of his body. He was fortunate not to have broken his neck. Behind him was the descent and in front of him were scrubs and some mangroves, and underneath him sand and just beyond was the crashing of waves on the shore. He realized that he had taken a wrong turn, that instead of going to the right towards the rocks and his fishing ground, he took the left and ended up in the scrub he had always avoided.

While he was thinking about this, he realized that in his right hand, he held the flower that he had been chasing. He opened his hand slowly and found a crushed pink flower. Despite being pulverized by his hand, Monkey was immediately taken aback by its beauty. It was perfect, he thought, more than perfect. There was a lifetime of wisdom in these petals, thought Monkey and he couldn't contain his happiness. If only he knew the name of the flower, he thought, and his little face was puzzled. He decided it must be a kind of cherry blossom when suddenly realized he was not alone. He turned around. It was his brother.

'What are you doing here Monkey?' he asked sternly.

'I'm sorry,' said Monkey. 'But I fell down the hill chasing this flower.' He held the flower up in his hand to show him.

'I saw you fall,' observed his brother.

'What are you doing on the beach?' asked Monkey. It was an odd place for his brother to be. He thought he would have been training with his grandfather as he normally did in the morning. His brother didn't answer him but rebuked him harshly for wandering to the beach as the waves were especially strong. Monkey turned his best ear to the ocean waves, but he could hear nothing amiss.

'The waves sound normal to me,' said Monkey. His brother seemed agitated. 'Is everything alright?' he asked with genuine concern.

'Everything is fine Monkey,' said his brother. 'I suggest you go back home now, back to your pebbles and beetles.'

Monkey did not like the tone of his voice and did not like to be told to leave so he said that he would stay and walk down to the beach for a while and do some fishing. His brother protested, telling him that he did not have any fishing line, to which Monkey retorted that it would be easy for him to fashion a line if he wished and didn't know why his brother was so irritable on such a bright and sunny day. Monkey assumed that his brother must have had an argument with his wife and had come down to the beach to sulk for a while.

They soon passed through the scrub and came to the edge of the beach which stretched out in both directions. The sand felt warm to his feet and the sun beat down on their heads. The ocean was a deep blue and stretched out as far as they could see. He breathed in deeply. He loved the smell of the ocean.

Suddenly, Monkey's ears pricked up, as if a bee had bitten him. His eyes were fixed on the far end of the beach to the left, just around the headland. There was something moving. Monkey could not see anything because of the glare of the sun.

Monkey's brother turned to him. 'It is only some of the warriors training, Monkey,' he said. 'It is nothing to be concerned about.'

Monkey felt the presence of another creeping up towards him out of the sun. Monkey could not see clearly but he knew the voice. It was his grandfather's general, a monkey by the name of One-Ear. He was clothed in the traditional armor of the clan and a sword was on his belt. The old general looked at the son of the high priest, and then at Monkey.

'I came to tell you that your grandfather is looking for you Monkey. He has something to tell you.'

'Where is he?' asked Monkey.

'At the Hall of Masks,' said the general. Monkey's brother nodded and looked at Monkey.

'Hurry along,' added Monkey's brother, 'you can go fishing later. Go and find my father.'

It all seemed quite reasonable to Monkey and so he turned to leave. He said farewell to his brother and walked back into the scrub. Had he continued along this path his life would have been completely different and it is quite likely that he would never have left the island alive. Looking back many years later, he didn't know what made him turn around once more and crouch down and hide, but he did, and it made all the difference. Perhaps it was his inbuilt suspicion or the fact that he didn't want to be left out and didn't like being told what to do and that it seemed strange that the general would be sent to the beach to find Monkey when Monkey didn't go to the beach with any real intention of going there and had only arrived by accident. It seemed too strange. Monkey turned around, crouched, and sat down out of sight.

Monkey peered back to the beach through the branches. His brother and the general had walked down the beach towards the other soldiers who were training near the ocean. He could not see them for the glare of the sun. It all seemed quite ordinary and normal, and Monkey was about to dismiss his suspicions and emerge from his hiding place when he heard a growl, a deep, guttural growl. Monkeys used to growl quite often during the Ancient Order of Things, but at the time of Monkey, it was an unusual sound, and not often heard in polite Monkey society. A figure emerged out of the sun on the beach, clothed entirely in black. The figure leapt and crept along the length of the beach and stopped only a few paces from where Monkey and his brother and the general had stood moments before. The black figure froze. It was as if time had stopped. There was silence. Monkey could hear his own little heart beating.

Monkey stared at the strange creature crouching on the sand. It appeared to be looking at something, its head tilted to one side. It was small and seemed to be a similar height to Monkey, his brother and the general. Monkey then realized he was also looking at a monkey. Perhaps it was one of the warriors who had been training in some new costume and Monkey almost felt like standing up, but it just did not seem right.

While he was thinking this, Monkey could hear other sounds on the beach. They were crunching sounds, like something was squashing pebbles. Monkey looked and realized that a boat had landed on the beach, digging itself into the smooth grey stones. It was soon followed by others that came to a stop, one to the right and the other to the left of the first boat. They were much smaller than the ones he found in the mangrove swamp. He could see other figures shrouded in black. Some stood in or near the boats. It was then he saw his brother and the general. They were talking with the creatures in black as if they were old friends. Monkey saw more black figures walking towards the forest near his fishing ground.

It was then that Monkey saw it. He could not believe his eyes and so he squinted and opened his eyes again, but nothing had changed. Monkey saw a ship moored offshore. Monkey was astounded for he had never seen a ship or boat like this in his entire life, and he found it difficult to describe, let alone explain to someone else. It filled him with wonder and fear. It is impossible, he thought to himself. He tapped his head and rubbed his eyes but when he opened them, the ship was still there.

While he was thinking this, another creature joined the one crouched on the pebbles. He was tall and large, wearing strange clothes that fitted loosely around his body and carrying two swords. He was too far away to notice any clear features. His face was the strangest thing Monkey had ever seen. It was not that of a monkey, nor was it the face of one of the masks in the Hall of Masks. This giant had long hair which was tied at the back of his head, small and narrow eyes, shiny skin, and a long nose. His skin was unlike anything Monkey had ever seen. It was smooth and it shone.

The crouching figure looked up at this tall one when he arrived. Monkey felt that the two creatures had little respect for each other. The crouching figure in black spoke first. 'They are here. I can smell their foul odor,' he said.

The other one laughed. 'You all have the same odor,' he said rudely.

The crouching monkey snorted. 'You don't know anything about us, we are all different. We are royalty, these are common village folk, and they smell.'

'I really don't care about your crude distinctions general,' said the tall figure. 'The weather is good, but it can change quickly. Do what you came to do quickly and bring your prisoners to the beach.'

'We didn't come for prisoners,' said the monkey grinning. 'We came for revenge.'

The other seemed a little surprised. He looked out to the ocean. 'What of the traitors? Will you kill them?' he asked.

'No, of course not,' said the monkey. 'We are not like your masters, the giants, we keep our word. But they will have a much smaller kingdom once this is all over. The unimportant we will use to sharpen our swords. Our captains have already placed wagers on how many they can cut down. I have bet a month's wages.'

'Yes, you are right,' said the tall figure, changing the subject. 'We have a poor reputation where honesty is concerned.'

The monkey spoke again. 'Fickle or not, your master, the so-called emperor of the Castle by the Sea has kept your word to us. My master, my beloved emperor will be pleased.'

The tall creature laughed aloud. 'Your master, the so-called emperor of the monkey kingdoms will now have no obstacle standing in the way of his unyielding support,' he said. The tall creature stretched himself as he seemed exhausted.

'Don't kill all of them,' he advised, leaning on his sword, still looking out to sea. 'They are your own kin. Convince them to return to the mainland as prisoners. I am sure some will fight, but most wanted to stay on the mainland if my memory serves me correctly. After all, the traitors can lead them. They have nowhere to go.'

'Nobody likes a traitor,' retorted the monkey. 'Once betrayed, you can never trust them again.'

The monkey crouching on the sand stood up and moved closer to the taller creature.

'You are certainly not a giant,' said the monkey. 'You are smaller than they are, thinner and your skin is not the same. You must come from a different place across the ocean. Are they all like you? How else could you pilot the boat across the treacherous waters? No giant could do that. Their reflexes are too slow. The currents tossed and turned us many times, but you knew how to overcome every wave. It is a miracle the giants arrived from over the sea. Where are you from?'

The tall creature said nothing. The monkey shrugged his shoulders and grinned to himself. He scratched his neck and finding a flea, he ate it.

'I will accept this wise advice,' admitted the general. 'We will not kill the prisoners. We are not entirely without honor.'

'You are not giants,' said the tall creature. 'You are just one large family at war with itself.'

The monkey looked up at him scornfully. 'You talk too much human,' spat the monkey.

He growled a command in a strange tongue and soon a large group of warriors joined him, all in black. They bowed in deference towards their leader. Monkey thought that odd. He had never seen that before. He was also surprised at the language used. It was formal and old fashioned, and it sounded like the way his grandfather sometimes spoke to his wife and the older monkeys. But the creature standing with his long sword puzzled Monkey a great deal. What was he and where did he come from?

The tall creature, the crouching monkey and the warriors were in deep discussion when they were interrupted by a sound in the scrub. Monkey looked down at his feet and realized he had trodden on a branch. It had snapped. He turned to run. He heard the crunching of pebbles on the beach as the black-cloaked warriors began to pursue him. Monkey ran as fast as he could through the mangroves. When he reached the edge of the swamp, he tried to scramble up the embankment.

His little heart pounded as he reached for every branch to pull himself up the steep incline, and grasped for weeds, dirt, or rocks or anything that would aid his ascent. He was soon at the top of the incline. Out of breath, he staggered to the nearest bush and fell in front of it. He was still in the open, but he was so exhausted he could not move. Every muscle in his arms and legs were aching. He could hear voices and warriors climbing up the rocks. He could hear them panting and growling and they were angry. His body refused to move. He turned his head towards the bush next to him only to see two red eyes staring back. Monkey's eyes widened in disbelief. The red eyes blinked. They were not from a monkey, or any creature Monkey had ever seen. This creature was large with a long tail and seemed hidden under the scrub, lying flat with its eyes piercing the darkness.

'Come in here,' said the creature. 'Come in here, out of the sun, it is cool here and safe.'

Monkey did not know why, but he did exactly as the creature suggested and rolled himself under the bush until he was concealed and lying only a few inches from this new face. The red-eyed creature blinked. Monkey froze. Both lay under the bush while the warriors in black all ran past. They did not notice Monkey, nor did they suspect he was hiding. In a few moments, all was silent, and birds began to sing again. It could have been any other day. Monkey looked at the strange creature under the bush, with its eyes staring at him.

Monkey thought it quite rude that he had not already introduced himself. He was about to say that he was Monkey when the creature interrupted him.

'I know who you are Monkey,' he said, in a voice resembling none other than his grandfather. Monkey looked at the creature bewildered. It felt to him that he had known this creature before, that he had always known him.

'Who are you?' asked Monkey.

'Why do you ask my name Monkey?' replied the creature. Monkey did not know what to say. He thought it was a strange answer to a simple question.

'Listen to me Monkey,' said the red-eyed creature. 'You must go to the Hall of Masks and warn your grandfather. Find a conch shell and blow into it to sound the alarm. Your brother has betrayed you, his father, and his clan. All those nights you thought he was going to meet his beloved. He was meeting to plot against you, even when he gave you the knapsack of ginkgo nuts, he already decided your fate. He did not care whether you lived or died. On the day of the tsunami, the day of your birth, he could have saved your father, but he didn't. He wanted to be the next high priest and he will be. He may even be emperor one day if he gets his way. But then you will have to die.'

The creature thrust two things in front of Monkey. He looked in the dark and saw the glint of a sword. He pushed it aside.

'I will not take up the sword,' he said defiantly.

'Then you will never be emperor,' replied the creature firmly.

'I do not wish to be emperor,' replied Monkey. 'Life is a gift to be enjoyed. I will not take it, even if all around me take up the sword, I will not.'

The creature laughed to itself. 'You are really a true monkey,' it said. 'It is just like before. The wheel, it turns again.'

'What do you mean?' asked Monkey. The creature did not answer but put something else into Monkeys hands. It was long and hollow, light, and smooth. It had several holes along the side. Monkey ran his hand along the edge and realized it was made from bamboo.

'What is it?' he asked.

'It is a flute, fashioned in the forest, by me Monkey, long ago for a friend of mine. Learn how to play it and take it with you on your journey.'

Monkey thanked him cautiously.

'The end is coming,' said the creature. 'Today is just the beginning. Soon, the one you laughed at will be here, all things will die, and all things will be made alive once more.'

'I don't understand,' replied Monkey.

'It is as it should be Monkey,' said the creature. 'Not everything should be understood.'

The creature paused and then it spoke again. 'Your grandfather will not believe you, so tell him this. Tell him, the answer to his question is yes, the giants do worship the one whose mask he hides in his inner chamber. Tell him that.'

'How do you know about the mask?' asked Monkey.

The creature smiled again and began to blow with its mouth and Monkey was thrown out of the bush landing in the scrub. He stood up quickly and looked back under the bush, but he saw nothing. Monkey picked himself up and began to run towards home. He passed the fort that stood by the edge of the forest that led the way up to the village. It had been destroyed and all the warriors there were dead. He stood over the still corpses, and then he saw that one of them was holding a conch shell. He had not heard it so the warrior must have been killed before he had the opportunity to sound the alarm.

Monkey tried to lift it, but it was very heavy, so he tucked the bamboo flute in his belt and lifted the shell with both hands. He had to prop the shell up on the edge of a large flat rock. He breathed in and put his lips around the shell and blew as hard as he could, but he made no sound. He panted heavily and breathed again, but once more he had no success. Monkey sighed and looked at the shell. There must be a way, he thought and breathed in again. This time, a weak sound emerged from the shell. This encouraged him and so with all his effort, he blew the conch shell again and a strong, deep sound bellowed forth. It seemed to rise into the air and was carried up the hill towards the village.

Monkey blew the conch shell several more times before he stopped, completely out of breath. He heard nothing but then suddenly he heard the bell ringing, the bell that was near the Hall of Masks, the only bell in the entire village. He had been successful in raising the alarm. When he was thinking this, an arrow flew past his head so close that it scratched the side of his face. Monkey turned around and far away, near the scrub was his brother, standing with the general and the warriors in black. His brother grinned at him and began to put another arrow in his bow. His warriors leapt forward on all fours, and Monkey knew he had to leave, he had to flee for his life. Monkey jumped over the fort ruins and ran on towards the village, never looking back.

7.

As he ran, his mind was full of confusion, sadness, and anger. His own brother, a traitor. It did not seem possible, but he could not dispute it, it was self-evident. But why? He had grown up with him and his brother did not seem to express any hatred towards him at all. Monkey thought he knew his brother, if he ever knew anyone, but now it seems he hid under a mask, a false face that hid his true feelings. Monkey thought it duplicitous and conniving and false, and with each step he wept for his brother, tears running down his cheeks.

When Monkey reached the edge of the village, the war had begun in earnest. The invaders and the defenders were locked in fierce fighting in the fields and along the paths. There was complete confusion. Monkeys were scattered, homes were on fire and Monkey could see fear on the faces of everyone he met. The older ones were protecting their families while the younger ones were taking up their swords and joining the fight. Some of them called out to Monkey for him to help them but he said nothing and did nothing to help them. He only had one goal, to get to the Hall of Masks. He ran into one of the priests, a monkey who had been there when he cut his hand on the sword. He grabbed Monkey with intense anger.

'You have brought calamity upon all of us!' he wailed and shook Monkey violently, knocking the breath out of him. Monkey wrenched himself free. The priest turned to some monkeys standing nearby. 'Here is the harbinger of death, as we all predicted, the one without name has still brought disaster upon our village. He is cursed!'

Monkey slapped him across his face. He was going to say something but decided to keep running.

'We are all doomed, thanks to the traitor Monkey!' wailed the priest and staggered aimlessly down the path until an arrow came out of the scrub and struck him in the chest. He looked down and saw the arrow. He staggered around and saw the one who launched it from his bow. His face was one of astonishment and horror. He fell to the ground dead. The son of the high priest sauntered towards him and stood over him.

'Soon, the old regime will be dead, and I will be in charge. Once we leave this wretched island, I will be emperor.'

He turned to One-Ear who stood next to him. 'Bide your time master,' cautioned the old soldier. 'This may take some years, so bide your time. We first need to usurp the pretender. Your father did not have the stomach for it, but I see that you do. You certainly do.'

Eventually, Monkey reached the Hall of Masks. He could not see his grandmother anywhere but was greatly relieved when he saw his grandfather standing on the top of the steps of the Hall. He was giving instructions to priests and soldiers alike. Monkey ran up to him and hugged his legs. His grandfather bent down and lifted him up.

'I am so glad to see you safe, young Monkey,' he said happily. 'Someone rang a conch shell and so we began to ring the bell. It seems the village is under attack,' said his grandfather. 'There is nothing for you to worry about. I think there must be a misunderstanding.'

Monkey wrestled himself free and fell to the floor. He was astonished at what his grandfather had just said.

'We are under attack!' Monkey blurted out frantically. 'They come from the mainland. There were several boats I could see on the beach and there was a much larger boat just offshore. They are led by warriors in black and by a tall giant, whose face I have not seen before. Your son is leading them as is old One-Ear, the general. Who knows how many he has on his side?'

The old priest laughed. 'I have never heard anything so ridiculous Monkey, and so outrageous, that my own son is trying to kill me.'

Another monkey overheard the conversation. It was the other general, One-Eye. He came up to the high priest.

'It makes sense to me,' he said to the priest. 'Old One-Ear and his regiment have disappeared, and your son is nowhere to be found.'

'My son is loyal to me, and he is not a traitor,' insisted the high priest.

'He has ambition, your son, you know,' insisted One-Eye. 'So did One-Ear, long ago before we came here, you remember, in the old days, he sought greater power. He must have convinced your son, and in any event, your grandson Monkey would have no reason to lie.'

'Of course, he does,' retorted the old priest. 'All monkeys lie.'

'Not your grandson,' insisted the general. 'He may waste his time with beetles and pebbles and fishing, and he may be unable to hold a sword, but he is not a liar. He is always honest. You know that and I know that. He wears no masks to hide himself from others. He is who he is, and he is the same to all, that is why you have always feared him. His honesty goes deeper than his bones. He would make a better priest than any who have gone before us.'

The old priest looked at his general and then looked at Monkey. It was as if his mind changed in mid-breath. He breathed out deeply.

'I stand corrected old friend,' he said. He turned to Monkey. 'I'm sorry Monkey, I did not believe you,' he said. 'I just find it hard to believe that my son is against us. He is my son, why would he do this terrible thing?'

Monkey appreciated the apology but didn't have an answer to this question. 'What do you want me to do?' he asked. 'I will not take up the sword, even in this battle.'

'And you don't need to,' interrupted the general who stepped forward. 'Listen Monkey, let me tell you a secret about war. A great general rarely uses his sword anyway. You can be the greatest warrior without even lifting one.'

'Not that peace-loving rubbish again,' said the high priest with contempt.

'I am not speaking nonsense. Use what you have,' he said to Monkey. 'What do you have?'

Monkey produced his bamboo flute and handed it to the general who took it and looked at it with admiration.

'It is a rare flute. I used to play one when I was young. It is a ritual flute, used for various ceremonies, ancient ceremonies –'

He stopped. He stared at the flute in amazement and handed it to the high priest. 'Look at the inscription,' he said softly.

The priest looked at it and then back at the general who was also astonished.

'It is impossible! It is a new flute. It looks like it was just crafted but the shrine where the flute claims to have been made was destroyed years ago when the forest burned, when the giants first came to this land, the days before the Castle by the Lake fell. In fact, this shrine, near the ocean, was where the war began. Where did you get this Monkey?'

'I was given it, near the beach, when I was hiding from your son and the invaders, a red-eyed creature gave it to me.'

'Was it a monkey?' asked the general.

Monkey shook his head.

'He sounded familiar, and he wouldn't give me his name.'

His grandfather crouched down and held Monkey. 'What did you ask him and what did he say?'

Monkey said that he asked him his name, but the creature replied, 'why do you ask me my name?'

Monkey's grandfather fell back and sat down, crossing his legs. 'He didn't give his name,' he said. 'Is it true? Are all things about to die?'

'What are you talking about?' asked Monkey.

'The old scrolls tell us the answer in poetry,' replied the general. 'All the kingdoms know these verses: 'when the air is still, a flute sounds by the sea, by the bridge no one can cross.' I think they are the words. They talk about the return of the One who named us all and whose name we do not speak. His return marks the end of all life and its renewal, so that it is not the same as before.'

Monkey suddenly remembered what the strange creature had told him to tell his grandfather. 'Grandfather,' he said. 'The one who did not give his name told me to tell you something.'

'He mentioned me by name?' asked his grandfather, surprised.

Monkey nodded. 'The strange creature told me to tell you that you were right. The one on the mask, with the red nose is worshipped by the giants.'

'What is he talking about?' asked One-Eye. 'Who is worshipped by the giants? I thought they worshipped only themselves.'

The high priest just sat there, staring into space, as if completely dazed. The bell continued to ring, and smoke began to rise into the air from dozens of homes now burning.

Suddenly, the door to the Hall of Masks slid open and a black warrior lunged forward towards them, his sword drawn. One-Eye snatched the flute from the priest and struck the cloaked warrior on the back of the head with such force that he was thrown down the stairs and hit the dirt. He staggered to his feet but held his head in pain and promptly fell dead. Monkey was speechless.

'That is how you fight when you don't have a sword Monkey,' he said, returning the flute to him. 'This is how our ancestors fought before the giants came, before swords, spears and bows.' He crouched down to Monkey's height.

'Keep the flute safe, go to the shrine and play the flute there and you may meet the One who will bring life again to this dying world. May you live to see the sunrise on that day and remember us.'

The general rose and turned to the high priest who was still lost in his thoughts. He hardly noticed the sudden attack by the cloaked warrior. One-Eye shook him roughly to rouse him.

'Old friend,' he said. 'You were banished because you became too much like the giants. You almost defeated them and drove them back into the ocean. I remember our forge and our foundry, and the secrets and skills those ocean monsters taught us. Our warriors smuggled as much as we could to this island in case this day ever came, and now it is upon us. Shall I go to the armory at the back of the Hall of Masks and find the black powder?'

The high priest grinned and looked up. 'Ah yes, the black powder. We were wise to bring some with us. It is dry, and in a barrel next to an old mask that has suddenly become important to me, but now, it is too late.'

The general laughed. 'We have no need of masks today. Let us face our enemy one last time, with our faces to the front, our eyes open and our hearts ready.'

'What about Monkey?' asked the high priest. 'He should be kept safe and far away from danger. He is the last of my line, the youngest of my blood.'

The high priest turned to his grandson. The news the red-eyed creature had given him had destroyed his faith and rendered null and void his pointless war against the giants who, for whatever reason, also worshipped the one who named the monkeys at the Great Mountain. Why didn't he consider this a possibility? In all those years pondering and plotting in the darkness of the Great Hall, why was his mind so closed to the idea that the one who named the monkeys might have also touched the lives of the giants? He was blinded by his beliefs that only his people were touched by the ocean spirit and for the first time in his life, he felt ashamed that he had taken up the sword.

He was grief-stricken that his youngest son was full of hate and a desire for power. One-Ear, the general was a malcontent and full of anger, and under his nose an old friend corrupted his son. He lifted his ears to the sounds of war. They were getting closer. This was his last battle. The invaders were about to overrun the entire village. It is likely that none would survive.

His only hope was to kill as many of his enemies as possible. This way, Monkey, and some of survivors might have a chance to escape using the boats his grandson found in the cavern. Swords, spears, bows were of no use. He needed to finish the war with the black powder. It had been given to him by one of the giants on the mainland long ago. Given might have been an overstatement. He had in fact stolen the powder from under their rather large noses once he realized what it had been used for and smuggled it to the island in barrels that were supposed to contain food. When lit, the powder would flash and explode and burn anything around it.

The high priest realized he had enough of the powder left to cause an explosion that would destroy the Hall of Masks and anyone inside. If the invaders knew about the secret passageway down the rock tunnel to the boats at the bottom of the cliffs, in the mangrove swamp, then it was certain that more would be climbing as he pondered what to do. Some of the boats must have gone around to the other side of the island and found the staircase leading up to the secret door in the Hall of Masks. He knew there was so little time left and so much to do, but his time had run out.

'Take Monkey with you to the old bell. Get our warriors to join me here. Our families will have to contend for themselves. Our enemy might show mercy. We will make our last stand at the Hall of Masks.'

'What will you do?' asked the general.

'I will get the black powder and then face my son when he appears. We have an unfinished conversation.'

The general grinned politely, with tears in his eyes. He bowed deeply to the high priest. 'It has been an honor your majesty to serve you all these years.'

'Your majesty?' asked the priest surprised. 'You have not called me that in years. My brother, the emperor was not blessed with such loyalty as I have enjoyed from you all these years my old friend.'

'Well, please hear it from me, one last time,' said the general. He turned to Monkey. 'You heard your grandfather's words: we have to go.'

Monkey looked up at his grandfather. After this is all over, can life go back to normal?' he asked.

'Of course!' lied the priest. It was the worst lie he had ever told. He knew that they would never see each other again. 'I just need to keep you safe and out of harm's way.'

Monkey nodded and hugged his grandfather and turned to leave.

'Monkey, I want you to hide there at the bell tower until morning. Do not come out for any sound. Wait until morning. Do not let anyone see you and say nothing. Can you do that?'

Monkey said that he could and that he would. He would stay there until the danger had passed. Monkey ran across the field and the long grass with One-Eye, and they arrived at the old bell. There were two warriors there still ringing it, but they stopped when they saw the general. He told them what the high priest had said, and they climbed down from the bell tower, put on their sandals, and picked up their swords and tucked them in their belts. They looked at Monkey but did not speak to him. They spoke with the general and ran off into the long grass towards the Hall of Masks.

'Listen Monkey,' said One-Eye. 'You are safest here at the bell tower. We will return to the battle now. I will come back here when the war is over.'

Monkey nodded. He left his sandals at the bottom of the steps to the bell tower and climbed up the small stone platform. He sat on the edge with his feet dangling over. Behind him was the sheer drop of the cliffs and in front of him was a field of long grass leading to the Hall of Masks.

'You should stay out of sight for the time being,' insisted the general, 'it is really too dangerous.'

He looked at Monkey. There was so much he wanted to say, but he needed to leave. He bowed quickly to Monkey and disappeared into the long grass.

Suddenly everything fell silent. There was no wind and the birds stopped singing. The bell had been ringing for so long that its sound still echoed in Monkey's ears. The smoke continued to rise from some of the buildings and Monkey could smell the burnt wood.

He felt sad. He was sad because his brother had betrayed everyone. He was sad because everyone was killing each other, and he was sad because his short life on the island was coming to an end. He did not want to leave but he also had no interest in fighting. He had no interest in taking up a sword and killing another monkey. He even had some reservation about hitting someone on the head with his bamboo flute. There was so much violence and it seemed all completely unnecessary.

The island had everything they needed. Why did his brother want to be emperor, whatever that meant? Why couldn't he just live a normal life and be content with what he had? He had a family who loved him, a wife and maybe children one day and a beautiful island where he could fish and run and explore. From the conversation he overheard on the beach, he didn't know his brother anymore. He had become a stranger. In his heart he was a different monkey entirely. The reality was that his brother, or his uncle had spent his life hiding behind a mask so deep that no one could see his real identity.

8.

Monkey continued to sit on the steps of the old bell. In early afternoon, clouds began to swirl in the sky above him. It was all quiet. The long grass began to sway in the wind. The sound it made was a rustling sound as if all the grass stalks were chattering to each other. Monkey wondered what they would make of the day's events. They grew here before the monkeys came and would be here long after they left, he thought. The clouds were gathering above him and not before long, there was a flash of lightning, a short pause and then a peal of thunder. It began to rain. He moved off the steps and under the bell tower where he could take refuge from the rain. He lay down as he was tired and soon fell fast asleep, though he tried to stay awake as long as possible.

Monkey awoke to a clap of thunder, and it startled him. For a moment he forgot where he was. He rubbed his eyes and remembered. It was strange to him that everything was dark. He must have slept past dusk and the twilight of the evening. He could not see the outline of the Hall of Masks. No lights shone through its sliding doors or in the courtyard. He heard no voices. The smoke coming from the village seemed to have stopped, though its pungent smell was still in his nostrils. There was no commotion, no sounds, nothing. He could see the tops of the grass stems blowing in the wind as the rain continued to fall. It made a nice sound as it bounced off the tiles on the bell-tower roof. Monkey looked out into the rain.

He was not sure, but for a moment, he thought he saw something, a movement, a shadow in the long grass. It must have been his imagination, he thought to himself. His eyes narrowed and darted backwards and forwards. There is something there, he thought to himself. Perhaps it was his grandfather walking towards him, or One-Eye. Yes, thought Monkey, that must be the answer. His grandfather was bringing him good news. Maybe the battle was over, the traitors had been captured and all was well. His anxiety disappeared. He sat back down on the floor of the bell tower.

A few moments later there was a flash of lightning and a roar of thunder. Monkey looked across the long grass and for a moment could see several black shadows only a hundred paces away. They were all crouched in the grass, creeping slowly towards the belltower. Monkey knew at once they were not his grandfather, or the general. They were not coming. If they were to come at all, they would have arrived by now. Monkey realized that the ones creeping in the grass must be some of the black figures he had seen on the pebbled beach, soldiers of the monkey who crouched beside the tall stranger with the long sword, the enemy.

He then realized that these creatures had somehow discovered his hiding place and they had come for him. He had been careless. He did not stay out of sight. His little heart began to pound. He looked around for another place to hide. There was none, no bucket, no hidden door, no tree, only a belltower surrounded by grass. He dared not enter the grass for the creatures could be anywhere. They could be waiting for him. He looked up. The bell sat above him, hanging from the roof. It was within reach, but he would have to jump.

He made his decision and leapt up to catch the edge of the bell and clung onto it with his hands. He did not realize it, but the bell began to sway, and it swung so far that it bumped the wooden stick hanging next to it. This was the wooden stick tied by rope to the roof, designed to strike the bell at times of celebration, remembrance or danger. The sound of the bell echoed in his ears, and it echoed across the island piercing the silence. If the enemy didn't know he was at the bell tower, they did now. Monkey turned his eyes back to the grass. It was difficult to see but he thought the figures were coming closer.

He climbed up the bell, using the ornate engravings of the bell as support and reached the top. The bell was tied by strong rope to a wooden cross beam that sat in the middle of the structure, covered by old clay tiles. Monkey reached up and tried to dislodge some of the clay tiles closest to him. Monkey could hear the creatures more clearly now. They were bounding now towards the belltower making strange grunts and growls. The tiles easily came apart and he moved them away.

In a few moments, he had made himself a hole large enough for his body to squeeze through and immediately the rain gushed through and splashed on his face. Eventually he climbed through it onto the roof. The rain fell on him strongly and he was surprised at its ferocity. He had never been in such rain before. When it rained in the past, he would always take shelter from it or if he were with his family, they would have an umbrella or raincoat. But this was torrential rain and it hurt his face as it fell like pebbles.

The very moment he pulled himself up, two creatures leapt onto the bell tower platform where he was sitting moments before, snarling, and growling, their claws scratching the stone. For a moment, Monkey felt safe on the roof. He peered through the hole in tiles which he had made, and the dark creatures prowled around the belltower calling to each other in words he did not understand. He was sure they were monkeys at the beach, but their strange speech and behavior made him question this completely. He saw one of them look up to the small hole he had made and previously climbed through. Monkey could see his eyes. This one motioned to the others. The two creatures jumped onto the bell and began to swing on it so they could climb up through the same hole Monkey made.

Suddenly there was a large crack as the wooden beam holding the bell in place fractured. All the bell ringing had weakened the beams. Monkey realized that he did not remember anyone ringing the bell so many times before. All the movement and excitement of the day must have weakened the joints in the tower. Monkey began to jump up and down on the roof of the tower to further weaken it. The bell suddenly rang again, its echo floating out across the grass field.

Two of the dark creatures were on the bell, moving it violently and unnaturally from one side to the other, eager to find leverage so they could climb up. There was a growl from below and in fright Monkey fell back onto the roof. A hand crept up through the tiles and Monkey came face to face with one of the creatures. His face was all but covered by a bandana made of cloth and he could see two little eyes which met his. Monkey grabbed one of the clay tiles next to him on the roof and thrust it into the face of the creature with all his strength. The creature howled terribly and fell back through the hole in the roof, onto the bell, causing it to ring once more, swinging violently and unnaturally. There were several more loud and awful cracks in the wood that shook the entire tower before the bell came loose and fell to the stone floor beneath squashing one of the creatures beneath it.

Suddenly, there was a growl in the mist and Monkey saw a shape rising into the sky, already swirling with dark rain clouds. It flew with its arms outstretched and landed crouching on the edge of the roof with a loud thud. The creature immediately discovered the perils of the roof, feeling the slats with its hands and looking up menacingly to Monkey. It began to crawl up the roof. Monkey reached around near his feet and dislodged a piece of tile. Out of desperation, he threw it at the creature on the roof, hitting him on the head. The creature wailed with a terrible cry. It clutched its head and lurched back. Monkey found some more tiles and then others. The more he loosened the more unstable the roof became. He found an unusually large tile and needing both hands he tossed it with force at the warrior on the roof.

The tile landed just a few feet in front of the creature but with a crack it dislodged several rows of tiles. They began to recede, just like the tide on the beach going out to sea. The creature clutched desperately at the roof tiles, but they were tumbling and soon so was the creature right off the roof and down to the ground. Monkey sighed with relief as it did not seem to move again. He fell back onto the roof exhausted.

He then looked up into the sky and saw something very strange. He saw the clouds joining and they seemed to be tying themselves into a knot of varying streams of grey and white. The clouds began to fall toward the earth in the form of a funnel as if a finger from the heavens was pulling them down. The funnel began to spin and spin and spin. Monkey quickly became dizzy just looking at it and it began to suck air into itself, drawing more of the sky towards the funnel in ever swirling fury.

It was a whirlwind.

This funnel of air, cloud and cold was gathering force and seemed to hover above the ground as if asking permission to land on the earth. But Monkey did not see what happened. He heard a sound beneath him and realized another creature was creeping up the other side of the roof, much more cautiously this time. Above them, the rain continued to beat down, but the wind was becoming more ferocious as more currents were caught up in the whirlwind.

The air itself began to cry out and Monkey wondered if he heard voices. Were they the voices of the past, ancient creatures long ago, or were they the voices of those fighting in the village beyond or perhaps they were voices from his future? He did not know. He was finding it more and more difficult to stand up. The wind forced him to his knees, and it seemed to be pressing him down further.

It was at this point that the creature had reached the top of the roof and crawled over the tiles so it could stand. It was only a few paces away from Monkey and due to the roar of the wind he could not see the danger he was in. The creature was ready to pounce. It stretched out its claws and licked its lips.

It was then that Monkey felt a tingling in his ears, a tingling that seemed to go right down inside to his very being. He shook his head and immediately there was a huge flash of light and heat followed by a pulse of power that went right through him. The creature behind him felt a searing hot beam burn into him and it killed the warrior immediately. His scream was terrifying as if he absorbed all the terrors of the night in one instant. As for Monkey, the full force of the lightning bolt struck the roof and Monkey was thrown forward onto the roof tiles face down and fell unconscious.

When he awoke, he found that he was not on the roof of the bell tower, nor was he anywhere he had known before. He was in a forest. There was an eerie silence. He was seated on what seemed to be a large stone, surrounded by other stones, some heaped together neatly piled on each other and others in the scrub, as if they had been tossed aside. Next to him was a fox or something else. He could not tell. Her image seemed to change. She looked tall with long flowing hair. She seemed similar in appearance to the creature Monkey saw on the beach that morning, leaning on the sword. There was a rabbit, with long, floppy ears, but he was wearing two swords tucked into his belt. He saw himself, but he seemed older, and he had his flute tucked into his belt, sitting on the rock. Everyone was happy and laughing. Monkey looked behind him and saw a tall creature with a long nose and round eyes and red face. It was the creature in the Hall of Masks, the one of whom Monkey's grandfather spoke. No one asked him who he was or what he was doing there, they simply accepted his presence with them.

Then Monkey saw the strange animal he met in the scrub that very morning, the one with the red squinting eyes. He smiled at Monkey.

'How swiftly do the seasons change, a morning of joy followed by an evening of sorrow. It is here you wander off Monkey and this is the day it all changes. This is the day your fellowship and friendship end.'

'What must I do?' asked Monkey.

'Don't wander off!' ordered the red-eyed creature, and Monkey looked, and he saw himself get up off the stone and walk into the forest. Monkey called out to himself to stop walking but to no avail.

He then woke up in a cold sweat and found himself back on the roof of the bell tower and the rain falling on him furiously. Next to him, the corpse of the creature who tried to kill him lay silent, half hanging off the roof. The sound of the wind was pierced by a huge clap of noise, and the sky lit up like the sun.

Monkey looked over and thought he saw the Hall of Masks explode into a thousand pieces or was it the whirlwind tearing it apart, throwing its wooden beams into the air? Monkey couldn't tell. In a moment, there was nothing left except ruins. The whirlwind changed course and started to move across the long grass towards him, but he didn't have the energy to move. The lightning bolt had rendered him virtually immobile, and he found even lifting one arm an impossible task.

The whirlwind reached the bell tower and shook it violently. The tiles on the roof began to scatter like leaves blown by autumn winds. Monkey was lifted into the air; his body limp and he was spinning around like the tiles. The whirlwind carried Monkey higher and higher into the sky. Monkey felt strange, but not dizzy. He did not feel cold, but he could feel the wind passing past his fur, through his fingers, between his toes, between the tufts of hair on his head. He was not spinning, though he thought so at first. He was floating, as if walking in the sky, though he was not moving his legs. It was a feeling that filled him with wonder, comfort, and fear, all at the same time. He had never felt these emotions all at once before, these emotions were normally so opposed to one another, but they felt in harmony, in balance, and in right proportion.

He relaxed his fingers that had been clenched together to form two little fists and for the first time opened his mouth and breathed in the air. It was cool and warm at the same time, and it felt like coming home, or enjoying a delicious meal, or watching something beautiful. He found that he was beginning to laugh. It was a happy sort of laugh, not the kind that pokes fun at another's misfortune, nor the kind that scoffs, but the kind of laugh one makes when doing something well or reaching a destination.

'Why do you laugh Monkey?' asked the voice in a deep, resonating tone that seemed to come from the heart of the whirlwind.

'I laugh because I am happy,' said Monkey.

'Why are you happy?' asked the voice, softly and gently.

'Because I'm home,' said Monkey.

Monkey opened his eyes, and he looked up. He realized he was being held in the arms of a tall, strange being and he was sitting on a raised platform in a room full of straw mats which seemed to go on forever. Monkey felt safe in his arms but did not know why. His face looked kind, and Monkey sensed that this was an important creature but did not understand why he felt this. He had never seen this creature before, nor could his eyes explain what he was seeing.

'The whirlwind,' he said softly.

'Yes, Monkey, the whirlwind brought you here. You are safe now.'

'How do you know my name? Have we met before?' asked Monkey.

'I knew you before you were born Monkey,' he said. 'Before the mountains filled with water, before the pebbles you collected took their smooth shape.'

Monkey was surprised, but also not surprised. It was the strangest feeling. The creature placed Monkey down on what seemed to be the ground. The floor was cool to his feet and as his eyes looked up, he realized that he was in huge hall, made of the newest wood, with that wonderful fresh smell. There were sliding doors all around the hall, some were open, but others were closed, and the sun was shining through the squares and the paper-thin screens. In the middle of the room was a stand and upon the stand was a scroll. It was a thick scroll, and it was open.

'Take a look Monkey,' said the creature.

Monkey ran across to the scroll and stood up on a stool to read the page. His little eyes traced the names down with his fingers, reading names to himself until he stopped.

'I have found it!' exclaimed Monkey 'Here is my name: Monkey!' Monkey looked closer and discovered some writing next to his name. 'What does this say?' he asked, not being able to read it.

'That, my dear Monkey, is your future, yet to be written,' he said.

'My future?' asked Monkey.

'So, is my future already written down?' Monkey asked.

'Yes and no, but only in the future, looking back will you understand it,' said the voice.

Monkey looked back to the scroll, but it was gone. He was standing on an open field of grass. He turned around and the grass field stretched out as far as he could see in every direction. He felt for his bamboo flute but when his hand came to his belt, he felt a sword tied to his waist. He recoiled in horror and tried to push it away, but as much as he struggled, the more it seemed to resist his efforts.

With all his strength he managed to wrest it free and with great effort drove it into the ground and stood back. It wavered tall in the grass. In the distance he saw a great army coming towards him. They all had swords tied to their belts and Monkey had just cast his aside. He felt alone, alone as he could ever be, but he did not feel sad. He felt that he needed to be here, that all his days led to this day, to this point, but beyond it he could see no further.

'Why am I here?' he called out to the wind. 'What do you want me to do?'

But no voice answered him. Everything around him was vanishing and he could feel again the warmth of the wind through his fingers and his hair and his toes. He had the distinct impression that he was moving downwards and looking down, he saw green, the color green and the color blue and he thought he heard a voice calling, and a splash and then all was dark.

9.

He was a Fisher, a creature of the swamp, the river, the mangroves, and the forest. The Fisher was green, with long legs, arms, and fingers. He had flowing hair and slimy skin. He spent so much time in the water since he was born that he was usually wet during most of the day. If he wasn't swimming in the river, he was wading in the swamp or walking in the forest and dipping himself in one of the many hot springs located there. He knew every tree personally, their age, their condition and the names of every bird and animal in the forest. They all knew his name as well, though none dared speak it. It was an ancient name, formed long before the kingdoms devised written word, it was more breath than form, more silence than speech, for his name was like the wind that blew between the trees at evening.

The Fisher himself had long since forgotten his name as it reminded him of events long ago, terrible events, events that the growth of trees, moss, fern, and flower could not extinguish. These events were engraved in their cells, burnt into their ancient memory. For the Fisher, it was just yesterday when the forests had been planted. He didn't know when that was, for he emerged out of the mist in the hills one day young and found the forest ancient in stature and beauty. But his forest, the forest he had tended for as long as he could remember was still young, and the trees were thinner and younger, while the moss, beautiful as it was, was tender and fragile.

The Fisher had been irritated for a long time. He expected the trees to be taller and thicker and their canopies wider and more abundant with birds. The migrations had been fewer and fewer for years, and many familiar faces and families never returned from the depths of the lands beyond. Deep inside his soul he knew the answer and it irritated him.

One such morning, he arose early as usual. The morning sun

broke through the canopy and enveloped him with warmth. It was not a day for fishing, he thought to himself, but a day for waterfalls. He decided to walk through the forest to his favorite waterfall. He had gone there often when he was younger. The sound of water rushing over the cliff into the ponds below made him feel relaxed. He loved to sit under the cascade and let the water fall on him.

Fresh river water, especially after a good rainfall was invigorating. He was thinking of the morning activities when along the forest path he noticed several large footprints in the dirt. His heart sank. He had hoped to go through at least the morning without remembering them, but not today. He looked around and sure enough, at the top of the hill was a giant, tending to some young trees.

He noticed that this giant was the shortest of the three, but he was a giant nonetheless and his grubby footprints were all over the moss. The giant had noticed him as well and immediately bowed deeply. The Fisher yelled some nasty words at him and went on his way quickly. Seeing the giant made him irritated all morning, even when he sat under the waterfall. He splashed the water in anger. He looked up at the forest. So young, he thought, so young. He remembered a time long ago when the trees were so tall and wide and strong, when the sound of birds could be heard in every space of the canopy, and the scurrying of little creatures and insects filled his ears.

He lifted one of his long, elongated ears to the forest and listened to the sounds. He could hear the eagle and saw it soar across the sky, surveying the ground for prey, he heard the crow, and he heard the owl. He smiled. The owl was back, he thought as he had not heard it for some time. But the sounds of these three birds made him lament the absence of other birds whose calls he had not heard for years. All the little birds were long gone, their chirping but a memory. The forest was like a deserted village where no one was home. He sighed to himself and dived into the pool of water at the bottom of the waterfall. When he emerged from the water, he heard a voice in the wind.

'When will you forgive them?'

'Never,' said the Fisher. 'Not until every tree is back in its place.'

'There are only three of them left,' said the voice. 'It is time to look to the future.'

'I cannot forget the past,' said the Fisher, ignoring the voice, jumping out of the pool. He went to a cave in the forest and brought out his fishing rods. He walked to the river. He decided to go fishing and wanted to forget that his day had been ruined by the sight of one of the giants. He had many different rods to catch various kinds of fish and he had many different strategies for catching them. He prided himself on being a good fisher, and all around knew him as such. He was not given to anger, but sometimes when his line was caught on a branch or he lost a catch due to back luck, he was known to huff and sigh.

After a few hours, the Fisher was able to catch some fish and he was content. He forgot the troubles of the morning and was sitting back in his boat, quietly humming to himself, and thinking of the great meal he was to eat in a few hours. He preferred baked fish on an open fire with some good vegetable soup. He looked up at the sky. It was blue. It had been a good morning fishing. Indeed, the entire day had been good, except for seeing the giant, and as he was pondering this to himself, he saw a bird flying across the sky.

He looked closer. It was a strange looking bird, and it was falling down to earth. But suddenly his line became taut, and he realized another fish was tugging on the line. He forgot about the strange sight from above and began to wrestle with the fish. It must have been a gigantic fish for the fish struggled with the Fisher. To balance himself he put one of his feet on the edge of the boat and the other in the center and pulled hard. Maybe the line was caught he thought, but then he heard a noise from above and the strange bird was plummeting towards the boat.

'Go away bird!' he shouted, motioning with his one free hand and as he did, the fish pulled away hard and the Fisher lost his balance. 'Oh no!' moaned the Fisher to himself and looking up, the bird hit the river with a splash just beside the boat. The wave caused the Fisher to lose his control and his foot tipped the boat up and all his fish fell back into the river and at last the Fisher felt headlong himself into the water.

When the Fisher reached the shore, he realized that he was carrying a strange wet and heavy creature. The creature had drunk a lot of water and was dazed, but otherwise all right. The Fisher looked back to his boat. It was now half submerged in the river, sinking fast, and all his fish were gone. He sighed. He looked down at the strange brown creature. He had seen one such creature like this before, but it was a long time ago.

He remembered it was called a monkey. A monkey had fallen from the sky. It was a wonder of wonders he thought. For several days he would often glance up into the sky at the slightest sound in case more were about to fall. For months afterwards he would always look upwards just before eating fish or casting a line on his boat.

The monkey seemed quite shaken from his ordeal and slept for some time. This gave the river creature plenty of time to catch some more fish by standing on the bank of the river. He cooked the fish over the open fire and prepared his evening meal of vegetable soup. He began to formulate in his mind what he would say to the little visitor from the sky, but he was quite worried there would be a language barrier. After all, he had met other animals before such as rabbits, frogs, and birds. While they all spoke a common tongue, the language of the forest, there were often variations of certain vowels and the meaning of certain words which often made for miscommunications and occasions for humor. He wondered if he would have to resort to hand gestures and was practicing such hand gestures for some time. It was at this moment that Monkey woke up.

'Hello,' said a weak Monkey with a faint smile. The river creature stopped gesturing and crouched in front of Monkey. He smiled. Monkey looked like a nice little fellow. And he seemed to speak the same language of the forest, a little dated perhaps, maybe an older version of the common vernacular. He was not sure of what to say and so he waited for another utterance from the small creature.

Monkey sat up and his stomach grumbled. The Fisher needed no interpretation. He handed Monkey a bowl of soup. It smelt good thought Monkey, a mixture of some kinds of vegetables with a new aroma, maybe a vegetable from the forest. Monkey drank from the soup and felt his strength return. Monkey thought about his current circumstances and the nice but strange creature crouched in front of him. He decided to introduce himself. He pointed to his small nose and spoke.

'I am Monkey.' He smiled and fell back to the ground exhausted.

The river creature was kind and gentle to Monkey, providing him with food, shelter, and a fire to sit by at night. It took a while for him to be restored to good health. During the days he spent walking in the forest, looking at the leaves changing and discovering the beauties and wonders of the undergrowth. When Monkey had fallen from the sky, the trees were still a rich green, but soon they began to transform into shades of yellow, red, and orange.

Monkey had never seen such beauty. The trees were splendid in their richness. The river creature caught fish and collected berries and fruit. Each night they enjoyed a banquet under the stars next to a campfire beside the river. He rarely spoke, using gestures instead, which Monkey soon understood. Monkey himself said little and learnt to listen to the sounds around him.

At first his mind was occupied by questions and thoughts, but soon he was able to listen to the symphony of the trees, the river, and the forest. He would lie awake at night listening to the wind as it whirled through the trees, and he could hear fish jumping out of the water. Monkey began to discern every crack of a twig, every movement in the bamboo, and from the sounds he began to hear patterns and voices. He soon understood that the river creature was quite unlike any creature he had ever met. He was not like a Monkey or a rabbit or even a bird. He was in a very real sense, the forest itself.

It had been at least a week since Monkey's introduction. They didn't speak but seemed to understand what the other was saying. Monkey appreciated that and it was a suitable time to think. He had a lot to ponder. He wondered what had happened to his grandfather and grandmother and the rest of the monkeys he knew on the island. Were they able to escape the terrible invasion of the black warriors? Where were they now? He hoped that his family were safe and out of harm's way and that all was well, but deep down in his heart, he knew that was probably not the case.

He remembered the destruction of the Hall of Masks by the whirlwind and wondered how extensive the damage had been. He was deeply disturbed by the betrayal of his brother and wondered what he would say to him if they ever met again. He didn't remember the dreams he experienced when the whirlwind took him upwards into the heavens. But, when he slept, fragments of those dreams returned to him, brief images only, glimpses, broken scenes, interrupted by images of the forest.

One morning, when walking in the forest, Monkey and the Fisher saw three giants on the path. They all bowed to the Fisher and went on their way but Monkey sensed something was wrong. The Fisher became irritable and mumbled to himself. Monkey was surprised that three giants would pay this strange creature such deep respect and that it was not reciprocated with not even a greeting. They saw no one else in the forest and Monkey thought that it was strange not even to say hello.

It was towards the end of their evening meal. The sun had set, and the fire was crackling. The Fisher began to sing. It was a haunting melody, melancholy and simple. Monkey said nothing but listened. At first, Monkey did not understand the words, but as the song progressed, he realized that the river creature was expounding the life of the forest.

The Fisher spoke in images and sounds and pictures. He said 'in the beginning an ancient being came out of the ocean. He made the forest with his breath and life came with abundance. There were flowers, trees, birds, and song. This world continued for so long as it was, rivers flowed, flowers bloomed, trees grew. It was a beautiful place. The first kingdoms came, the rabbits and foxes and monkeys and others. They all lived in peace. There was the occasional dispute over trivial things, but they were moments compared to what seemed to be an eternity of peace.

'Then suddenly the giants came. They had destroyed their own world and so came looking for another to consume. They killed many animals of the forest. Few survived and those who did were not the same, their free spirits had been crushed with fear and everything was thrown out of order. Those who survived became like the giants, copying their dress, carrying their weapons, and molding their kingdoms after the ones who came to destroy. Soon, instead of one destroyer, there were its offspring, rabbits with swords, monkeys with spears, a new language of hate, discord, and anger.'

The Fisher paused in his song. He looked at Monkey. He sat quietly. It was one reason the Fisher liked Monkey. He was different. He did not carry a sword and while he wore strange clothes, he didn't say much and that was a blessing. The only thing Monkey had was his bamboo flute and he never played it, but perhaps he did not know how. The Fisher didn't know either, but he remembered that the flute was common among the kingdoms in the days before the giants came. He began to sing again.

'The forests burned as the result of the giants and the Fisher pleaded with the heavens for help, but it came in the form of a terrible fire. The fire burned the forests and killed the giants far and wide and in the smoldering ruins of their citadel, trees sprouted and grew again. Three or four giants were spared despite his prayers, and they lived to serve the forest until it returned to the beauty of the past. He could not, however, forgive them for what they did.

The tragedy was that the monkey, raccoon-dog, fox, and rabbit kingdoms never returned to the old ways. They never put down the sword or the spear. The giants were gone but they lived, spoke, and copied them in every way. This the Fisher could not understand. It made no sense to him that the animal kingdoms did not return to the Ancient Order of Things because the reason for their sadness was gone. One day, another wave of giants came from across the seas, smaller and fatter and worse than before. They had little to change on the island, for the world welcomed them and was already resonating in their image. Their Castle by the Sea was an abomination but at least it was not in the forest. He could not understand why these new giants feared the forest until he realized that it was probably a divine joke, it had to be.

'Only the deep forests where the Fisher lived, over the mountains, away from the world of giants, was safe and would always be. Monkey fell from the sky. What did this mean? He is the first monkey the Fisher has seen without a sword and that was a good sign. Did it mean things were going to change?'

Monkey listened to the song as it was sung. He did not know what to say to such a tale, but he smiled. The Fisher sat there, his long arms reaching down to the ground and his strange but kind face glancing towards the fire. He smiled at Monkey and threw another branch on the fire. He continued to hum his song and it drifted into the wind as it blew across the surface of the river.

Soon Monkey's eyes were heavy, and he fell asleep. His last memory was the stars above. He thought that the next day he could ask the Fisher some questions about his song and the forest, but the next morning the river creature had disappeared. Monkey searched for him all day, but he could not be found. Monkey would never see him again, but he heard the song in his heart every day for the rest of his life.

Monkey tidied up the place he had lived for the previous few weeks, and he left. He found it hard to leave. He had grown accustomed to the earthen bed and the sky above for his canopy.

He was now in good spirits, having eaten well from the fruit of the forest and the river. He stopped by the edge of the clearing which had been his home and said a little prayer of thanks and a blessing for that place. After bowing deeply, he turned around and entered the forest.

Monkey had not gone far when a tall creature passed across the forest path, as tall as the trees themselves, garbed in old robes, a belt, barefooted, his long hair tightly pulled back, his skin a bright reddish color. He crossed the path a few steps from the place where Monkey stood transfixed, but then as if noticing him in the corner of his eye, turned around and stared directly at Monkey.

Monkey could see that it was one of the giants he had encountered earlier. This filled him with apprehension and anxiety, but the giant did not seem threatening and so he walked right up to it, bowed, and gave his greetings. In response the giant lifted his head and laughed out aloud. His breath was so strong that it seemed to sway the nearby branches as well as ruffling Monkey's fur. Monkey could smell the forest in that breath, the smell of wood and nuts and berries. This made Monkey feel relaxed as whoever communed in the forest could not mean him no harm.

Two more giants appeared, one who had walked on ahead and the other who was following. They all shared the same appearance. They were tall and powerful, with budging muscles, dark hair, and red skin. They were taller than anything Monkey had ever seen, and they carried in their arms long black sticks. Their skin seemed as wrinkled as old trees. They all stared down at Monkey who stood still on the forest path.

'Look' said the one following to his brothers. 'It is the friend of the Fisher.'

The three of them laughed loudly.

This seemed to occupy their minds for some time, and they continued to laugh amongst themselves. At some point, the giant before whom Monkey bowed interrupted the laughter and spoke.

'Don't worry little Monkey. We mean you no harm. We saw you before. We were surprised because the Fisher treated you so kindly.'

'Why was that strange?' asked Monkey.

'He has never accepted another. We know of him, and he knows of us, but we have never spoken. He was here before any of us came to dwell in the forest long ago.'

This intrigued Monkey, so he climbed up on a rock that was beside the path. The position brought him closer to the giants, but he was still only as high as their knees.

He looked at all three of them. 'You bowed to him, but he did not bow to you. Why?'

'He is as old as the forest itself,' replied the tallest of them. 'He is the forest. We are but those who are passing. We enjoy its fruits, we sit under the shade of its trees, listen to the sounds of the birds in his branches. He is the undergrowth, the vines, the brush, the trunks and the branches, the changing leaves, and the new life in spring. He is the forest itself. Each day the forest bows to us and pays us respect, allows us to dwell in its places of beauty, and gives us the gifts of life. Do you not feel the forest around you?'

Monkey looked up at the trees that stood all around them. They were indeed beautiful and full of color, their branches long and their canopies wide. He could smell fruit and berries in abundance and in the distance, he could hear the bubbling of a small creek emptying into a small lagoon. Through the trees and the leaves, Monkey could hear the song the river creature sang the night before. It was faint as it whispered through the trees.

'I can hear his song,' said Monkey.

'He has sung since the days when the forest was young,' said one of the giants.

'Why did you laugh at me?'

The giant sat down on the path. The one on the left crouched on the hill and the one on the right leaned on his staff.

'We came here long ago with our brethren from across the seas, from an ancient kingdom at war. Those who were left scattered around the world and our families were those who came here to this island of forests, for it was in those days, from the beaches to the mountains, one giant forest, lush and green.'

'Who are you?' asked the giant leaning on the staff, interrupting his brother.

'My name is Monkey,' he replied.

The giants did not seem impressed with his answer.

'What are your names?' Monkey inquired.

The three giants had puzzled expressions and looked at each other and then back to Monkey.

'Names?' asked the seated giant. 'Why do you wish to know

our names?'

Monkey was taken aback by this strange response. This was the answer the red-eyed creature had given him. Monkey wondered if they were related.

The giant who lent on his staff spoke.

'You must understand Monkey, that we do not have many visitors to this forest, in fact to be honest with you, we never get visitors.'

'Why not?' asked Monkey. 'It is a beautiful forest. What about the monkeys or rabbits or foxes? Why don't they visit?'

'Yes, it is,' replied the giant. 'It is a beautiful forest, but we don't see any of the larger animals here anymore. Some of the birds come of course and fish swim in the rivers but not the others. In any event, we don't remember our names because we know each other very well and have no use for polite pleasantries.'

'Besides,' said the one crouching on the hill. 'We are almost as old as the forest itself, bar one distinction, which is that I can remember the days of my youth which means I must be the youngest, whereas these other two are so old they cannot remember when they were young.'

'It is sad you cannot remember your youth,' said Monkey.

'Some things are best forgotten,' replied the giant.

'So young Monkey,' asked the seated giant. 'Do you serve the emperor?'

'I don't know of whom you speak,' replied Monkey. He had heard that word a few times before when he was on the island, but he did not know what was meant by it. He heard the general refer to his grandfather as 'your majesty' but that made no sense to him at all.

'No,' he replied, 'I don't think so.'

The giants laughed together. The one bending on his staff spoke.

'You don't think so?' he asked. 'What a strange thing to say. You either know or you don't, I would imagine. The emperor of the monkeys is not someone easily forgotten. He is not a giant but walks like one, eats like one and burps like one.'

The other giants laughed. 'We know of him even in this forest.'

'I'm sorry,' said Monkey. 'I know of no such emperor, nor have I ever met him, nor would I be likely to know him if I did.'

The giants looked at each other in amazement. 'It is not possible,' said the seated one. 'He must know, we all know, it is common knowledge, and he is after all a monkey.' The others concurred.

'Maybe he bumped his head,' said the seated giant.

'No,' disagreed the one leaning on his staff. 'He is just probably hungry. Maybe we should give him something to eat.'

The others nodded in approval. The seated one reached into his pocket and pulled out four pieces of fruit. They were orange in color, polished and smelling ripe. He tossed one to each of his companions and leaned over and gave one to Monkey. Monkey received the piece of fruit graciously and as was his custom bowed in politeness. Monkey looked at the fruit. He had never seen it before. It was slightly soft to touch and felt good in his hand, as it was just the right size.

For Monkey, the feeling of a piece of fruit was as important as the eating of it. Texture, taste, flavor all played their part in his estimation of its quality and ranking alongside the other fruit that he had eaten in the past, but the first test of quality was how it fell in the hand. He had thought of examining it further but with three pairs of eyes staring at him he decided to let his custom pass and bite the fruit. The flavors invaded his senses, and he was so surprised at its taste that he almost jumped for joy, part of the fruit falling out onto the forest path. The giants laughed. After Monkey had wiped his mouth and swallowed, he told the giants how much he was enjoying the fruit.

'So, if you don't know who the emperor is,' continued the seated giant, 'where do you come from?'

Monkey thought for a moment. He didn't know what to say. He really didn't know where he came from at all. 'I came from the sky, like a bird,' he said. 'I fell out of the sky and landed in the river near the one who lives in the forest.'

'His answer is even more inexplicable than the first,' said the standing giant.

'And he has already eaten some fruit,' said the seated giant.

'I came from the whirlwind,' continued Monkey. 'I was living on an island far away, off the coast and there was a terrible storm and the whirlwind lifted me up and brought me to this forest.'

The giants didn't say anything for a long time, pausing to ponder what Monkey had said. 'So,' said the giant seated. 'You are not from here; you do not know the emperor and you came from another island?'

Monkey nodded.

'It's possible,' said the standing giant. 'We all came from a different place.' They nodded to each other. 'But look what we did,' said the seated giant. 'This Monkey hasn't done anything.'

'Yet,' said the standing giant. 'Who knows what he will do?'

It then suddenly occurred to Monkey that the giants were right. This wasn't his home. He was in a new place, a new world, and he was a visitor. What did he want to do? Did he want to try to find his way back to the island and to his grandfather, or did he want to continue along this new path and find out where it led? He had not thought about the future at all until this conversation. He decided to ask the giants for their opinion. They all stared at him in amazement.

'Why are you looking at me like this?' asked Monkey.

'Monkeys are not known for their conversation,' said the standing giant. 'Eating, fighting, sleeping perhaps are more important to them, but it is very strange to engage in conversation with a monkey.'

'This is my first conversation with a monkey,' said the seated giant.

'A special occasion then,' blurted out Monkey.

'Yes,' they all replied in unison.

There was silence for a while as the three giants digested what Monkey had asked. 'The story you tell Monkey is a strange story and one difficult to believe,' said the seated giant.

'Why is it strange?' asked Monkey.

'We have not heard a story like this before. As we told you we do not meet many creatures in the forest anyway as we live so far away from the edge of the kingdoms, especially the kingdom of the monkeys. We know of the emperor and all he has tried to do. We hear rumors and stories from the birds and other animals, and it grieves us that monkeys try so hard to be like our people, the giants, or rightly speaking the giants who came after us. We have never met a monkey who fell out of the sky, nor a monkey who lived for a while with the Fisher, for he seems to have the life of a hermit. We didn't know there was another place where monkeys could be found. Tell us Monkey, is there a forest there, and what is it like?'

Monkey thought for a moment.

'Well, it is a beautiful place. There are beaches there and each beach has well positioned rocks for fishing, and the fish of the sea is abundant and varied. I make fishing rods from young bamboo stalks and fishing line from the twine of vines and get bait from the river or from under the soil, as the soil is rich and deep and good for planting crops of various kinds. The sun is hot in summer and warm in winter, it snows around the time for New Year and the trees change their color during Autumn, the moon shines brightly at night and the air is clean and fresh. The forests are deep and lush and were it not for a small village built there years ago, long before we arrived, there is nothing but pristine beauty.'

It was the mention of the village that got the giants attention.

'What do you mean 'a village,' Monkey? Who built it and when?' inquired the giants.

'We don't know,' replied Monkey. 'I was born after my grandfather, the high priest and his relatives and friends arrived on the island. The houses and halls were large, and there was a Hall of Masks with a dozen mask on the wall, all with strange appearances, noses, and faces. One of the masks was of a creature with a large red face and an incredibly long nose.'

This got the attention of the giants even more, and their eyes widened.

'What happened to those who lived there?' asked the seated giant eagerly, his eyes quivering.

'I got lost in the Hall of Masks one day and made my way down a very dark tunnel only to discover that the original inhabitants were all dead. We thought they might have left the island long ago, but it seems they all died there.'

The faces of the giants fell. The seated one sighed deeply. 'So, it is true,' he said. He turned to the others. They nodded.

'Dear Monkey, this is most troubling news you bring us. Let us discuss this among ourselves for a while and then tell you our response is. Is this acceptable to you? Please find a place to sit and please enjoy some more of the fruit, until we are ready to speak again.'

Monkey gave his assent and sat down on the path. The giants gave him a small cloth which contained the fruit. Monkey was tired, so it was good to sit down and happy to eat some more of this lovely fruit without the distraction of speech. What occurred next surprised him.

The giants did not speak to each other, but they whistled to each other. Their whistling was unlike anything Monkey had ever heard. The sounds were deep and seemed to drench the forest with their melody. The tune was melancholy, but ordered and with structure, and with closed eyes, the three giants continued while Monkey munched on the orange fruit as softly as he could. It seemed like such a long time before the giants spoke again.

The seated one spoke for the three.

'My brothers have chosen me to speak on behalf of the three for I am the youngest. My memories are clearest. We were deeply saddened to hear of what happened to our brothers on your island. Yes, they were our brethren, one of many groups of families who left our people in the early days. They wanted to be free of the constraints of living with us and did not want to help build our Castle by the Lake. They did not want to live under its shadow and instead wanted to return as much as possible to the earth.

'We, and our ancestors, feared the earth and sought to conquer it. We were successful, and the world burned with fire and what we did not burn we changed. The monkeys changed first and became like us. They went and conquered the rabbits and the foxes and the racoon-dogs. It was the monkeys who first forged swords and spears and built foundries based on our designs and wore clothes based on our fabrics and weavers. They changed their entire society, so it became like ours.

'We were a people of war. Long ago, our ancestors came to this land from across the seas. Our old world was in ruins. Centuries of war destroyed our land and burnt our forests and poisoned our waters. Those who survived found this place. It was perfect. Following our customs and practices, we soon corrupted everything. Even I remember the twilight of those days. At this time, the great forests were hewn down and used to build a castle based on the castle our ancestors built across the sea.

'We found the most sacred and beautiful space in the land. It was near a lake of exceptional beauty. Our soothsayers told us that this was the best place for prosperity and good fortune. We were superstitious and brought our faiths with us, our idols, and our gods made in our image. We heard about the beliefs of the monkeys, of the cycle of life and death, of growth and decline, of decay and renewal. We dismissed it as nonsense.

'We discovered that some of the kingdoms held to an ancient belief in a spirit who brought the worlds into being and who brought life to the world. A small group of heretics sought out the stories and the legends, spoke to the faithful ones in the various kingdoms and went to their shrines. We laughed at them. We mocked them and said that any spirit of the animal kingdoms is not as powerful as our gods of fire and war and death.

'But the heretics wanted a different path and a separate way. One day they came back to us with a mask. This image was apparently of the creature the kingdoms worshipped as the one who brings life to the world. They explained that the world moves in a cycle, like the seasons, that death is but the door to new life. They said all that was, is changed into what could be. This creature is the one you describe with the red face and the long red nose.'

'That's incredible!' exclaimed Monkey. 'So how did the mask end up on my island?'

'The story is a sad one, especially as you have told it. Now that we know the truth then it all makes sense. We rejected the pleas of this small group of heretics and didn't want their ideas polluting everyone and so we banished them to an island on the edge of our new home, surrounded by treacherous currents.'

'My island,' whispered Monkey, finally realizing the answer to the riddle that consumed all the monkeys who lived there.

The giants nodded. Everyone was silent for a long time. The giant continued.

'With the dissenters out of the way, we built our Castle by the Lake and sought to stretch out our hand to consume the world. But this was an illusion. The very creature the heretics feared came out of the ocean from an ancient shrine and destroyed the castle and all who dwelt there. We sought to know everything and so he gave us what we asked for. We could see into the hearts of our brothers and sisters. What we saw horrified us, and so we turned on each other. We sought truth and he brought revelation. We sought to see, and he brought light into our hearts.

'There were four of us who were far from the chaos when it began. We relented long before the battle and decided to leave our brethren. A deep mist fell upon the land, and we wandered far from the field of battle. The sounds of war and the screams of death grew fainter until we could only hear the wind. When the mist cleared, we found that we were here. It seems the madness that fell upon our brothers and sisters extended even to your island and the heretics too were consumed by his wrath, so none escaped. It grieves us that even they died. Until today we held out hope, however slim that the heretics might have found peace far away. But they did not. Their bones turned to dust long ago, and their voices have been still. There are a few others like us, who dwell in the deep mountains. When the revelations came, we also saw them, but they did not drive us to kill but drove us to tears, for beyond the veil of politeness and masks lies a heart of fear and deception. This truth filled us with shame.'

Monkey looked at the three giants. They were all that were left of an entire civilization. All their dreams and desires and stories and songs were all carried by these three tenders of the ancient forest. Their castle, emperor, wars, and swords were all gone. Their role was to tend to the forest and return it to its original beauty. The giant who was standing looked at the trees around him and leant to touch the trunk of a tall cedar tree, standing nearby.

'We tend to the trees and try to repair the damage we did, but even now our footprints remain, and the destruction we wrought does not disappear.'

He looked down to the ground with sadness.

'There is something I do not understand,' pondered Monkey. The giants looked at him again, waiting for his question. 'If, as you say, the creature with the red face brought death and renewal, then everything must have gone back to the way things were, surely?'

'He is a smart one, this Monkey,' said the seated giant.

'I mean,' continued Monkey. 'If your people all died, then the monkeys would have returned to the forest and put away their swords and gone back to doing what monkeys did before the giants. If there was renewal and new beginnings, surely this must have happened.'

'You are right Monkey,' said the seated giant. 'You are right, they did. The monkeys gave up being like us and they put down their swords and went back to the forest, to the kind of life you described earlier, and they were good days for them, happy days. They did from time to time fight their ancient enemies the racoon dogs but with their claws again. Even the foxes grew in number and moved around openly, and the rabbits flourished. The three great kingdoms lived in peace for what seemed a long time.

'Then one day, the Fisher let out a howl that woke us from our slumber. We called to the birds, and they took our concerns to the far shores, over the mountains on the other side of this great land. It was then that we learnt the truth. A fleet of ships had arrived on our shore, and it was full of a new race of people, giants like us, but from a different land, an ancient and seafaring people.

'We were from ancient stock who dwelled inland and preferred the mountains and the forests, fearless and brave. The new arrivals preferred the ocean and the coast and were naturally suspicious of the forest and the glades and the glen. They knew nothing of this land. They came to a world rejuvenated, replenished, and renewed. The scars of the war had long passed from view and vines and creepers, and the wearing of time hid the errors of the past.

'They seemed too small to be noticed and they were industrious and productive. They tilled the soil and were careful not to disturb the forest. They avoided it deliberately and started to build a castle, not by the lake as we did, but by the sea, a huge citadel with stone walls several times higher than us, with a port and a moat that stretched inland, which involved reshaping the land and redirecting the rivers and the estuary.

'When we heard that they were building the Castle by the Sea our hearts sank. We heard that the monkeys sent a delegation from their emperor to tell the giants not to build near the ocean because of the frequent tsunami that affects the coastline. They even offered the ruined castle in the forest. The giants just laughed at them and said that they would build a castle that would be the envy of the entire world and nothing and no one would be able to knock it down.

'We saw in them the same poison that existed in our hearts which led to our destruction. The new giants reached out to the monkeys in the forest and sought an alliance with them. They quickly became like the giants and began to rule the entire forests as their own kingdom. Using newly formed swords and spears they fought against the foxes and the rabbits, the only two kingdoms who could oppose them. We don't know too much about these wars, as we did not want to fall into despair, but it seems to me that your presence of the island might have occurred because of one of these disputes with the current emperor of the monkeys. He rules the forests next to the Castle by the Sea all the way to the mountains. The giants do not venture into the forest.

They fear the forest and its power and entrust control of the forest to your kin.'

Monkey continued to listen to the giants and their conversation went on right into evening, past dusk. The stars shone in the sky above and still they talked, and Monkey asked many more questions as did the giants. They all watched the sun rise the following morning.

He told them of the bamboo flute, and they had examined it. They had never seen one before, nor did they know to play it. They preferred to whistle, and the flute was much too small for them to play. They encouraged Monkey to whistle but he could not and so he listened to their haunting tunes in the evening. They did not know of the shrine by the sea where the flute was alleged to have been made, nor what or if any significance the flute had. But the giants did know of the possible existence of ancient ruins up and down the coast, created by those who left them, and they said that if Monkey was to find further answers, then he might consider trying to find the ruins.

Monkey spent the night also wondering about the fate of the monkey kingdom. He could not understand the attraction monkeys had to become like the giants. What was it about the giants that so attracted them and why would they give up a simple life in the forest to be like them?

Monkey as this stage in his life, knew little of ambition since he had simple pleasures and simple choices to make. He did not know the power ambition had over most creatures, especially creatures with the ability to change the lives of those around them.

Monkey also wondered about the creature with the long red nose and why he felt it necessary to bring about such terrible destruction and wrought renewal on the earth. Surely, thought Monkey, there was another way, where all creatures could live in peace. He was also amazed that there would be a being with such incredible power and might with the ability to destroy so much of life. He could not understand why this being would behave in this manner, even to the most miserable of creatures.

These thoughts stuck with him in the morning, and they made him restless. He would find no answers here in the forest. So, in the morning, as the sun rose, he told the giants:

'I deeply appreciate your time and consideration, but I will find no answers in the forest. I must continue my journey, but I do not know where this path will take me.'

'You are fortunate Monkey,' said one of the giants.

'How can you say that?' asked Monkey, his eyes wide open.

'Most have their lives plotted out before them Monkey. Few have an opportunity to think about the path they are to follow, and even fewer have the experiences you have been given. You were plucked up in a whirlwind and taken to the heavens. You have spoken with the custodian of the ancient forests and survived, and you have met three of the ancient ones who were once as numerous as the stars in the sky. These are memories to cherish in your heart and ones to dwell upon during cold nights along the forest path or times of loneliness in the mountains. I do not know where you should go or what you should do. But go in peace.'

The other giants nodded.

'The sun is now above us Monkey. If you begin to walk now you will reach the edge of the forest by dusk. It will take a day. There are no dangers in this forest as it is under our protection, but the same could not be said for the forests beyond the first river which marks the boundary. There should be a small bridge for you to cross and beyond that there are three paths. The first takes you to the castle of the giants, the Castle by the Sea, and the second takes you to the interior and to the old ruins of the Castle by the Lake. The third is the one you should take for it delivers you along the coastal paths. There may be shrines along that path built long ago, but we never found them maybe because we were never looking.'

Monkey stood up and brushed off the dust from his bottom. He looked at the three giants. He bowed deeply to all of them individually.

'I thank all of you for your kindness to me,' said Monkey. 'Your words and encouragement will not be forgotten. I will cherish this meeting in my heart until we meet again.'

The giants all arose and bowed to Monkey. One of the giants spoke again.

'Dear Monkey, we also will remember this day and recall it when the rays of the morning sun come through on a cold winter's day. Your words have warmed our hearts and given us hope. We wish you a safe journey along the path and hope that you will find your questions answered.'

Monkey turned to leave but the giants continued to speak.

'It has been many years since a monkey stood before us in the forest. Most of the world fears us with dread but we fear the one who accepted you. The custodian is the forest and under his tutelage we have sought these many years to restore part of it to its former glory. So, Monkey, we bid you farewell, and when you meet others, they will tell you that nothing but evil lurks in our hearts, that we were the vilest of monsters, hidden in the dark places of the earth. That was our past, it is true. We are all the same kin but not the same spirit, at least not anymore.'

'There is always the possibility of change,' said Monkey. The giants nodded.

'We spend our days here to protect and preserve the forest. Its song lightens our burden, and its words give us strength. It is our life. May you find yours.'

Monkey bowed to them again and walked away.

As he passed around the corner, the tall, long figure of the Fisher stepped onto the path. His eyes surveyed the forest around him, the three giants behind him and Monkey walking off into the distance. Tears filled his eyes.

The Fisher turned to a figure standing beside him. The figure was tall and strong, with a red face and a long red nose. 'All of the same kin, but not the same spirit,' he said. 'The forest is well my friend. It is as strong as the day you first arrived. You cannot hate them forever. Let it go.'

The Fisher nodded slightly and bowed deeply to the figure before him. There was a sudden rush of wind in the trees and when the custodian lifted his head, he was alone.

10.

Monkey walked all day until he reached the small bridge at dusk and decided to sleep on it. The next morning, he crossed it and found three ways in front of him. He decided that the road going south along the river must have been the one towards the ocean for the river was flowing in that direction. The next day he fished, fashioning a rod and he caught a few fish which he ate raw. He didn't mind raw fish. He didn't want to attract too much attention with a fire. He was also very hungry.

He found some wild white radishes in the field near the river. He didn't mind eating them raw as well, as he had sometimes eaten these radishes on the island. It wasn't the most ideal situation, but he needed to eat to keep up his strength. He drank from the water in the river. As he walked, the ground sloped downwards until the river emptied into the ocean itself. He reached the ocean at dusk on the second day. He had hoped to search for signs of his island, but the sun had already set.

He awoke at dawn and walked along the ocean path until it began to rise upwards and so he climbed the path until he reached the cliffs. The waters extended out to the horizon, and the path along the coast was narrow and precarious. He walked along the path, stopping to eat some fruit that he recognized in the trees. From time to time, he stopped and looked out across the ocean, but he could see no island, only a vast expanse of blue.

He reached the end of the path by the end of the third day. It simply stopped. It went nowhere, overtaken by scrub and bracken. It was as if the forest had decided that the path was no longer to be used and closed in around it. He wondered how long it had been since the three giants had even been this way. The trees that obscured the path were tall and strong and the scrub was so thick that Monkey found it quite difficult to cross.

He was a monkey and therefore adept at climbing trees, but he didn't like to climb as it made him dizzy and weak in the knees. After a few hours of pointless wrestling with vines and thickets, he succumbed to the inevitable and climbed up the nearest branch. He then jumped across to the next tree and hugged the trunk precariously. When he felt secure, he climbed up it till he reached a fork in the bough and jumped again. The more he jumped, the more confident he became. His jumps became longer and bolder and soon he was travelling quite a distance, certainly a lot further than he would on foot. But Monkey, being Monkey, kept pushing himself too far and there was eventually a branch just out of reach. He missed it and fell to the ground with a thud.

Monkey awoke to the sound of leaves moving. He sat up and realized he was sitting in the middle of a clearing. He looked around and saw a small mouse nibbling and foraging for food in the undergrowth. He looked up for the sun. It was still the early hours of the morning and the rays of sunshine had just broken through the canopy. Monkey yawned and fell back onto the soft grass, half-asleep. He felt a rush of wind from the sky and the sound of a brief struggle.

He sat up again. The mouse was gone, but leaves were still falling back down. He looked around for the mouse, but it was nowhere to be seen. A branch snapping high above alerted him. At the top of a tree, sitting perched on a branch was an owl, the mouse caught securely in its claws. It looked down at Monkey. Monkey looked up at the owl. He stood up quickly, brushed off the leaves, grass and dust and left the clearing. He kept his eyes on the owl until he was out of sight. The owl, however, turned its face away.

Monkey walked through the forest for hours. He decided not to climb trees for a while as he didn't want to fall again. It was a pleasant stroll over tree trunks, and through scrub. Being rather small, it was easy for him to find his way forward now as the terrain was changing. He was also a little disturbed about the owl. He had never seen one before and the sight of the limp mouse in its claws made him shudder. He was glad that he was larger than a mouse, but then he began to think that perhaps in the forest was also a creature large enough to be interested in him. This thought made him ever more worried, and he began to be more suspicious of his surroundings. Every sound, every snap of a branch made him concerned. Soon he was sure that there were many creatures lurking in the forest waiting to snare him. Fortunately, his stomach distracted him, and he started to think instead of finding some food.

Towards the end of the day when the sun began to fall behind the trees of the forest, a dark shadow descended. Monkey noticed the light dimming in the canopy above and around him and the undergrowth became more obscure. The sounds of the forest began to wane, first the birds, then the scurrying of small creatures and finally, the chirping of crickets and frogs echoed through the trees. Monkey did not mind the dusk at all, in fact it made him a little cooler to walk, but he became anxious about where he might sleep. He sometimes looked above to see if the owl had returned to perch in one of the high branches.

The next day he awoke and rubbed his eyes. He ate some radishes and found some berries and munched on them. It was about this time that he thought he saw a flash of white on his left, darting through the undergrowth. He thought it strange that it was the color white and so he rubbed his eyes. He must have been tired because the color white was very unusual in the forest. He looked around and not seeing anything unusual, kept walking.

Monkey did not think about it until he heard another strange sound. His first thought was that it was his stomach rumbling and so he patted it, reminding himself that he should find something to eat. His stomach rumbled again, but this time, it seemed to rumble so much that his feet lifted off the ground. It had not happened to him before, but as far as he could remember, he had never been this hungry before, so this must be what happens when one is extremely hungry, he thought. Monkey kept walking and found himself in a small clearing.

Suddenly, his feet lifted off the ground again and he realized to his surprise that it was not his stomach at all. The earth and the entire forest around him shook. He looked at the tree branches. They too were still swaying. The earth shook again and then again, each time the sound was louder and louder. He turned around to face the sound. He could hear the snapping of many branches and then it burst into the clearing full of rage.

It was a giant.

The creature was enormous, standing almost as tall as some of the trees. His face and skin were a light reddish color and he had large open eyes and a fat nose. He had no hair to speak of, but he was too tall for Monkey to see clearly. He was dressed in a blue robe, tied at the waist and white-collared leggings. He wore no shoes, but his feet were huge, and his toes larger than Monkey's arms. The giant roared and the sound made the branches quake and Monkey's heart pounded rapidly. Monkey could see the reason for the giant's anger: a wooden arrow was lodged in his left thigh. It was causing him considerable pain and he was furious. His large eyes found Monkey cowering in the middle of the clearing. Monkey turned and ran into the forest, pursued by the giant.

Monkey, despite being very hungry and scared, was not devoid of his wits and quickly realized that he had two options. The first was to find some place underground to hide or some safe place high in a tree. He quickly surmised that the giant being so heavy could quickly jump on anything on the ground, so he realized the only safe option was high in a tree. Monkey searched frantically for a large, tall tree, while behind him he could hear the raging giant. Most of the trees were thin or too short but soon Monkey saw a strong, tall, pine tree with huge branches and thick bark. This was an excellent place to hide.

Monkey ran straight past it and then darted back out of sight and scrambled up the trunk as fast as he could. In moments he had reached what he thought was a safe location tucked behind a strong branch. While he was thinking this, the trunk of the tree shook him violently and threw him out onto one of the branches. At the base of the tree, the giant thumped the trunk with his fists. Each thump placed Monkey further and further out on the limb. He grabbed at the branch and tried to find something to hold onto.

The giant thumped the trunk with his hands, and it knocked Monkey down the branches. It was then that he saw it. What he saw astonished him. It was a creature perched on the branch in front of him. It saw him tumble from the branch above. It had a long face with ears, brown fur and legs which hugged the branch. Its eyes were red, and it had long sharp claws that hugged the branches. It seemed to shiver in the dusk, one moment visible, the next invisible, as if it too were hiding. He knew immediately who it was. It was the creature under the scrub he saw back on the island, the creature with the red eyes, the one who gave him the flute.

'You!' exclaimed Monkey loudly. 'What are you doing here?'

The creature looked puzzled and said nothing. Monkey called out again. The tree shook once more. The creature spoke. 'Can you see me?' it asked.

Monkey nodded.

'How strange,' said the creature. 'I have not been noticed here before.'

'Why not?' asked Monkey.

'I do not belong here,' said the creature.

'But I noticed you at the beach on my island,' said Monkey.

'Ah yes,' said the creature grinning. 'You have my flute I see. Can you play it?'

'Can I play it?' asked Monkey. He wasn't thinking about the flute or his ability to make a note.

The giant had ripped off several branches and was getting closer to where Monkey had fallen. 'I will play the flute for you if you help me!' he pleaded.

'No, it is best to fall Monkey. The giant will not kill you. He is too busy dying. But know this. The one you seek is close. You will see him and rejoice in him for a while and then you will lose him, but you will see him again at the end. He is coming to bring death to all and then life, so why worry about falling today?'

Monkey had no idea what the strange creature was talking about, but the tree shook again, and Monkey was thrown into the air, falling through the branches, and landing in the undergrowth at the foot of the giant. The giant roared with anger and looked down at Monkey. Monkey covered his eyes. All went dark. The next thing he heard was the giant shrieking in pain. He opened his eyes. The giant had staggered back and was holding his face. An arrow had struck one of his eyes. Another flew and struck his chest. The giant was in agony.

The flash of white appeared again, and Monkey could see a small but determined white clothed creature land on the shoulder of the giant wielding a short sharp sword. There was a brief flash, the giant groaned in pain and fell backwards. His body shook and shivered in the undergrowth and then lay still. Monkey could not understand how such a large and terrible creature could be brought down by an arrow and a few slashes of a sword, no matter how sharp.

Monkey looked behind himself and saw a fox. She stood tall and was holding a bow. She extended her hand and pulled Monkey up. A rabbit soon joined them. He was dressed in a white robe and a short sword was tucked into his belt.

'Is it dead?' asked Monkey pointing to the giant.

'It soon will be,' said the rabbit, jumping up onto the chest of the giant and sitting down.

'Is it safe?' asked Monkey.

'He won't do anything,' said the rabbit, pulling a piece of straw from his pocket and putting it in his mouth.

'Those arrows are poisoned,' he informed Monkey. Monkey was shocked. Poison! How terrible, he thought to himself, but he remembered that the giant was trying to kill him, so he felt a little better. He must have been visibly shaken because Fox came and put her arm around him.

'Don't worry. You are safe now,' she reassured him.

'My name is Rabbit,' said the rabbit munching on his straw. Rabbit was only small, about the same size as Monkey. He was more a hare than a rabbit, and Monkey thought it strange that this hare would be a kind of warrior. He thought to himself that he had never met a hare or a rabbit before and while he did remember hearing about them at some point, he never thought that he would meet one. His grandfather's stories told of rabbits who were gentle and weak. This one had the air of confidence and strength. It must have been this rabbit which darted past him in the forest before the giant attacked, thought Monkey.

Rabbit pointed to the Fox. 'This is Fox.'

Fox smiled. She let go of Monkey and bowed before him.

'I'm pleased to meet you,' she said. 'We are honored to make your acquaintance, especially on this happy occasion.'

Monkey was a little surprised. 'What occasion is this?' he asked.

'This day,' said Rabbit proudly, 'marks the twelfth giant we have slain and the anniversary of our first meeting, one year ago.'

'A truly precious event,' added Fox. 'It is quite a blessing from the ancestors that you came to meet us on this day.'

Monkey thought that it would be appropriate if he also introduced himself. 'My name is Monkey,' he said. 'I come from an island far away from here and I was brought here by a whirlwind. I spent some time with a kind fisher of the river last week and met some friends of his and then I continued my journey in this forest until our paths crossed.'

Monkey thought it wise not to tell them that he had met three other giants. They had been so nice to him, and he did not want his two new friends to go hunting for them.

'We are most pleased to meet you Monkey,' said Fox. Rabbit gave his assent. Monkey continued, 'I am forever in your debt. I thought I was about to die.'

'Think nothing of it,' said Rabbit. 'One less giant in the world is a good thing.'

Fox nodded. 'Two today, and maybe another tomorrow. It is a good season so far.'

Monkey was shocked. 'Do you hunt giants?' he asked.

They both nodded.

'As long as I can remember,' said Rabbit.

'Why?' asked Monkey.

'You are from far away aren't you,' said Fox looking at Rabbit a little concerned.

'Giants are the enemy of the entire forest,' said Fox. 'They are the curse of the land. My people, the foxes, once lived all over the forest and on the plains and the coast. We were hunted to extinction, our elders massacred, and our young captured for sport. The giants did this, or at least organized it.'

'All the creatures of the forest suffer because of the giants,' continued Rabbit. 'The raccoon-dogs, the bears, the rabbits and even owls are not safe. Some of us are feared by the giants because of ancient superstition. That is why seeing a giant in the forest is such a rare thing.'

Monkey noticed that they did not mention monkeys. It seemed to him that they were either being polite, or they were hiding something. 'Where do the giants live?' asked Monkey.

'Along the coast in their city, the Castle by the Sea, and in some smaller towns, on the edge of the forest they also dwell, rarely entering the forests or going inland for any purpose,' said Rabbit.

'How did you find this giant?' asked Monkey.

'Most of the giants never leave the city, but there is a sacred shrine located just a few hours from here, by the ocean, a beautiful place. No one knows who built the shrine. The ruins predate the giants, and we didn't build it.'

'If the journey is so dangerous, why do they go there?'

'For pilgrimage they come,' said Fox.

'Why?' asked Monkey.

'They want to pay homage to the spirit of the shrine. They believe that by coming here, they and their family are blessed, by the ocean spirit,' said Rabbit.

Monkey was astonished. What the creature said to Monkey under the scrub, and the three forest giants was true. The giants also worshipped the one with the red face and the long nose.

'Do the rabbits and foxes also go to the shrine and have festivals there?' asked Monkey.

Fox shook her head. 'As I said, I am the only one left. As for Rabbit, he can speak for himself.'

They looked at Rabbit. 'I'm sorry,' he apologized. I was just waiting for the giant to finally die, and we can move on.'

'What do the rabbits think of the shrine?' asked Monkey.

'Who cares?' said Rabbit. 'We used to believe in something long ago, but the giants came, and they destroyed everything that was beautiful. All I know is war and how to kill giants. Nothing more.'

'Is it possible that we all celebrate the same spirit, the spirit of the ocean or whatever he is called?' asked Monkey.

'Maybe,' said Fox.

'Impossible,' said Rabbit.

The giant suddenly interrupted them and spoke.

The sound of his voice frightened Monkey and he jumped away from him. Rabbit didn't move.

'Your ocean god won't save you now,' said Rabbit.

Monkey moved closer. 'He is trying to say something,' said Monkey.

The giant spoke. His voice was strong and gentle. 'I am the last of my family,' he said.

Rabbit smiled 'That is good news to hear,' he said.

The giant smiled. His large eyes bulged with the pain of the poison as it seeped through his body. 'The path of the pilgrims will now run dry. You have slain all my brothers who walked the path before me. The rest, my cousins, those in the city…'

'We will slay them too,' interrupted Rabbit.

The giant smiled all too painfully. 'We are all gone now. They will not venture into the forest as we did.'

'Then we will lure them in,' said Fox.

'Ah,' exclaimed the giant. His eyes looked up into the tree above followed by the watchful gaze of Fox, Rabbit, and Monkey.

'What do you see?' asked Fox.

'He is standing in front of you, can you not see him? The one who has no name but who is known by all. His herald is in the tree above you.'

Rabbit and Fox searched the area branches with their eyes, but they could see nothing but branches and leaves. But Monkey's eyes were fixed on one branch and the creature the giant could see he could also see most clearly, his claws stretching out across the branch, his tail dangling in the breeze and his eyes red with fire. Monkey was terrified. The creature put his claw up to his mouth and motioned for Monkey not to say anything.

'I see the ancestors,' the giant said slowly.

Fox turned to Rabbit. 'This one is unusually talkative,' she observed.

'What do you see?' asked Monkey quietly, keeping his eyes on the creature staring at him from above.

'They are all there now, calling me home, even your clan old Grey Ears.'

Rabbit's ears pricked up. He had not heard that name in a long time. 'How do you know my tribal name giant?'

The giant laughed in pain. 'You father told me, just now. He is here with me.'

'That is impossible' said Rabbit angrily.

Monkey realized the giant made no more sounds.

'He is dead,' said Fox. She moved forward to the giant and sat near his silent head.

She prayed silently.

Monkey looked at Rabbit. He sat munching his straw.

Fox stood up. 'One day, giants and the forest will live in peace. Until that day, we are enemies,' she said.

'What about monkeys – am I the only one?' asked the Monkey. Rabbit and Fox looked at each other with puzzled expressions.

'Your dialect is a little strange,' said Fox. 'It is as if you speak an older language of the forest,'

Rabbit nodded. 'You speak a little like my grandfather's generation,' he said. 'You are not like the monkeys of today. You are also polite and friendly which suggests you are not from around here.'

'You also haven't tried to kill us,' added Fox warily. 'You

forgot to mention that.'

Monkey was shocked. 'Why would I want to kill you?' he asked. Both Fox and Rabbit laughed aloud.

'You are certainly not a local,' said Fox.

'There is an alliance between the emperor of the monkeys and the giants,' said Rabbit. 'Being a monkey, I thought you might have known that fact.' Rabbit looked at him suspiciously. 'I have never met a monkey who wasn't like the rest, devious and conniving.'

Monkey was surprised. He had never thought of monkeys as devious or cunning in that way, though individual monkeys may have had traits of personality that were less than ideal. He repeated his earlier question. 'Why would a monkey want to kill a rabbit or a fox?' he asked.

'It's obvious, isn't it?' said Rabbit, 'It's part of the alliance. The monkeys stay away from the coast and keep the giants safe from the forest by ensuring that rabbits and foxes, the other two kingdoms, are not a threat.'

'As I said earlier Monkey,' continued Fox. 'My family, the foxes, were all killed by monkeys sent from the emperor, and I was the only one who escaped.'

'You still have not told me how,' interjected Rabbit. 'It has never made sense to me.'

'I have told you Rabbit, but you have never believed me. I was sent on an errand by the empress to fetch water from the brook and when I returned, she and the entire retinue had been killed. When I returned to our home, I realized I was the only fox left in the entire forest.'

'How awful,' sympathized Monkey. 'You must feel very alone.'

'I do,' replied Fox. 'But I have Rabbit and he is a good friend.'

'I cannot imagine being the only monkey left in the world,' said Monkey. He then realized that he was, very much, alone, in the real sense of the word. He was away from the island, away from his grandfather and his family. He also had discovered that the only monkeys around were completely different, and for them, war was a way of life. 'So,' said Monkey, 'the giants stay away from the forest because of their fear of the forest. Why do they fear the forest?'

'I don't know,' said Rabbit. 'The pilgrims we have met, and killed, have all told us the same story. The giants seem to fear the forest for some reason. Maybe it is a place of running streams and flourishing trees, different from their ordered streets and neatly built castle by the sea. But I think it is something different.'

He chewed on his straw and looked at Monkey intently, his eyes narrowing. 'I think that the monkeys fed them a pack of lies about their religion and the giants were taken in, some of them becoming devoted worshippers while the rest just live in superstition and fear. After all, all the kingdoms, both animal and giant, have their own understanding of how the world works. The giants probably brought their own idols or religion with them, but it doesn't work here. This is a new land and the monkey emperor, seizing his opportunity, told them a lot of nonsense about the forest, and the giants being a superstitious lot, fell for it. The forests are deep and mysterious places Monkey. Even the strongest rabbits can be overcome with emotion if they enter. The monkeys must have spun a clever tale.'

'I have heard this before Rabbit,' said Fox. 'I am not convinced. The monkey emperor, like us, believes in the old stories. We all share the same history and read the same books. I don't think that it is all a pack of lies. These pilgrims, including the giant we just killed, obviously believed the stories in the scrolls, otherwise why would they risk such a perilous journey? No, I think the monkeys warned the giants, which is true, but I also think the stories are true and the forest should be feared and one day that the guardian of the forest will return and renew the whole land.'

'Absolute nonsense!' quipped Rabbit. 'Don't listen to her Monkey,' he said seriously. 'Her blind faith in the old scrolls will get her killed and you if you are not careful. There is no god of the forest, no ancient being, no renewal of the lands. There is only the here and now. Al that matters is that we kill giants and don't stop until they are all dead. What do you think Monkey?'

Both Rabbit and Fox looked at Monkey. He didn't know what to say. He scratched his head and turned it to one side trying to think of what to say first.

'I really don't know what to say,' he began. 'As I said, I am not from around here. I come from an island and spend most of my time fishing or writing poetry. I know that there were stories of the past, but I had no interest in them, a little bit like Rabbit. I think, I saw no use for them, and I was never really allowed to read them, they were left for other monkeys.'

Monkey realized that it might be better not to tell Rabbit or Fox that his grandfather was a high priest, or that the old general called referred to him as 'your majesty' on the day of the whirlwind. He decided to keep those pieces of information to himself.

Monkey continued, 'I don't want giants to rule the world or destroy it again. I think they do have to be stopped, but I don't support violence. We can surely reason with them. I also think that if there is a god or a guardian of the forest, then he wouldn't come to destroy everything, but he would want to be our friend, after all, the forest is a beautiful, wonderful place and surely this guardian would be like the world he created.'

'They cannot be reasoned with, the giants that is,' said Rabbit.

'You haven't read the scrolls then,' said Fox.

'Then maybe you are just reading the wrong ones,' replied Monkey. 'This is a beautiful world and we have gone and spoilt it, but if the guardian came, I am sure he would just want to be our friends.'

'You are the strangest monkey we have ever met,' said Rabbit. 'You talk more than any I have ever heard, and you don't carry a sword, which is a surprise to me. A monkey without a sword is a fish without water.'

Monkey realized that talking reasonably with Fox and Rabbit was pointless. They were both set in their ways, and their consciences seared no doubt by the blood they had shed along the way. Fox was full of mourning for the past and Rabbit was only interested in killing giants.

'The fact is,' said Fox. 'Things are reaching somewhat of a climax. The racoon-dogs have come out of the far hills and engaged the monkeys in open warfare. They are the ancient enemies of the monkeys and the emperor, a wily and clever monkey, has lost the last three engagements. The whole forest is worried because the monkey emperor might go and ask the giants for support and if he does, then the whole forest will burn, like it did before.'

'The forest never burned,' interjected Rabbit. 'But you are right, if the monkeys lose again, the wily old emperor will ask the giants for support and then they might enter the forest. Which is why we are killing as many of them as we can. Perhaps with enough supporters, we can launch a surprise attack on the Castle by the Sea itself.'

Fox laughed. 'Rabbit, you are dreaming again! Even if we had a thousand rabbits like you and ten thousand monkeys, the walls of the castle could never be breached. It would take a tsunami to destroy it and generations of war to kill those who survived.'

'Then we better make a start,' said Rabbit angrily.

'A tsunami killed my father,' said Monkey.

Fox and Rabbit looked genuinely sad. Rabbit felt a twinge of guilt. 'I'm sorry Monkey, our silly arguing brought up the sadness of the past.' Fox nodded.

'It is alright,' said Monkey. 'It happened when I was born. I never met my father and was brought up by relatives. But I am who I am because of what happened to me. I wouldn't change who I am because then I wouldn't be me. But do not please Fox, think about the tsunami as a tool of the ancestors. It is a terrible thing, it's indiscriminate and it doesn't show partiality. Everyone in its path dies.'

There was a long pause. Nobody said anything for a long while. Fox offered Monkey some nuts she had in her bag. Monkey accepted them and munched on them. Rabbit scratched his chin and spat out the straw. All the time, Rabbit kept his eye on Monkey. He had never met such a creature before. He was a monkey but didn't speak like one. He spoke like a rabbit and had the values of a fox. It was all very strange. This Monkey was someone to keep on his side.

'We are going along this ocean road to an old shrine that was built long ago,' said Rabbit. 'You are welcome to join us if you like, we could use a travelling companion. After that, you can decide what you want to do, whether you want to join the monkeys or stay with us. What do you say?'

'Please join us,' insisted Fox. 'We would love the company and I would enjoy the conversation. I weary of Rabbit's long diatribes and laments, so it would be a pleasant change.'

Monkey agreed. This was the only path forward. Rabbit and Fox could become friends, though Rabbit was grumpy and would probably irritate him eventually. Fox led the way, and within moments they had disappeared into the undergrowth.

11

Monkey, Fox, and Rabbit reached the shrine by dusk the next day. The building was worn and weathered. The paths were covered in leaves and the shrine creaked in the wind. The structure sat entirely on the edge of the ocean, with long verandas stretching out on both sides. In the middle of the bay sat two giant wooden pillars with a wooden beam across the top. The wooden gate sat in the ocean, unreachable by land unless swimming was involved. Fox said something about the inconvenience of the place. Rabbit was more impressed putting his hands on his hips and talking about the architecture.

Monkey looked at the writing on the shrine gate. The weather had worn most of the letters away, but they were the same characters as the ones written on his little bamboo flute. Monkey didn't know the significance of this and why he would have been given a flute which came from this shrine. They all found a room behind the shrine and slept there for the night, but Monkey fell asleep clutching the bamboo flute in his little hands wondering what it all meant.

Later that evening, Monkey awoke with a fright. He sat upright. The room was dark, but the moon was shining through the cracks in the wooden panels. The wind was only a breeze, and all was silent. It must have been a bad dream, thought Monkey, falling back again to the floor. He could hear Rabbit snoring loudly. It would be impossible to fall asleep again, he realized.

Monkey thought he saw a shadow pass by the wall. He must have blinked because there was no sound of someone walking but he was sure that a shadow fell quietly by the narrow crack in the wall. He fixed his little eyes on that narrow opening and waited. He waited and waited, and his eyes began to become weary, and his eyelids tried to fall, and Monkey wished he had two little sticks to keep them open. Monkey was just about to fall asleep when he thought he saw two eyes peering through the wooden slats. His heart jumped and he closed his eyes quickly. There was someone out there, Monkey realized. He was terrified. Maybe it was someone wandering through the forests by the ocean shrine on a moonlit night, he asked himself, but it seemed highly unlikely. There were at least two of them and they were creeping around.

Monkey decided to look outside and investigate. He tiptoed around Rabbit and Fox and walked slowly across the wooden floor of the shrine. Maybe he had imagined the eyes he thought to himself. Maybe he had been dreaming. He was after all in a strange new place and the memories of the last night on his island had not fully passed. Monkey walked over to the nearest sliding door thinking how cold the floor was to his little feet. As he opened the sliding door, a gush of wind hit his face and he squinted for a moment. He opened his eyes. He looked down on both sides of the veranda. He saw nothing but an empty blackness.

He walked out onto the veranda, leaned on the railing and looked up. It was a beautiful sight. The moon sat high up in the sky, radiant in the evening, and the little stars sat roundabout, twinkling, and shining. The ocean was still, and the waves gently washed the shores. The wooden gate in the ocean stood still and Monkey thought the water was so still, someone could walk across to the gate and back again.

As he thought about this, Monkey looked back to the end of the veranda. It was almost as black as the sky itself, an old wooden structure, washed and worn by the waves. He felt its surface with his hand. It was smooth to touch. As he ran his hand along the beam, he decided that the figure he saw at the door must have been a dream, a nightmare, the memories of that fateful day on the island still lingering. For the first time since he left home, he felt calm and at peace.

Monkey felt something brush his ear. It felt like the tickling of a mosquito. There was a dull thud on the veranda further down in the darkness as something hit the wood.

Fox grabbed Monkey's arm. 'We are in danger!' she said and pulled him back to the wall of the shrine, away from the openness of the veranda. Another arrow whizzed past their faces and hit a wooden post. A shadow ran towards them on the wooden floor. Monkey could see the glint of a knife reflected by the light of the moon. Why do they all carry knives, Monkey asked himself. Fox pulled an arrow from her pouch and put in her bow, but she didn't get to release it because there was a terrible crash and the sliding door of one of the panels was thrown across the veranda, knocking the shadow off his feet, over the railing and into the darkness, onto the sand below. It was Rabbit. He had kicked the sliding door off its hinge. He was armed with his two swords and fully dressed.

'You were not the only one awake,' he barked at Monkey. Fox lent over the railings and released her arrow, meeting its target who was getting to his feet on the beach holding his head. The arrow struck him in the chest, and he fell back, dead. Rabbit ran down the veranda to join Fox and Monkey. Monkey looked out to the wooden gate standing in the ocean. A mist had fallen over the waves and he could not see the water anymore.

'It is too dark. I cannot see their number,' said Rabbit, drawing his long sword. He looked at Fox and Monkey. 'Monkey,' he said. 'Find a safe place to hide. Fox and I will try to stop them.'

Fox patted Monkey on the head. 'Don't worry Monkey!' she said, 'We have been in worse situations!'

With that, they both disappeared into the night. Fox ran down the veranda and Rabbit jumped over the railing onto the sand. Monkey was alone again. He looked around and could not find a good place to hide so he decided to follow the veranda to its end, furthest away from danger. He ran quietly to the end of the veranda. He was sure it had ended at this point. They had walked around the shrine when they arrived earlier in the evening, but this section was unfamiliar to him. It looked new. It was not worn and weathered. It smelt like newly cut wood, and it was polished. He looked at the mist over the ocean. It had grown thicker and soon it enveloped him and the veranda completely. Monkey had a distinct feeling of unease, like how he felt just before the whirlwind took him into the air. Something was happening beyond his control, and it had nothing to do with the shadows.

He decided to walk on and found himself on an open veranda which seemed to have no walls on either side, only a small railing that stretched out into the darkness. As he walked, he felt the freezing wind of the ocean brush against him, and he thought it strange that he could feel it. He walked to the edge of the veranda and looked out. He could not see anything, but he felt the drizzle of rain. It was very cold, and he wrapped his arms around himself and continued to walk. In front of him the mist obscured his sight, and all was quiet.

He realized that he had walked a fair distance from the shrine out onto the ocean. Beneath him were the waves of the ocean. Looking back, he could see the outline of the shrine in the moonlight, but he could see no one. He was convinced that this veranda was not there earlier in the day. It simply was not there, so what was he walking on?

While he was turned away, looking back to the land, a sound could be heard coming from further down the veranda, deep in the mist, where he could hear the waves of the deep ocean. The sound was of someone walking, as if they were wearing wooden shoes. The steps were even and measured and they seemed to carry a creature of considerable weight. Monkey wasn't sure what to do, so he went as far to the left of the walkway as he could and crouched. Perhaps the creature would pass him by and not notice him.

Meanwhile, Rabbit threw another shadow across the veranda onto the sand. He had been hopping up and down from the railing to the beach, cutting down any shadow he could find. He was very agile for his age, and full of excitement. He had not enjoyed this much killing for months. He lent down to a body which lay in front of him and took off the disguise. He was not surprised to see the face of a monkey. They bore the mark of the emperor's imperial guard. They were not ordinary warriors but true zealots for the empire. He had hoped that they might wear the mark of his old nemesis, the One-Eyed Dragon, but he was, once again, disappointed. Fox joined him and nodded after she saw the corpse.

'These are probably the ones who have been tracking us the last few days,' she suggested.

Rabbit agreed and tucked his sword back into his belt. 'Where is Monkey?' he asked.

'He went this way! Follow me!' she beckoned, pointing in the direction of the wooden veranda of the shrine leading off into the mist. They reached the section of the shrine where Monkey had noticed the new wood, but architecture was furthest from their minds. Suddenly, Fox was knocked off the veranda by one of the shadows. She struck her head on one of the wooden beams and fell to the beach below. She tried to pick herself up but felt that she was no longer on the beach but back in the forest with her family. These were the most painful memories of her life, memories that she wanted to forget. Rabbit called to her several times before drawing both his swords and inviting the shadows to come forth. He could not help her as he was being attacked from all sides.

'You must know your place,' said another fox, tall and beautiful, draped in robes of assorted colors.

Fox looked up and saw the empress of the foxes. 'I cannot show you favoritism even if we are related,' she said.

'Please forgive me' said Fox, bowing deeply.

One of the imperial advisers moved forward. 'You have always been too kind to your sister, your highness.'

The Empress smiled. 'I am the empress. I can make my own decisions,' she said and dismissed her chamberlain. She looked down at Fox in a condescending fashion. 'Sister, tomorrow you can redeem yourself and we can put your many lapses of memory and failures in duty behind us. You will escort me to the great tree in the middle of the forest where we will light our lanterns for our ancestors. It is a short journey. I trust you will not fail me again?'

Fox bowed even more deeply. 'I am gracious that your highness has such faith in me.' In her memory, she felt the imperial advisor shaking her. This shaking became more vigorous, and she began to shout.

'Wake up! Wake up!'

Fox sat up and looked and the imperial advisor had two long grey ears on either side of a very anxious face. It was Rabbit.

'I cannot do this on my own,' he insisted. She realized that she was dreaming about the past. Her mind quickly returned to the present and rubbed her bruised forehead. 'Where is Monkey?' Fox looked at Rabbit. They both turned and looked down at the wooden railing that now stretched out into the ocean. They could see and hear nothing. They looked behind them and more shadows had climbed up onto the shrine and were advancing toward them. The veranda was black. They had to forget about Monkey for the time being.

'We must be important, if they sent a whole regiment on foot to kill us,' said Rabbit. Fox grinned. 'I would have thought two regiments at least but let us send a message to the emperor that he will not forget.'

'Get behind me,' insisted Rabbit, wanting to protect her.

'Don't be silly,' said Fox and pushed past him, drawing her short sword from her belt. 'Don't ever say that to me again,' she said to Rabbit very seriously, turning to him. He apologized with a nod.

Further down the wooden path, deep in the ocean, Monkey could hear the steps coming closer. They echoed across the sea. He stared into the mist. He saw the feet. They sat on two wooden shoes. Then he saw the body, tall and strong, in a blue gown, tied with a red belt. The figure had two swords on his belt. Monkey looked up at the creature which appeared before him. The face was hidden in the mist.

'Who are you?' asked the creature.

'I'm Monkey,' said Monkey.

The mist cleared. The face was revealed. It was red as was his hands and neck. His eyes were huge, and his chin stuck out. But Monkey's eyes were glued on his nose. It sat on his face as if it did not belong there. Monkey stood up and staggered to the middle of the bridge and looked at the creature which stood before him.

There was silence.

Suddenly Monkey laughed aloud.

He laughed so loud he thought his heart would give out. He fell on his back holding his stomach.

'Why do you laugh?' asked the creature genuinely surprised.

'Your nose!' shouted Monkey. 'It is so big! It is so huge! It is enormous!' He could not contain himself and fell back again, his legs shaking in the air. He had never laughed so long or loud or deep in his life.

'You are Mr. Big Nose!' shouted Monkey in absolute delirium.

The tall creature looked down at Monkey and for a moment his eyes glistened. But then, a grin appeared on his face and a sound began to rumble deep in his chest which exploded with a roar of laughter. He put his hands on his hips and laughed out loud. After they had laughed for what seemed like a long time, Monkey thought it best to ask his name.

'You can call me Mr. Big Nose Monkey,' he said grinning. He noticed that Monkey was holding his flute. 'You have a flute,' said

Mr. Big Nose.

Monkey nodded.

'May I have a look at it?' asked Mr. Big Nose.

Monkey nodded and reached up and gave it to him.

'What a beautiful piece of bamboo,' said Mr. Big Nose. He looked at it and turned it over, seeing an inscription burnt into the wood. His eyes lit up.

'Why, it is my old flute,' said Mr. Big Nose. 'I had it last time I was here. Why, it hasn't aged a day. Where did you get it?'

'I was given it,' said Monkey. 'From a strange creature on my island far away, he just gave it to me and said that it came from here.'

'Stole it more likely,' said Mr. Big Nose. 'Not you of course, but the one who gave to you, he was always taking things. His job is to keep an eye on things while I am away. You mean the one with the red eyes and claws and so on?'

Monkey nodded.

'He gave it to you so you could give it to me.'

Mr. Big Nose looked at Monkey, through his incredibly long nose. 'I shall have to play it Monkey. It is difficult to play, but there is not a sound like it in the entire world.'

It was then that Monkey realized that he had forgotten Fox and Rabbit.

Mr. Big Nose laughed aloud. 'You are thinking of your two new friends, the rabbit, and the fox. Rabbit says I don't exist. He is in for a shocking surprise!' he said laughing loudly. 'They will be here soon, once they finish killing the monkeys who had been following you ever since you left the bridge on the edge of the forest.'

'Following me?' asked Monkey.

'Yes,' he replied. 'A scout on a routine journey thought it strange that you appeared out of the forbidden forests as no monkeys dare cross that bridge nor have done so since I last came. He sent word to the emperor of the monkeys and a regiment of imperial guards were dispatched to kill you and everyone you were with. They followed you even when you were leaping across the branches and fell in the clearing. They were going to kill you the morning Rabbit and Fox turned up and were astounded that they had also found the two most wanted fugitives in all the land, who had by themselves, killed over a dozen giants. Rabbit and Fox fight like giants though much faster and they are almost as skilled with the sword as one other, long ago, who also caused trouble for the emperor. He was banished. They say that this one trained Fox, but who knows? You don't carry a sword, do you?'

'I don't believe in violence,' he said.

Mr. Big Nose just smiled.

Mr. Big Nose and Monkey walked along the railing back to the shrine. They walked out of the mist, off the bridge and onto the older, weathered, wide veranda of the shrine. Fox and Rabbit could only stare in wonder. They had just finished killing all the assassins. Rabbit put down his swords and bowed deeply. Fox prostrated herself on the ground, keeping her eyes to the floor.

'What are you doing?' asked Monkey, wondering why the others were showing such respect. 'This is Mr. Big Nose!'

Fox cautioned Monkey to bow as well. 'Bow quickly!' she insisted.

'Leave him be Fox,' said Mr. Big Nose.

Fox was astonished, her eyes wide.

'Do you know me?' she asked with trembling in her voice.

'A monkey, a rabbit and a fox,' he said looking at all three of them. 'I know all of you.'

Monkey could not take his eyes off the tall creature. Fox bowed even deeper on the ground. Rabbit saw her trembling and was puzzled. He had never seen Fox perturbed in any way, or fearful, let alone trembling.

Later, Monkey, Fox, and Rabbit sat on the veranda of the shrine, their feet dangling over the edge. Below them, the gentle waves of the morning sea washed against the old wooden pillars encrusted with oyster shells and wrapped in various kinds of seaweed. The tall wooden gate stood deep in the water in front on them out of reach. The morning rays of the sun shone over the surface of the ocean, its light blinding them and warming their fur. A small fish leapt out of the water, climbing high into the blue sky, until it fell back into the deep with a little splash.

'There was a bridge' said Fox finally.

'Yes, I saw it,' said Rabbit.

'I was on the bridge,' added Monkey.

'It was as real as this wood,' said Fox, knocking the planks next to her gently.

'And cool to my feet,' added Monkey.

'It is gone now,' said Rabbit.

'Where did it go?' asked Monkey. He looked at Rabbit and Fox. Rabbit was munching a piece of straw. Fox was sitting with her eyes closed. Rabbit took the piece of straw from his mouth and looked at it.

'I have been munching you for far too long,' he said and with that, let it fall between his fingers into the ocean below them. It sat on the surface for a moment, teased by the foam, until it was thrown against one of the wooden pillars only to be pulled under. Rabbit reached into his cloak and pulled out another piece of straw, putting it into his mouth. He turned to Monkey.

'Fox was right,' he said reluctantly.

'On which subject?' asked Fox, her eyes still closed.

'There was a bridge, one that extended from this veranda over to the huge wooden gate in the ocean and it vanished in the mist,' said Rabbit.

'That we all agree on,' said Fox. 'It means you can use your eyes.'

'I still don't believe my eyes,' said Rabbit. 'But even if it is what I saw, it doesn't mean he is some kind of forest guardian or god or whatever, he is just like us, it is just that he knows how to travel further than we do, and he has an incredibly long nose.'

'So, you agree its long,' said Monkey still laughing.

'It is an important day,' said Fox. 'The one foretold has returned to save us from the giants.'

'Save me from Fox and her ravings,' spat Rabbit.

'I am not raving,' insisted Fox. 'It is an important day, because he has returned.'

'I don't know whether this day is important or not,' said Rabbit. 'Maybe it is. Maybe this is the day your Mr. Big Nose was supposed to return, but I have no idea.'

Fox turned to Rabbit her eyes opened. 'This is no accident, Rabbit. We are here the same time Mr. Big Nose arrived, and Monkey is holding a flute that belonged to him last time he was here, and we decide the following day's destination by chance, by whim, by fancy. There was no plan to come here.'

'We came at the right time,' said Monkey. 'We did not come late or too early. If we arrived today, we would not have met him at all.'

Fox was still adjusting her eyes to the sun. The force of the sun's reflections blurred her vision, and she felt a dizziness of spirit. She rubbed her head. The bruises will come out, she thought, and she had a terrible headache. She had to close her eyes again because the sun was too strong. When she fell and bumped her head, the past seeped into her active memory and she recalled the trauma of the past. She rubbed her head and in the morning sun, she drifted back into a dreamlike state.

Fox remembered the day that haunted her, the day her world ended. The foxes marched in procession through the forest, led by an advance party of soldiers, followed by the imperial guards and the palanquin of the empress, reinforced from behind by another party of warriors. They wore blue and red, the colors of the royal house. Fox led the advance party. As they turned a bend in the road, she noticed something amiss. It was a smell, faint but certain.

She shouted a command to the others, but as the words left her lips, an arrow grazed her face, burrowing into a tree on the other side of the road. Two more arrows found their mark, bringing down two of the advance party. Before she could pull an arrow from her pouch, another soldier fell. She reached instead for her short sword. Instinctively, she knocked away two arrows which sought her, and she leapt into the underground. She came face to face with a smallish crouching figure, clothed all in black, except for a small slit for the eyes. She did not give him time to react but struck him down. It was a monkey. He or she was an assassin, there to do the bidding of the giants.

Her eyes scoured the surroundings and caught the glint of an arrow high in one of the trees. It was just within reach, so she threw her sword. Before the second black figure could utter a sound, he was dislodged from the branch and fell into the scrub. She leapt back to the road. The advance party had taken up defensive positions and reinforcements had arrived from the rear. Fox noticed the imperial advisor approaching. She was furious.

'The empress is safe. Two more of the enemy have been stopped further back along the road.'

The advisor looked at her contemptuously. 'If you had done your job properly, we would never have encountered them. Let us pray we have no further distractions on the road.'

Fox remembered her surroundings and her memories of the distant past faded. Rabbit was still munching his straw and

Monkey was looking at the flute. Her heart felt suddenly heavy, as if she were carrying a deep burden. It felt too heavy for her to hold, and it seemed to be pulling her downwards, towards the ocean. Her hands gripped the edge of the veranda, squeezing tight, draining her strength. She began to breathe less, feeling a strain across her chest. She felt herself slipping and falling forward into the ocean. Maybe it was for the best, she thought.

The strong hands of Mr. Big Nose grabbed her shoulder and pulled her back to her original position. He whispered into her ears. 'Not today, Fox, not ever, there is always light, even in the darkness.'

She woke startled. She looked behind her. Mr. Big Nose was nowhere to be seen. She was alone with Rabbit and Monkey. Monkey had closed his eyes for so long that he had fallen asleep and was lying back on the wood, snoring loudly. Rabbit continued to munch on the piece of straw, his eyes still open.

'Where did Mr. Big Nose come from?' asked Fox to herself. She was sure that she had not spoken aloud but Rabbit seemed to answer her.

'He came through the gate,' said Rabbit, still staring in that direction. 'Did he come from his world into ours or maybe this is his world, and we are just visiting. I don't remember much of the old scrolls Fox. I was fighting as soon as I was young, first in the early civil wars and then for the emperor, our emperor, or so he called himself, then the later civil wars, wars against the raccoon-dogs and then the monkeys and then the raccoon-dogs again and finally, the great forest wars which brought us to this pathetic situation of having to take on one giant at a time.'

Fox said nothing. She had heard Rabbit rattle off the list of battles so many times so could not remember.

'We can ask him,' said Monkey who had woken up, rubbing his stomach. 'If he can make bridges then maybe he knows how to make food.'

Rabbit laughed. They helped each other up and walked along the veranda to find Mr. Big Nose kneeling before the bodies of those who died attacking them the previous night. He seemed to be praying. Fox joined him and knelt beside him. Monkey sat on the steps of the veranda, but Rabbit walked down onto the sand, past them and towards the water.

After their prayers, Mr. Big Nose turned to Fox and Monkey.

'While you were sitting on the veranda, I caught some fish for us. It should be almost ready.'

Monkey jumped to attention, his nose seeking out the smell of baked fish. He could not remember a time he was hungrier than this morning. In his haste, he slipped on the wooden floor landing on his back. At this Fox laughed and even Mr. Big Nose grinned. Fox went off to get Rabbit who had wandered further down the beach, with the shallow tides washing his feet.

Mr. Big Nose had prepared the morning meal on the other side of the shrine. He had also gathered the fallen masked intruders for burial. This made Fox, Rabbit and Monkey all felt a little guilty because they had not helped him in any way. Monkey noted to Fox that Mr. Big Nose had not asked for help so perhaps he did not need any. This provoked a rebuke from Rabbit who told him that the absence of a request did not imply a lack of responsibility. He added some cursory remark about Monkey's upbringing or perceived lack of it. Monkey responded by asking why Rabbit was wandering along the beach when he could have lent his assistance to Mr. Big Nose and made some comment about Rabbit's ears being too long. They continued to bicker until they reached the campfire whereupon Fox told them both to desist from their quarrelling.

The campfire sat in the middle of the beach and its warmth and good aroma filled their nostrils. Monkey realized that he had not eaten well since he left the company of the Fisher and the pungent smell of baked fish topped with salt, sitting on long wooden skewers in the middle of the fire reminded him of one of his greatest pastimes he had neglected in recent days.

'What are you thinking about?' asked Mr. Big Nose.

'I remember eating baked fish, back home with my family,' he answered. 'I felt safe and warm.'

'That is a good memory Monkey,' noted Mr. Big Nose. 'You should cherish it.'

Mr. Big Nose reached into the fire and pulled out a skewer of fish and gave it to Monkey. Monkey looked at it. It was a small ocean fish, well cooked, partly black with charcoal and covered in salt. The fish seemed to look up at him and for a moment, he felt sorry that he was about to eat it. This little fish, he thought, had started the day with expectations and plans, places he wanted to go, things he wanted to say and other fish to meet. On any other day, Monkey could have spent the entire morning pondering the philosophical aspects of this most remarkable encounter, but on this day, his stomach triumphed, and the skewer was all that remained. Monkey smiled at Mr. Big Nose and asked for another, being careful to be as polite as possible, so as not to incur the wrath of Rabbit. Rabbit was, however, thinking of other things. Looking at the fish, he lent forward on the stone where he was seated.

'Who were those creatures which attacked us?' Monkey asked.

'They were assassins from the emperor of the monkey kingdom,' said Fox. 'As we said before, the monkeys and the giants signed a treaty. How they found us is a mystery to me.'

'Ask Mr. Big Nose,' said Rabbit sarcastically. 'If he is a god then he would know.'

'They were following Monkey,' said Mr. Big Nose. 'You are indeed right Rabbit, I do know but not because I am a god but because I had someone tracking Monkey, keeping an eye on him, as he left the old forest and some old friends of mine. Monkey, for whatever reason, was able to see this friend of mine, a strange and ugly creature. This creature gave Monkey a flute, my flute. I lost it last time I was here. He saw that Monkey was being followed and he was worried about the situation and so he informed me.'

'So, you came to the shrine to collect your flute?' asked Rabbit trying to start an argument.

'Would it make more sense to you Rabbit?' asked Mr. Big Nose. 'I came to thank Monkey for returning my flute to me and for being able to see you all here. The bridge you saw last night extends to many places and many islands. I often walk along these bridges from this world and mine and last night I walked out of the mist to find Monkey laughing his head off when he saw my nose. No one has ever laughed before.'

'I don't believe you,' said Fox, interrupting. 'The ancient scrolls say that you are here to bring destruction to the giants and return harmony to the world.'

'You don't need me Fox,' replied Mr. Big Nose with a smile. 'You have Rabbit who is doing an outstanding job killing giants. All he must do is raise an army and attack the Castle by the Sea and overpower it, throwing the giants into the ocean.'

'It doesn't work,' retorted Rabbit. 'We have tried it, the walls are too high and too thick, no one can penetrate them.'

'You are surprised therefore, that the monkeys forged a treaty with them?' asked Mr. Big Nose. 'Fearing their own destruction, they negotiated with their enemy.'

'They betrayed the forest,' insisted Fox.

'Sometimes we all do desperate things for the right reasons,' replied Mr. Big Nose.

'I do not blame the monkeys for their treaty,' said Fox. 'But what they did afterwards was too horrible to talk about. They killed the foxes and became too much like giants.'

'Too much like you,' added Rabbit contemptuously.

'I am not a giant,' said Mr. Big Nose. 'There is only one of me, and I can choose whatever form I desire.'

'So why don't you wipe out the giants and let us live in peace,' said Rabbit.

'So, you now believe that I can do what only a god can do?'

'I don't care if you are a god or not. I just want the giants dead, all of them. It is the only important thing in my life. Everything else is unimportant,' replied Rabbit.

'I don't believe you,' said Mr. Big Nose.

'Nor do I,' said Fox. 'Rabbit just likes the sound of his own voice.'

'But Rabbit is right,' said Mr. Big Nose.

'How so?' asked Monkey.

'In the beginning, all the kingdoms lived in peace with one another for an extremely long time. They called it the Ancient Order of Things. The animals squabbled from time to time, but it was over food or family, and if they did fight, it was with their bare knuckles and it always ended in a celebration with both sides making peace. When the first giants arrived, they soon began to move into the forests. The monkeys were the most inquisitive and curious of all the animals which dwelt there. They learnt many things from the giants; things which were good to learn, things which were not good to learn and things which should never have been taught even to giants. In time, whatever good they had copied was replaced by the bad and they in turn inspired the other animals.'

Rabbit looked at the fish skewers and frowned. Mr. Big Nose saw this and said, 'I have something special for you Rabbit,' and turning behind him produced a hot bowl of vegetable soup. Rabbit bowed in politeness and accepted the bowl with gratitude.

'The monkeys spend so much time thinking they are something they are not. They are putting on a mask that belongs to someone else,' said Mr. Big Nose.

'Sometimes masks are essential to hide what you are really feeling but don't want to share,' said Rabbit. Fox nodded.

'I don't like masks,' said Monkey. 'I learnt that my brother was a traitor, and he led an army against my grandfather because he wanted to be high priest. I never suspected him of betraying me. The last time we met, he planned to kill me. I don't like masks.'

Fox and Rabbit looked at each other. 'Hence your distaste for swords,' said Rabbit.

'No,' corrected Monkey. 'I have always hated them.'

'They are essential in this world though,' said Mr. Big Nose. 'Or at least, that is what Rabbit would say, wouldn't you Rabbit?'

'We agree on something then,' said Rabbit with a smile.

Monkey, Fox, and Rabbit met Mr. Big Nose at the end of Spring. Already the cooler winds were coming, and the world was preparing for the advent of colder weather. Mr. Big Nose told them that he would stay with them for as long as it was needed to train Monkey to play the flute. Rabbit insisted that Mr. Big Nose contribute to the fighting and Fox wanted to learn more about the ancient scrolls. Monkey was happy just to get to know the tall red creature with the long nose.

For the rest of Spring until the first autumn leaves fell, the four of them had some remarkable adventures. Together they visited many places and spoke with many creatures, Monkey had never met before. They met some white snakes in the forest, bears that sat by the rivers catching fish, some racoon-dogs trading barley and sugar as well as other creatures. Monkey would run ahead of them and introduce Mr. Big Nose. The days were long and arduous, but they could enjoy each other's companionship and for Monkey, it was an adventure.

One night, Monkey and Fox had gone off exploring in the forest. They had been told that honey could be found from one particularly large tree. Rabbit and Mr. Big Nose remained in the camp, sitting near a small fire gazing up into the sky. It was a still night, with no clouds and the stars shone brightly.

'The moon is clear tonight,' said Mr. Big Nose.

'I have never noticed it before,' said Rabbit.

'Why is that?'

'I have spent my life hiding from giants or killing them. I have never had time to look up.'

'That is sad,' said Mr. Big Nose.

They sat and looked at the moon.

'What do you see?' asked Mr. Big Nose.

'I see nothing,' said Rabbit.

There was silence.

'The raccoon-dogs told me that they see a rabbit,' said Mr. Big Nose.

Rabbit looked intently at the surface of the moon. 'I can't see anything,' he said.

Soon Monkey and Fox joined them. Monkey had honey all over his face and hands and looked especially happy. Fox brought back some honey on large banana leaves for the others to enjoy. After several hours of eating honey, they all lay back on the grass looking up at the moon, the embers of the fire flickering in the breeze.

'I can see it,' said Monkey.

Fox agreed. 'There is definitely something that looks like a rabbit.'

'A fat rabbit,' said Monkey, laughing.

'He is doing something,' said Fox.

'Eating something tasty,' added Monkey.

'No, no, quite seriously,' said Fox. 'He is making something.'

'What is it?' asked Monkey, 'Rabbit, what do you think?' he asked.

Rabbit said nothing. 'I can't see anything,' he finally said. 'There is nothing there.'

Fox and Monkey continued to talk well into the evening, but Rabbit soon fell asleep.

Mr. Big Nose listened but was silent.

12.

Meanwhile, at the same time, far away at the giant's citadel by the sea, in a shrine that was located on the outer wall of the castle, overlooking the ocean below and the waves that crashed into the wall, there was a giant who was a priest, a high priest, the most important priest in the kingdom. It was only a small shrine, containing the wooden figure of an ancient god, the one whom the priest believed would protect the castle from calamity.

The wooden figure was incredibly old and had been brought with the priest when he had travelled over the ocean to this land. He had instructed the architects on the design of the castle and especially on the location of this shrine as it needed to be in a place that the first rays of the sun could touch in the morning. The wooden figure had been passed down to him by his father, the high priest before him and his father before him. It was the only significant idol he salvaged from the great calamity which befell his people, and which brought them to the land they now lived.

The rest of the idols, small and great, were consumed in a conflagration as the result of war between his people and another race who had invaded their lands. It was the only idol he really cared about, and it was the faith of his heart. He feared the sea and feared the ocean gods and was careful to perform many ceremonies on behalf of the people to appease the deities, lest they break out against them and destroy them and their city.

But that morning, as he held the ancient idol in his hands with deepest reverence, he realized that, so few believed in the old ways and the old stories. They believed in the Castle by the Sea and the power it gave. His faith, the faith of his ancestors, was slowly being overtaken by a new and dangerous way of thinking.

He could not believe why his emperor would bother making an agreement with monkeys, no matter how devious or cunning they were. In the lands they had left across the oceans, animals and people had nothing to do with each other, each knew their place and there was no thought that a monkey would ever know a giant. It astonished him that monkeys were walking upright and writing and fighting and reasoning philosophy. He could not explain it with all the wisdom at his disposal, but he concluded that for some reason, life was more abundant in this new home of the giants, far away from their world of fire and death. Maybe it was the soil, or the air, or the water, or maybe all three, but there was something rich beyond description, not in terms of wealth, but life itself. He kept his conclusions to himself. It did not help that the emperors of the giants were becoming increasingly insane, the natural result of generations of inbreeding. The current emperor was even more insane than his father and his grandfather. He was more obsessed with threats and dangers and becoming more paranoid by the day.

The emperor's claim to power, if it was anything, was the ownership of three great sacred objects. The high priest knew that the reason this emperor was emperor was that his grandfather was the last one standing in a vicious inheritance dispute. The story was, at least, that the gods of old had agreed that the emperor's grandfather was the one to lead his people forever and that his leadership would bring peace and prosperity. The gods gave the old man three sacred objects: a mirror, a sword and necklace. These items of great worth were passed on from him to his son and then to the current emperor. They were said to contain great power. If they were destroyed, it was said, the giants would all vanish from the face of the earth.

The priest knew that this was of course nonsense. He knew that those in power often invented stories to cover up their brutal ascension to the throne. The one to whom the three sacred objects were given died shortly afterwards, poisoned by his son and then the son oversaw foolish negotiations with a new race of people who arrived in their territory. These negotiations involved clever but terrible betrayal which may have worked if the new race was without allies, but they were not. The allies joined with them and pushed the emperor and his people to the ocean where there was a great and terrible slaughter. The remnant, including the high priest, the imperial family, and a few dozen families, fled in ships to the land they now call home. Along the way, the necklace was lost, and the sword perished in the war. Only the mirror remained, and it was the greatest treasure of the emperor and his people.

Most of the emperor's subjects also knew this and had long given up any sense of devotion to the old faith. The imperial house had fallen into decay, propped up by a series of violent repressions. The most recent uprising had resulted in the destruction of many of the shrines and important buildings in some of the outlying towns on the edge of the city. The priest, as a member of the imperial household, remained impartial in the affairs of state, partly because he wanted to survive, but also, he was conscious about the small number of people who still believed in the old ways. He was responsible for them. The local people whose shrines had been burnt asked him to visit one of the outlying towns to oversee the repairs of the local shrine.

The chamberlain, the closest advisor to the emperor wanted the priest to go because he was widely respected by all sides of the conflict due to his wisdom and maturity. But the chamberlain had another goal in mind. The priest was also to meet up with the cousin of the emperor, the last surviving relative, the only not to have been purged, a prince in his own right, though none would dare utter that title openly. It had transpired that the emperor's cousin had somehow embroiled himself in a local controversy which may have involved taking more than passing interest in the recently concluded civil war. The priest protested that this task lay outside his official responsibilities, but he had no choice, and with a small group of assistants, soon arrived in the town.

The town officials greeted him warmly and explained to him the situation. The cousin of the emperor had indeed participated in the recent conflict, aligning his banner with a giant who gambled and lost. The prince had decided to usurp his older cousin but failed. The war had brought devastation to the town and one evening, soldiers from the now triumphant general, loyal to the emperor, had ransacked some merchant warehouses. One of the warehouses caught alight. Many died in the blaze, and more were badly burned. The priest and his assistants treated as many as they could.

The town officials were deeply concerned that the prince's disloyalty might incur the wrath of the emperor. More disturbing was that this behavior of the emperor's cousin was completely out of character. He was a large, fat giant, taken by many indulgences and not given to helping anyone. This complacent, selfish giant suddenly and abruptly changed after he returned from a trip into the forest. He said nothing, only murmuring to himself and asking for strong drink. He locked himself in his residence and spent the time wailing and drinking. When he emerged, he immediately plotted the ruin of the Castle by the Sea, or so the officials alleged.

The priest entered the room. Two soldiers guarded it. The room was bare, made of wooden flooring and in the middle sat the cousin. The priest bowed deeply and sat down in front of him.

'Excellency, I pardon this intrusion,' he said. 'I am a humble servant of your cousin the emperor and I have been asked to...' he was interrupted.

'They think I have lost my mind,' said the cousin, looking up.

'Have you?' asked the priest directly.

The cousin smiled slowly. 'I am still royalty,' he said. 'A direct question like that in the city would result in harsh punishment, even for a priest.'

'Yes, excellency,' said the priest. 'But as you said they all believe that you have lost your mind.'

The cousin grinned insincerely and leaned forward. 'I am quite mad,' he said calmly.

The priest said nothing.

'I never believed the stories you see.'

'What stories?'

'As a boy, in class, about the old times, the old writings, your area of expertise,' he said, pointing at the priest.

'Has this changed?'

The cousin grinned again, and his eyes filled with tears. 'I saw him.'

'Whom did you see?'

'The one who gave the first emperor the mirror and the sword the one in the old stories.'

The priest leaned forward intently. 'What did he say to you?'

The cousin's eyes turned dark, as if in despair. 'Our time is at an end. Very soon, all of us will be dead. The Castle by the Sea will fall.'

The Castle by the Sea, or the Palace of the Dawn as the giants called it, was the greatest building the giants ever constructed in their new home. In fact, it was much larger and more extensive than anything they had built before. The city of the giants was on the coast, the main castle drawing the water for its moat directly from the tides. The bay was protected from the full force of the wind and the sea by the headlands through which ships came and off-loaded their cargo. The giants had originally come from a distant land and despite their long sojourn, had for reasons of tradition decided to dwell on the coast. There were of course several small towns inland, but most hugged the coast and because the roads were so poorly developed, they relied heavily on local shipping.

The city was also a reminder to the giants of where they had come from. They were as they believed, the last survivors of a calamity, arriving in a small fleet of ships. The castle was built to survive and survive it would. It would take an unnatural calamity of a terrible tsunami to scale the walls of the castle, and even if it did, most of the outlying towns would survive.

The cousin of the emperor was quite mad, concluded the priest, noticing the prince's frantic eyes shifting back and forth and endless fidgeting. The priest spoke with him some more and the more he said confirmed it. He was rambling and quite insane. He mumbled, was unable to finish sentences, sighed often, and wept. The priest took notes and tried to make sense of the mental chaos of this deeply troubled heir to the throne.

The priest quickly returned to the city after the strange conversation with the emperor's cousin and soon sat inside the throne room in the castle by the sea. He had not changed since his return. This displeased the chamberlain who saw to all the affairs of the imperial household. He sat opposite the priest in a large room with a polished wooden floor. Sliding doors extended around the wall except in the front. There was a raised platform, and it was veiled by a long bamboo curtain.

Behind this curtain were two more curtains hiding the sitting figure of the emperor. It was impossible for anyone to see his face and rarely did others hear him speak. The priest realized that this was the first time he had ever been in this room, and he felt uncomfortable in his worn clothes. Both the priest and the chamberlain bowed deeply when the emperor made his presence known.

The chamberlain spoke. 'My Lord, we apologize for this intrusion, but we have a matter of some importance which we would like to bring to your notice.'

The emperor said nothing, so the chamberlain continued.

'Your cousin is indeed in a troubled state, as we feared.'

He motioned to the priest to speak.

'My Lord,' said the priest. 'I spoke to your cousin a few days ago. It is the prince's belief that he had an epiphany in the forest while walking there, a vision. As to the more delicate matter of his participation in an incident of scandal, the allegations exist, but I found no direct evidence other than a complete loyalty to his excellency and to the Palace of the Dawn. I believe any actions subsequent to his epiphany need to be understood in that context.'

'Please explain what you mean by 'vision,'' insisted the chamberlain.

'I will do my best,' replied the priest cautiously. 'Your cousin, the prince saw a woman walking in the forest. She was not a giant, but smaller and slenderer than our women. He had not seen her kind before, and he followed her to a place where there was a monkey, rabbit, and a tall giant with a long red nose. He was told that a calamity would befall this citadel and lead to its complete destruction.'

There was silence from behind the curtain.

The chamberlain said nothing. The priest sat waiting for an answer. He would soon get it in the form of a raspy whisper from across the room.

'Autumn has already arrived, there is snow on the peaks, it cold in the nights and my cousin needs an extension of his stipend. He doesn't need to bother me with silly stories of calamity,' said the emperor. 'I forgive my cousin and wish him to return to the palace, he has been away too long.'

'My Lord is too gracious,' said the chamberlain.

'As for the vision,' continued the emperor. 'I believe you saw my cousin with a sickness of the mind. He had, after all, been involved in the last rebellion and I suspect my neglect of him was the reason for his alienation. His loneliness must have led him to experience this epiphany as you call it, and I concur that we can dismiss the proposition of ill-intent. Please return to my cousin immediately and convey to him my deepest love and entreat him to return home.'

The priest bowed, thanked the emperor, bowing deeply to the

floor. He bowed to the chamberlain as well and left the room. As the instructions meant right away, he had no time to wash and reluctantly set off on his journey at once. He did not know it at the time, but he would never return to the Palace of the Dawn.

With the priest gone, the chamberlain sat in the hall, silent.

'Nothing to say?' asked the emperor in his proper voice, a deep, resonating tone of abiding authority.

'I am a little surprised,' said the chamberlain 'We have heard rumors of the return of the long-nosed god of the ocean.'

'There is no god,' said the emperor firmly.

'Whatever he is,' corrected the chamberlain.

The emperor spoke. 'As you know chamberlain, my grandfather and father were both fools. They failed to protect themselves against their enemies and my grandfather lost us the kingdom. You remember our great citadels and ramparts, the way the world trembled at our feet. That war was against people like us, well-armed with regiments and cannons and fire. We now fight superstition and false gods, whether it is the crazy monkeys and their quest for power or the others who believe in this red-nosed monster who flies. It is all complete nonsense. My father did not understand this, and his death paved the way for our treaty with the forest. He made a treaty with these creatures, and I intend to use this treaty as a trap and lure them to their complete destruction.

'We must take away their hope, convince them that they are alone and without help. If we do that, then they belong to us, and we can do with them as we wish. Since I ascended the throne, we have revised the treaty my father made with the monkeys, and they have on our behalf exterminated the foxes and the owls and any other animals of religious significance in their eyes. We decided not to kill all rabbits because they are too busy fighting each other. As for old legends, the so-called 'Tale of the Three Friends,' the return of the ocean god and so on, that is fine. We will make sure that this legend cannot be repeated.'

'What shall we do now, my lord,' asked the chamberlain.

'First, kill my cousin and the priest. It is time to end the traditions of the past. With one cut, I can sever the last vestige of imperial competition, and the last relics of that foul religion we brought from across the sea. Burn the shrine and destroy the wooden idol. Throw it into the sea. Second, the human will arrange for the capture of the red-nosed imposter and will die at his hand. After that we can rest in the land forever with no more curses, no more legends, and no more fear.'

'If the human kills the mountain creature, the curse will pass onto him and his people,' added the chamberlain. 'His race is the same one that forced us to leave our home and come to this forested world. My lord, you are all wise and knowing, truly a god yourself.'

The emperor laughed and stared at his chamberlain through the curtain, his eyes narrowed and his face emotionless.

The priest did as he was ordered by the emperor and returned to tell the prince the good news. He went alone. He dismissed his servants so they could attend to their own affairs. He did not believe his journey would take as long as before and he was happy to be able to convey the good news to the emperor's cousin. He also felt a great relief for if what the emperor said was true, then the cousin's mind would soon be at rest. The town was as he found it in his previous visit. The local officials were glad to hear of the emperor's proclamation of forgiveness as they had feared some retribution because of the prince's involvement in the recent rebellion. The cousin was said to be resting in one of the tea houses. The priest spoke with the officials for a while before entering the gate to the tea house.

He walked along the stone path until reaching the veranda. He took off his sandals and stepped up. He looked down at his feet. His clothes and feet were filthy. He longed for a nice cup of tea and some place to lay his head for a while. Upon entering the room, he saw the prince asleep on the floor. He bowed deeply, with his head to the floor, and made his introduction, but something seemed out of place. He approached and crouched down. The cousin of the emperor was dead. A cup lay on the floor. He had been poisoned.

'Treachery!' shouted the priest and ran out of the tea house, across the stone steps to the veranda of the main building 'Murder!' he called.

No sooner had the words left his mouth than an arrow scratched his face, only to become lodged in one of the frames of the veranda.

A town official appeared. 'We are under attack!' he said

frantically. 'Hide! Please hide yourself!'

The official's face looked surprised and fell into the priest's arms, an arrow in his back.

The priest took the officials sword. He ran back into the room and burst through the paper screen. In moments he was in the forest, and he began to run. The priest ran with determination through the trees. His first duty, he thought was to report the death of the cousin to the imperial house as soon as possible, but he dared not use the roads, so he kept to the undergrowth.

After two hours of fleeing, he felt comfortable enough to rest by a stream to drink and think over the events. He sat down on a large flat stone which was beside the stream. The forest air was cool, and he sighed deeply. It was then that he saw her. A woman stood on the other side of the stream, dressed like a traveler, in red and blue. She had a bow over her shoulder and a small sword at her waist. The priest thought for a moment that he had found the assassin. His hand reached for his sword, and he stood up facing her. She was beautiful.

As soon as he faced her, the priest heard a sound in the undergrowth behind him and turned around quickly. Four giants appeared dressed in black and attacked him without provocation. The priest drew his sword and quickly cut one down. The others waited for a reaction, but the priest went to the stream and stood in it. He looked to find the woman, but she was gone. The second giant lunged forward, but the priest side-stepped him and knocked him into the water. The third attacked but the priest caught him unawares and brought him to the ground. The priest turned to the fourth assassin, who had climbed to his feet.

'Who is your master?' demanded the priest.

The assassin said nothing. The two dueled in the stream. The black shrouded assassin had great skill and soon the priest was knocked down. He looked up to see the giant standing above him. The giant raised his sword and stood still. The priest was puzzled until the giant fell into the river, two arrows in his back. The priest looked up to see Rabbit and Fox standing on the other side of the stream. He was speechless.

Rabbit was munching on straw, his hand on his sword. Fox put her bow around her shoulder.

The priest stood up. Rabbit and Fox came closer.

'Are you spirits of the forest?' asked the priest genuinely. Rabbit and Fox looked at each other quite surprised.

The priest looked at the figure in the stream, with two arrows in his back. 'Thank you,' he said to Rabbit and Fox.

'Happy to help,' said Rabbit. He was about to say, 'killing giants is what I do,' but stopped himself.

The priest was still amazed that he was talking to a rabbit.

'You can call me Fox,' said Fox. 'This is 'Rabbit,''

Rabbit nodded.

'I am honored,' said the priest. 'I am a priest from the Castle by the Sea. I am now a fugitive, I guess. I believe now that the emperor wants me dead because I told him the story that the god of the ocean has returned.'

'The one of whom you speak has returned to us,' said Rabbit.

'Is he real? I never thought it possible. Where did he come from?' inquired the priest.

'From the ocean,' said a small voice on the other side of the stream. The priest turned around to see Monkey standing next to Mr. Big Nose. When the priest saw Mr. Big Nose, he fell to his feet as a sign of respect.

13.

Monkey saw the ruins first. He ran ahead of the rest. Behind him were Fox and then Rabbit, followed by the priest and Mr. Big Nose. The two had been in conversation for a long time. By the time they had reached the clearing, Monkey had climbed up the stone walls and reached the top.

'What is this place?' asked Rabbit. He had, like everyone, heard of the ruins of the old fortress, but he had never been there, and was surprised how extensive the remains of the castle were.

'It is old,' said Monkey pointing to the stones all covered with undergrowth and moss. The stone walls stood side by side and covered what seemed to be two small hills and the remains of what was an old stone bridge which crossed them. Trees grew where the castle once stood. The glen was shrouded by a dense canopy. Rabbit and Fox were amazed. So was the priest. It didn't seem possible that this place of beauty was once the site of the most fearsome castle in the land. He turned to Mr. Big Nose expecting an answer.

'It all began here,' said Mr. Big Nose. He motioned for them all to sit on the rocks. They all listened to him.

'Just over the hill is a lake, a beautiful lake and beside the lake are ruins much like this. This is a fort that was built on the outskirts of a great city. The ones who built the city long ago burnt most of the forest to build it and killed many of the animals who lived in it for food and for clothing. Their wanton destruction of the environment caused a rebellion across the land with the smaller creatures, the monkey, the rabbits, and the foxes rising against them. This fort fell first.'

'So, were the rabbits, and monkeys and foxes, long ago, peaceful creatures?' asked the priest.

'Yes,' said Mr. Big Nose. 'As it was in your lands across the ocean. This land was full of life, abundant life. All the kingdoms lived in peace and kept to themselves. They do not belong in the cities, nor should they carry swords and fight. They belong in the forests, in the mountains and in the hills. The giants changed all that. The land was cursed by their selfishness. The giants tried to destroy life itself, but you cannot destroy life. It is impossible.

One day, their forest burning was so great that the entire mountains were on fire, but they didn't understand. It was in the middle of summer. The undergrowth was dry. Any spark was dangerous. The wind changed suddenly and because the citadel was made of wood and stone, it burnt easily and burn it did. It took only a day for the castle by the lake to be incinerated. Those giants who were left were furious with each other.

'They came to me and demanded that I restore their world and their power. I refused. They didn't care about the world around them. I told them to search their own hearts and they refused to do that. So, I opened their minds so they could see each other clearly, so they could see each other's true feelings. They did not like what they saw and so they turned on each other and killed each other.'

'So, you destroyed them,' said Rabbit.

'They destroyed themselves, and besides Rabbit, you don't believe a word I am saying, so why do you care?' retorted Mr. Big Nose.

While they were speaking, no one noticed that Monkey was no longer with them. He was bored with all the talk of the past and he was hungry. He was gone. He had wandered off.

Fox thought she heard Monkey call out for help. She looked up but he was nowhere to be seen.

'Monkey!' she called out and jumped off the rock into the undergrowth. A sound alerted her of the galloping of a horse through the dense scrub. She looked down and saw someone carrying Monkey off in a large net thrown over his shoulder.

Monkey saw Fox.

'Help me!' he cried as he, his kidnapper and the horse disappeared.

'Rabbit!' Fox screamed as she was in pursuit.

Rabbit ran to tell Mr. Big Nose and informed him of the situation.

'Monkey will be taken to the Castle by the Sea,' he revealed.

'They know about you,' said the priest.

'So, it is a trap,' said Rabbit, 'they are after you.'

'Your emperor at the Palace of the Dawn thinks he is very clever,' said Mr. Big Nose.

'He loves power,' said the priest. 'What shall we do?'

'Rabbit and I will go to the city and rescue Monkey. I want you to stay in the forest. Your leadership will be needed here. Reach out to the other animals and tell them that the end is coming, and they are all needed to gather when Monkey returns. He will know what to do.'

'As you wish my Lord,' said the priest, bowing deeply. 'I will gather the tribes.' Mr. Big Nose nodded and smiled. 'I know you will,' he said warmly.

Fox pursued the rider through the forest. He was always too far ahead for her to use her bow, so she tried to get as close as she could. The giant could not travel as fast as he wanted to because Monkey was making such a fuss and the undergrowth was so dense. In what seemed like only moments, the rider reached the outskirts of the city. The horse crossed the stream and the rider turned back to see who or what was pursuing. Fox was exhausted but she took her bow and affixed a poisoned arrow. She took aim just as the kidnapper turned his face. She looked into his eyes. He looked at her. She could not shoot. She relaxed her grip. The man rode into the city with Monkey.

Hours later when Monkey awoke, he found himself in a small room. The floor was wooden and polished. In front of him was a thatch of steel bars. The only light in the room was seeping through the metal grate on the wall. He felt sore all over and had a lump on his head which was painful to touch. He climbed to his feet and walked slowly over to the thatched steel. There was a small door, but it was locked. Monkey placed his hands on the bars and peered into the darkness. At first, he thought he was alone as there were no sounds in the room, but as he stood there, he smelt smoke emanating from the far side, below the window. Monkey stared into the void, and he could see the orange color of fire like a small ball glowing and then disappearing at regular intervals.

Above the orange fire, Monkey could see the white of two eyes staring at him. He let go of the bars and walked back slowly. The giant in the shadows said nothing but continued to smoke slowly. Monkey stood still and returned the stare. Time seemed to pass until the slits of light in the far windows turned color and they too fell to darkness.

'Who are you?' said Monkey.

There was no answer. Monkey walked back to the steel cage and rested his arms on the bars.

'I am Monkey,' he said. 'I know it is an unusual name for a monkey, but I have no other name.'

With no answer or response forthcoming, Monkey decided to continue speaking, partly because he was scared but also because he could think of no better way to pass the time. It occurred to him while he was standing and staring that his capture was no simple coincidence. But he was not entirely sure who had captured him. But he was sure that it wasn't a fox or a rabbit.

Rabbit and Fox!

Monkey's heart leapt because he realized that both would be on their way to rescue him. At some point in the future, one or both would burst through the door. No doubt they would have seen the identity of his captor. This brought him a great deal of comfort and since the stranger in the dark had nothing to say, Monkey sat down and then curled up against the wall. There would be no talking tonight, and with that he fell asleep.

When Monkey woke the next morning, he felt some rumbling in his stomach. He rubbed his eyes and looked up. The sun's bright rays were shining through the narrow window on the other side of the wall blinding him. He stood up, holding his hands to cover the light. Monkey walked across to the edge of the room, and held onto the bars, peering through to see what had become of his captor.

To his surprise, the figure appeared to be a giant of some kind. He was dressed in a grey cloak, its hood pulled over his face. The giant appeared also to be slightly disturbed, his face moving slightly from side to side and emitting some guttural sounds. He must be dreaming, thought Monkey. The giant shuddered, and called out 'No, I beg you!' his arms frantically trying to push away some imaginary threat. He lost his balance and half-fell onto the ground, the prison keys falling from his hand, clanging to the floor. The giant regained his composure, picked up the keys and returned to his seat. It was then that he noticed Monkey staring at him.

'A dream?' asked Monkey. The giant nodded.

'A nightmare. Every night the same,' replied the giant. He

pulled back his cloaked hood to reveal a most unusual face. He was a giant but there was no hair on his face and his skin was polished and long, his eyes narrower and had long black hair. Monkey decided to remark upon it.

'You do not look like a giant, and you are no monkey. Where are you from?' he asked politely.

The man looked over to Monkey. 'I have no home,' he replied.

'Everyone has a home,' said Monkey slightly surprised. 'We all come from somewhere.'

'Not me,' insisted the giant.

'Then why are you here?' asked Monkey.

'I serve the giants. I am useful to them,' replied the strange looking giant, but the way he said 'useful' was full of sarcasm.

The giant stood up, collected the keys, and walked outside. The prison was at the top of some stairs that ran down the outside of one of the walls of the castle on the ocean side of the citadel. For prisoners to escape they had to break out of the prison and swim out to sea and down or up the coast, which would have been impossible given the fierce waves and ocean currents. They could also try and go down the staircase and out through the courtyard and the several gates and moats that led to the city beyond. It was, therefore, virtually impossible.

The warden thought it was pointless to even guard the prisoner as there was no hope for anyone who might have been trapped there. He walked over to the other side of the courtyard and lit his pipe and sat down. Next to him on the seat was a charcoal stove and the remains of some fish he had been roasting there the night before. He picked up the remains of one piece of fish. The birds had been nibbling it, so he threw it away. He leaned back on his seat against the wall of the castle and took a long breath in with the pipe and his mind drifted back to the nightmare, but his mind couldn't dwell there and so it took him to the beginning, memories of pain and suffering.

It seemed like so long ago, but it was only a few years since he arrived at the Castle by the Sea. He was an outsider, a foreigner. He could ride through the city and go past the barracks. The troops all knew him, and ignored him, though some greeted him with politeness. The road from the castle to the forest passed through the neighborhood, past tiled roofs and plastered buildings, shop fronts and children of the giants playing. The man had lived among them for two years, walked along the streets, ate in the inns, drank their wine, but he was not one of them and never could be.

It was easy to capture the monkey. He had wandered off and left the group gathered at the old castle ruins. The man did not have to use his sword or bow. The monkey was light, and it was only the woman who followed him, and he was able to elude her. Her presence with the enemies of the giants settled a question that had been on his mind for a while. If he saw her again, what would he do? Now, he could do nothing. He did not want to forfeit his position, wretched as it was. He needed to maintain good relations with the giants, at least until something better came along.

But the capture of the monkey made the man think of the past, his past. His mind went back to the day he left his country and his family and was forced to flee. On that day, long ago, he rode his horse across a wide green plain, the animal stretching and pushing with every gallop, fear in every tread. The man dared not look behind, but they were gaining. The hooves of the horse dug deep into the soft earth, kicking up the green grass. The sun shone high above, and the sky was a bright blue. It was too much of a beautiful day for such sadness. The morning brought him home from a journey only to find his wife and children dead, killed at the hands of the men now pursuing him. He was the first son of the highest elder in his clan, one that fell out of favor with those in power. A question of politics, ceremony, nothing more, perhaps the wrong gesture, or an impolite remark, or a simmering feud, he never discovered the reason.

The enemy struck quickly. His wife died in his arms just as he saw his only brother slain before his eyes. He barely escaped, knocking a warrior from his mount, and riding off into the forest. He was making for the coast and another village, inhabited by members of his clan. Perhaps they too had been destroyed, or maybe they did not know of their impending doom.

His thoughts turned to his father and mother. He did not know if they were alive or dead. The tread of the horse changed as they reached the edge of the beach. Before them was the grand expanse of the ocean, deep and blue stretching out as far as he could see. He had never been to the ocean before, spending most of his life along the rivers and in the forests. As a child he was most at home with such a life, walking along the forest trails, wading in the stream, feeling the pebbles between his toes. He dug his feet into the belly of the horse, and it made its way along the beach towards a small gathering of dwellings and fishing boats.

As the man rode closer, smoke could be seen billowing into the air from most of the houses. People lay motionless on the beach and in the boats. He realized the worst. His eyes scanned the village for signs of life. He did not believe that all could be dead. He gripped the reins of the horse and looked back. His pursuers were coming, but he had made a little headway across the green plains.

A small sound alerted him. Hiding beneath a pile of stacked wood was a child. He dismounted quickly and ran across to where the child was sitting and crying. His little eyes were wide and full of tears, and he could not speak, so the man lifted him up into his arms carrying him to the nearest boat. As soon as he placed the child in the boat, a sound brought him around and he saw a young woman. She was cowering at the doorway of one of the houses.

The man looked in the distance at the approaching riders. They would arrive at any moment. It was too difficult to rescue the woman. She was too far away. He could not save them both. He could push the boat into the water, put his strength into the oars and in a few minutes be far from harm. He looked back at the boat and thought for a moment to flee. It was after all impossible to save her. He glanced back and discovered she was staring at him, holding the door of the house. He felt a combination of guilt and fear and instinctively ran towards her. She went to meet him, and they met in the middle of the beach, in the open. They said nothing and both turned to meet their attackers.

The other warriors dismounted and approached. As they came closer, he noticed that they were clansmen of a distant relative as they wore a distinctive emblem. He realized that he might know some of them if only by name. The one who seemed to be their leader moved to the front.

'So, you are the last of the traitors,' he boasted to his comrades. They all laughed amongst themselves. At this time, the man realized the fate of the rest of his family.

'Nothing lasts,' said the man to himself. He spoke to the woman but did not take his eyes off the leader.

'Stand behind me,' he said. She nodded, said nothing, and hid behind him. He dug his shoes into the sand and stood in a defensive position, his hands on the hilt of his sword.

In a few moments, all of them lay dead on the sand. The man sheathed his sword, grabbed the arm of the woman, and took her to the boat. They sailed in the boat for days until they reached the shores of a distant land. The young woman was beautiful but frail and she didn't survive the journey. He buried her on the beach. He and the boy made their way inland until they found a beautiful valley. It was like a paradise. The soil was rich, and the food was abundant. He built a makeshift dwelling out of timber, branches, and leaves. He felt happy for the first time in months.

One day, the forest woke him early. He arose to the sounds of his adopted son playing outside. He got up and walked over the wooden floor, stepped down into his sandals and washed his face in the local stream. The morning air was fresh, and he rubbed the stubble on his chin. He looked down at his reflection. He could not see his face clearly, but he was older.

His son called out to him. The man met his son in the garden. Their house sat in a large clearing in the middle of the forest. The tall trees enveloped the edge of the clearing. A small creek ran past the house and various vegetables were planted in the cultivated soil. The man had cut down the trees himself, building his home. Life was difficult but they could enjoy the fruits of the forests and the fish that swam in the streams and creeks.

'Yes, my son?'

His son was crouching behind a pile of wood in front of the house. He pointed to the edge of the forest.

'What is that?' asked the boy.

The man stared. At the edge of the forest was a figure. It stood hidden by the shade of the canopy, still and motionless.

'Stay here,' cautioned the man, going inside to fetch his sword. When he came out, he walked towards the silent figure. After he crossed the stream, he looked again. He was surprised because he saw the figure of a woman. A tall woman with long black hair. A snapped twig on his left made him halt; he drew his sword and turned around. It was nothing. When he looked for the woman, she was gone. He looked back at his son hiding behind the wood. It was too early in the morning, he thought to himself. He sheathed his sword and retraced his steps.

'Son!' he called when he reached the house once more. His

little boy had left the wood pile and was nowhere to be seen. He walked around to the other side of the house. It was then he heard the bellow of a horn. It sounded like it was made from a conch shell deep in the forest. He heard the shrieking of lots of creatures and the banging of swords and spears together. He had not heard those sounds before. They sounded like some kind of animal.

The man was hit on the back of the head, and he found himself falling. When his eyes opened, it was night. He felt the pain in the back of his head and tried to reach for it.

'Easy friend,' said a figure crouching over him. The man opened his eyes slowly and he could see himself as if he were looking into a mirror. Was he dreaming? How could he be seeing himself?

'You were struck from behind,' said the figure. As his eyes cleared, the figure became easier to recognize. He was a man dressed in black armor from head to toe, with cloth armbands and leggings. His feet were filthy, and blood was splattered across his breastplate. As the man looked closer, he realized that the soldier had a larger face, with more pronounced features and facial hair. His eyes were bulging and shone in the moonlight.

'Where am I?' asked the man. He tried to remember the events of the previous day, but he could not. There were images and thoughts, but he could not find in himself the right words to utter. The man was about to speak, when he heard a sound, he had not heard for many months. It was the panting and strutting of a giant horse.

His head turned and another warrior approached. The crouching soldier turned and bowed deeply.

'My lord, he is awake, but badly hurt. They struck him on the head.'

The man looked up at the warrior on the horse. He too wore black armor and a black helmet with a mask covering most of his face. The mask was terrible, like a nightmare. The warrior seemed to stare at him through the mask, and dismounted, throwing the mask to an aide who was nearby. He came and stood over the man and then crouched down. He called to a figure standing in the mist and he arrived quickly with what appeared to be a flask made from bamboo full of water. The warrior lifted the man up higher so that he was sitting upright.

'Lean on me and drink,' said the warrior. The man took the flask from his hand and drank slowly. The water sat on his tongue before sliding down his throat. With the first gulp, the second became easier and a few mouthfuls later, he felt his strength returning, though the back of his head continued to pulse. As he sat propped up against the warrior, another aide approached and crouched down.

'My Lord, what are your orders? The forest path is clear again.'

The man looked around him as his strength returned slowly. 'Let me help you to your feet,' said the warrior and put his arms under the armpits of the man and pulled him up.

His legs felt as if they did not belong to his body, but in a few awkward moments, his feet found the ground and he could stand. The warrior released his grip but held onto his shoulders. The aides stood in front to catch him in case he fell, but the man steadied himself as best he could, though his entire body was wracked with pain and his head was throbbing.

His memory also returned to him, slowly at first and then all at once and then he remembered his son. He turned to the warrior who stood behind him, his eyes full of fear but tainted with a glimmer of hope.

'Have you also found my son?' he asked in desperation, running his hands through his hair.

The warrior was full of compassion and held onto his shoulders tightly, shaking his head. 'I am sorry, but we believe that he is dead. We saw a monkey carry him off into the forest. They do not take prisoners. They probably saw him as a threat. They have killed everyone in their path,' said the warrior, his voice drifting off into the night.

The man fell again to his knees and wept. The aides looked at each other and at their master. One of them, a tall and thin soldier with a patch over his eye dared to speak.

'My Lord,' he said quietly. 'How did they survive so deep in the forest?'

The warrior said nothing, so he turned to his associate. 'It is impossible, the monkeys would have killed them long ago.' His associate nodded in agreement.

'Then my lord,' continued the aide with the eye-patch. 'Who is he, for he is not one of us. He is...'

'Different,' finished the aged warrior. 'The main thing is that he is not one of them, so he will find in us an ally.'

The aides nodded to each other.

The man rose to his feet, his eyes drenched with tears and his face red with anger.

'Who is responsible for this crime?' asked the man.

'The monkeys,' replied the warrior. The man looked surprised.

'Monkeys?' He turned to the other soldiers.

They all nodded.

'But they live in the forest, eat berries and wild nuts and they are not capable of such an atrocity. This is the work of evil. It is the work of men.'

'Where are you from that you do not know of the ferocity of the monkeys?' asked their leader. 'We have been at war with them for at least three weeks, and they have laid waste to all of dwellings right up to the edge of our city.'

'City?' asked the man. 'What is the city of which you speak?'

The aides and the warrior were speechless. 'You do not know of our city?' the warriors asked.

'No, I arrived here only a while ago, maybe a year, and moved into the forest to plant crops.'

'But where did you come from if you did not come from the city?' asked their leader.

'I came from across the seas,' replied the man.

There was silence. In the distance a screaming could heard. It was the sound he heard when he was struck down from behind.

'It is the enemy,' said the warrior loudly. 'It is time for us to leave. Come with us, to our city, you will be safe there.'

'But who are you?' asked the man.

'Who is this?' asked the warrior with one eye. 'This is the general of our imperial army, the bravest and the best of us. Count yourself lucky. The monkeys have just killed the Fox empress and all her court as well. We found their bodies just near your house along one of the old roads. The monkeys have also marched against the rabbits and routed them and the racoon-dogs in the hills just beyond here.'

'Come, son,' said the general. 'Let me show the safest place in all the land, the greatest wonder of the world, the Castle by the Sea.'

So, the man went with the imperial general and what was left of his regiment, and they returned to the Castle by the Sea. The next week, the monkeys and the emperor of the giants signed a treaty of peace in return for a clear demarcation of boundaries. The monkeys also received technology to enable them to forge their own swords and spears and technical skills to construct their own houses.

The man was adopted into the family of the general despite some opposition and a wife was sought for him, but he could not marry any of them. In his mind, he could only see his wife in his arms, his dead son, the young woman who died on the beach and the battered body of the child he brought into the forest. His heart was too heavy for love. The wise general saw this and sent the suitors away.

The man often thought of the woman he saw the day he left the forest. He had not seen her since he had arrived in the city. He thought that she must have been an illusion, a dream or maybe a memory of long ago. He spent most of his time with the soldiers for he too was a warrior and they often sparred in the barracks.

One morning the general visited him. 'Good morning!' he said cheerily.

'My Lord,' said the man, bowing deeply.

'You don't have to call me that. I am your father. I adopted you, remember?' laughed the general.

'What would you like to see me about?' asked the man.

The general sat down next to him on the veranda. 'Today the Lord chamberlain asked me about you, what you will do among us. I may have adopted you, but the others see you as an outsider,' he said.

'We are different,' said the man. 'At first, I thought we were the same, but the more I am among you...'

'Yes,' said the general. 'I don't know how or why, but you have many different customs. You don't eat meat, your skin is a slightly different color, you are not as tall or as strong as we are, and you spend much time in the river.'

'Yes,' said the man. 'I came from a different island, far away. We don't have 'giants' of any kind. We are all my height and complexion, and we share the same habits, or we did.'

'Why did you leave you people?' asked the general.

'There was a war,' said the man. 'Our family lost, and everyone I knew and loved, died. I escaped with a girl and her son, but she died on the beach and the boy, well, you know what hell awaited him in the depths of the forests, all alone. I lived in the forest, and I liked it there, but I did not realize how dangerous it was.'

'How long did you live there, in the forest?' asked the general.

'About a year or so,' replied the man.

'That is longer than any of us,' said the general. 'For some reason, the forests are dreadful places. Perhaps it is why we built the castle here and not in the forest. We are sea people, not people of the forest, but you are comfortable anywhere and that is the message I have taken to the emperor. I believe the land is cursed and it goes back generations. Nothing is as it should be. It is like a kind of madness. Everything is out of place. You spoke of the monkeys when we first met. I agree, their place is in the trees.'

'It was the same in my land,' said the man. 'Among my people, the animals know nothing of our lives. They go about their business in the forests, and we go about our business in the towns. We do not understand each other, nor do we have anything to do with each other.'

'That is part of the problem here, which brings you to my original reason for coming to you,' insisted the general. 'The Lord chamberlain does not completely trust you, but he realizes your value. You can be important to us. We need someone to be an intermediary between the giants and the forest, someone both sides respect. We are entering into a difficult and dangerous time. You are good with the sword and with the horse and you have lived in the forest, you know it well. We need as many allies among the lower creatures as possible.'

'They killed the boy in cold blood, he was just a boy,' said the man angrily. 'I will never forgive what was done.'

'You will have your revenge,' replied the general. 'We will move against the monkeys when they have eradicated all other threats. The plan is complete extinction. We will expand the city well beyond its current limits until we reach the lake in the middle of the forest and have extensive roads between the two locations. We are planning industry and forges and furnaces and factories. We have lots of ideas and we want to live in a way that does not see us cower from trees and monkeys. Will you help us?'

The man looked at his adopted father. 'Until my dying breath,' he said with full conviction.

'Each of us has a purpose for being, even if we do not understand it,' said the general. He held out his hand in friendship.

The man didn't realize what he had promised when he received the hand in friendship. He spent months in the forest talking with the monkeys and learning as much as he could from their strategies and ambitions. He often went on errands for them in return for certain favors, usually food that he could not find in the city. He found that he came to respect the monkeys and could see in their adoption of the ways of the giants a fear that the giants were a threat to them. He wondered if there were no giants whether the monkeys would all just go back to being what they were before. The line between civilization and savagery was so thin and the man thought that he was unsure who was the savage and who was the civilized.

One of his errands took him to an island off the coast where he was to capture and return a group of fugitives who had escaped punishment. Apparently, they were related to the emperor of the monkeys, but had fallen out of favor for some reason and he was asked to provide a boat to transport them to the mainland. In return, the emperor of the monkeys would lay waste to the last city of the racoon-dogs.

The secret invasion of the island turned out to be a disaster, though apparently it had been well-planned. The battle was progressing nicely when there was a strong counterattack by the defenders, leaving many of them dead. This was a trick to lure the invaders all to the top of the island and to a large wooden hall. Most of the invaders ended up there, including one general of the monkeys who had special hatred for those who had been banished to the island.

Back in the village, the man suspected foul play and ran to stop them going into the Hall, but he was too late. There was a huge explosion. The defenders had rigged the building with black powder, and they were all killed, including most of the attackers. He did not know monkeys were adept with explosives and this event convinced him to urge the emperor to hasten the plans for the extinction of the monkey kingdom.

Nothing was done. The settlements near the edge of the forest continued to be attacked and the emperor did nothing. As a result, there was civil war among the giants. The emperor's grip on the city was fading. Fear was growing in the town over the power of the forest and the lack of food and water, and the civil war was led by none other than the emperor's cousin, a weak man but the last surviving royal relative.

The man was not hopeful for the future when he captured the monkey because he was pursued along the path by the same woman whom he saw in the forest, the day the boy was killed. He didn't like being superstitious but her appearance on the road was a sign of evil tidings to come. He smoked on his pipe and then realized he needed some water, so he got up, walked out of the courtyard, down the steps outside the castle wall and through the gate to the nearest well.

While the man had reflected upon his life up to that day, and had gone to get water, Monkey had fallen asleep in the prison. When he woke up, he heard the songs of birds whose voice seemed to come from far away. The sounds were accompanied by a few narrow shards of sunlight which peered through cracks in the roof. He stretched and winced. His arms and legs felt even more bruised in the morning. He tried to stand and began to pace up and down the room.

He walked over to the wooden frame and pulled at the lock. It was fastened in place. He found that he could stick his head through the spaces between the wood and was able to look down the corridor. It was dimly lit, and he could neither see nor hear anyone. It was a mysterious place, he thought. Just as he thought to pull his head back in, he heard a sound at the end of the room.

'Hello?!' he called out. He wondered where the warden had gotten to. But there was no answer. He pulled his head back in and walked to where he had slept the night before. The space which was only a few moments ago warm had become cooler and he felt a chill up and down his body. He turned around again and found himself looking at Fox. He felt the urge to call out, but she cautioned against it.

'Time to go,' she said, unlocking the wooden frame.

'How did you find me?' he asked, hugging her.

'Mr. Big Nose found you. He and Rabbit are outside. It is early morning and most of the giants are still asleep. Their locks are so easy to open.'

She seemed nervous, but Monkey was elated to be free and so he followed her out of the prison and into the courtyard. It was quiet. They walked out of the gate and down the steps outside the castle to another gate at the bottom. Monkey didn't have time to look at the ocean. Another gate awaited them which opened to a long series of stone steps winding downwards. Monkey looked behind him and was shocked. A huge castle tower stood out of the ground almost to the clouds, with about five levels of floors and windows and a variety of roofs and ornaments. It was plastered white.

'Monkey!' said Rabbit, who quickly held him and then felt embarrassed and let him go. Monkey was overjoyed to see him as well. They quickly began to walk down the stone stairs. All was quiet. Monkey wondered what all the giants could be doing at this hour. He was thinking that they must have been quite lazy when they found two giants dead on the ground. Next to them was a third gate guarded by Mr. Big Nose. Monkey ran up to him and hugged his legs.

'It's time to go Monkey,' he said. 'Rabbit, lead the way!'

Just as he said these words, they came face to face with someone. He was holding a bucket of water in one hand and a cloth in another. Monkey recognized him as the prison warden. Fox knew him as well. She had seen him twice, once in the forest the day her family were killed, and she recognized him as the one who kidnapped Monkey. She drew her bow and shot him in the shoulder with an arrow. She cursed to herself, for she was aiming for his chest.

The man cried out in pain, throwing the bucket of water at Fox, knocking the bow out of her hand. As he staggered back, two giants appeared at the gate behind them. They shouted warnings to other giants who seemed to be located nearby. Very quickly more voices could be heard.

'We are discovered!' said Mr. Big Nose. 'We must hurry! Rabbit, lead the way. I am right behind you!'

Rabbit, Fox, and Monkey ran quickly down the stairs, but Fox kept glancing back until they passed another turn. Mr. Big Nose turned to the man struck with the arrow. He lay against the wall and had already turned pale due to the poison. Fox never used arrows without poison, and it would have been better if she killed the man outright.

Mr. Big Nose grabbed the arrow with his left hand and pushed the shoulder of the human against the wall, ripping the arrow and the arrowhead out of his body with one stroke. Mr. Big Nose threw the arrow to the ground and placed his right hand on the wound. He closed his eyes and prayed.

The man woke up suddenly and realized that the wound was

completely healed. Mr. Big Nose smiled at him and then jumped over the wall.

Rabbit, Monkey and Fox soon found themselves at the bottom of the stairs. A host of sentries and guards now pursued them. Before them was an open space and in front of that was the final gate of the citadel fortress that led to another compound and another gate. That was the gate the little group had entered stealthily a short while before. A quiet exit was no longer possible. That gate was full of soldiers all running towards their position, and other giants seemed to be emerging from other locations.

'We must reach the gate together!' said Fox.

She took aim at the closest giant. Her arrow found its mark and the giant fell face first into the dust. She quickly placed another arrow in her bow and struck down a second. Monkey wondered what had happened to Mr. Big Nose when he landed in front of them. Rabbit looked up in the sky, a little perplexed wondering where Mr. Big Nose had come from. Mr. Big Nose looked down and realized one of his sandals had broken in the fall. He took it off and threw it at one of the giants, knocking him senseless. He took off the other and cast it aside.

He bent over and thumped the ground. The whole area shook, bringing most of the giants to their knees. Some of them turned to run. Mr. Big Nose picked up Rabbit, Fox, and Monkey and with one jump, flew over the last gate to the other side. He took a few more strides and leapt again, jumping clear over the final gate, well over the large bridge that linked the citadel with the city.

They found themselves in the town itself. Around them, giants were going about their morning chores and activities. Mr. Big Nose seemed to resemble a giant, but that Mr. Big Nose fell out of the sky with Rabbit, Fox and Monkey caused them great consternation. Near the castle wall was a grass field upon which some giants were preparing to launch a kite. It was no ordinary kite, but a huge paper and bamboo kite stretching almost as large as the field itself. Rabbit looked at Fox and then at Monkey.

'There is our means of escape!' exclaimed Rabbit. 'Let us hope the wind picks up!'

They all ran to the field. Mr. Big Nose walked up to the giants holding the kite in place. The wind was not strong, but without their assistance, the kite would've taken off into the sky. The giants walked over to greet him, but he quickly knocked them senseless.

'Monkey!' he called. 'Find a position and tie yourself to the kite.'

Monkey ran and tied himself to a rope on one side of the kite. Rabbit found another position on the opposite side and Fox took the middle. Mr. Big Nose smiled and released the ropes holding the kite to the ground. He breathed on the kite, and it lifted off the ground. He prayed silently to himself, and a huge gush of wind came over the ocean, over the castle and across the field. The kite launched itself into the air going upwards at great speed.

As Mr. Big Nose let his hands go, Monkey realized that he was not going to join them. He felt his feet lifting off the ground and tried to undo his knots. His fingers could not find the end of the rope as he had tied the knots too tightly. He looked down and the ground was further and further away.

'Mr. Big Nose!' cried Monkey. 'Mr. Big Nose! Mr. Big Nose!'

He tore at his rope and tried to squeeze through it. Rabbit called to him. 'Monkey! We are too far from the ground! Don't break your bonds! You will fall!'

But Monkey called out even more and more, tears flowing from his eyes. Soon, the kite lifted above the clouds. The castle seemed so far beneath them, and the giants seemed smaller. Monkey looked for Mr. Big Nose, though he could not see very well with all his tears. The last he saw was Mr. Big Nose drawing his swords from his belt and hundreds of giants running towards his location. Then he disappeared from view. Monkey was beside himself with grief.

The man lifted himself up again. He reached for the wound on his shoulder. The red-nosed creature had indeed healed him. He had felt the poison of the arrow run through his blood like water down his throat. If he ever saw that woman again, he swore he was going to take his revenge. The arrow lay on the ground, broken and further up, a soldier lay dead in front of the gate. The bucket of water was near his feet. He leaned against the wall and in the distance, he heard some strange sounds. Was the castle under attack? They were probably warriors trying to prevent the fugitives from escaping. He staggered over to the nearest slit in the wall. It gave him an excellent view of the field and the outskirts of the city. He could see some giants lying still on the dirt and many soldiers gathering near the first entrance to the castle. There seemed to be a great commotion.

'Human,' said a voice behind him. 'What are you doing here?'

He turned to see the chamberlain with his personal guards. He tried to bow. He explained the situation as best he could, though he could not remember much. The chamberlain looked at him in disgust as did the other guards, and they rushed down the steps towards the commotion.

The man returned to the window in the wall. He squinted his eyes and saw a tall figure by the first gate, just after the bridge. He had a red nose, but he was alone. The rabbit, woman and monkey were nowhere to be seen. The red-nosed creature was walking with a drawn sword, comfortably and determined. A soldier moved to stop him but was killed instantly by one thrust of his blade. A second came from behind, but he too fell, as did a third and a fourth and a fifth. As he watched, a group of twelve soldiers rushed the tall figure, only to be cut down as if they were rushes in a pond. He then saw the chamberlain on the field, his personal guard running ahead towards the figure. They all looked so small from the window, thought the man. More guards fell and then more until the ground was covered in bodies.

The personal guards of the lord chamberlain were cast aside quickly but they were replaced by more and more soldiers pouring across the field from the barracks. The man had never seen so many soldiers in such a long time. There was a terrible slaughter. He turned his face away. He had seen battles like this across the sea, in his home, the day of the uprising. The sounds of death grew stronger and louder and so he covered his eyes with both hands.

In his mind, he held to the image of the tall, red-nosed stranger smiling at him. He could not forget it. He then thought of the woman. His feelings for revenge disappeared the longer he realized the poison had truly left him. It was strange that he saw her. He had only seen such beauty twice before in his life. The most recent time was by the stream when he had captured the monkey. But the earliest memory was so long ago, well before his life in the castle, a sad time, a time that he had tried so hard to forget, a previous life.

As he thought this, he realized that the sounds of death had ceased. He looked up and realized that the fighting had stopped. To his disbelief, the stranger had thrown down his swords and surrendered. This seemed inexplicable to him. The chamberlain was there, as were a few remaining soldiers. The red-nosed creature had wiped out half the garrison with relative ease and surrendered on his own accord.

Later that day, the man was called to see the chamberlain, from whom he expected a stern and public rebuke for failing in his duties to protect the captured monkey. He had spent the rest of the morning resting and thinking in his room, on the outskirts of the castle. His room was bare except for a few books which belonged to his adopted father. The old general had died only the previous winter due to a chill.

The chamberlain took him aside and surprised him. 'You will soon be asked before the emperor,' he said looking at his humble clothes.

'You look too plain, but I suppose it will have to do.'

'It is an honor,' said the man, still dazed that instead of a rebuke he was going to have an audience with the emperor. He had never met the emperor before, nor had most people. It was the highest privilege even for the noblest rank. The chamberlain pulled him closer.

'We need you to attend an execution,' he whispered.

The man nodded.

'This morning we captured a villain, a rogue, a criminal. He is responsible for many of the crimes committed in our city of late.' The chamberlain glared at him seriously. The man was surprised but said nothing, only nodding.

'The emperor asked for you personally,' said the chamberlain.

'Why?' asked the man.

'It is not your place to ask why,' snarled the chamberlain sternly.

The man apologized.

'I'm afraid that in the last few months we have not shown you the kindness you deserved. For that, I take full responsibility. It is difficult for us to accept you, as you know. But we will all make more of an effort in the months ahead.'

The man bowed deeply. 'I appreciate all your kindnesses.'

The chamberlain put his arm on his shoulder. 'This morning, when we met you at the wall, you looked very pale. What happened?' he asked quietly. The man told him the events of the morning in as much detail as possible. The chamberlain listened quietly, his arm gripping his shoulder. As the man spoke, he realized that the chamberlain was holding him not for secrecy, but for support, for he was old.

'I don't know what to make of it,' said the man finally. 'For some reason he saved me and healed me from the effects of the poison. Now, I must kill him.'

The chamberlain nodded slowly and seriously. 'Ours is not the place to ask the reason why,' he began. 'Even I follow the orders of my master, but I am not surprised at what you told me.'

The man looked surprised. 'Why do you say so?' he asked.

'Your arrival at our castle was no accident. If the prisoner healed you, it suggests he has incredible power. He can also control the wind and the waves. I am not convinced that killing him will change anything, but the emperor must be obeyed. There is something wrong, I can sense it. I wish I had the advice of your adopted father. He would have given me the wisdom I surely lack. He and I are the last of those who came here so long ago.'

He leaned closer to the man, so that their faces were almost touching.

'You must tell no one about the events of the morning. Your life will depend on it. We will speak again tonight after the execution. I will do my best to protect you. I promised this much to your father.'

The chamberlain led him into a wide courtyard, one of the special execution places. There was a large sand garden with a few rocks jutting out in various places. On the veranda sat several officials and hidden by the curtains sat the emperor. The chamberlain bowed deeply and took his position on the veranda.

An official spoke. 'Judgment and deliberation have already been heard. Bring in the condemned.'

From the left came Mr. Big Nose, his hands bound behind his back. He was wearing a white robe. Two guards followed him. They placed him in the center of the sand garden and told him to kneel, which he did. The man approached.

Mr. Big Nose did not look at him, but kept his eyes fixed on the curtain, behind which came no sound. The man drew his sword, and then a guard poured water on the blade. The man gripped the sword tightly in his hand. In a soft voice he spoke to Mr. Big Nose.

'Please forgive me. It is my duty to perform. I appreciate your kindness to me this morning.'

'I forgive you.'

In a moment, it was all over. The man held the sword in his hand. He looked down at it and then at the silent body of Mr. Big Nose. He did not sheath the sword but stuck it in the sand. Sliding doors closed the veranda and the officials returned to their duties.

The man stood in the courtyard alone. He reached into his robe and pulled out a bandana. He carefully and respectfully wrapped the head in the bandana. Four guards came with a stretcher and placed the body of Mr. Big Nose on it and took it away. The man looked for the sword to sheath it, but it was nowhere to be seen. Perhaps one of the guards took it with the body, so he followed them. The courtyard was silent, except for the blood sinking into the sand.

14.

The chamberlain paced up and down the corridor. The emissaries were late, and he was impatient. Time was of the essence. The man had executed the major threat to their domain only moments before. Whatever the monster was, he was dead. He was not a god. Gods do not bleed. They do not die. The emperor was overjoyed. The prince was dead, the rebellion was crushed, the ancient religion was abolished, and all the priests had been slaughtered. The emperor was in the banquet hall celebrating.

But for the chamberlain, it was all too easy, too simple. Why did the red-nosed creature surrender in the first place? Why did he bother to set the monkey free? Who cares about one, single monkey? This action made little sense to the old official. His job was to observe the meticulous, to embrace the details of the court, to monitor every expression of every servant and visitor, to ascertain and prevent every threat to the Imperial House. As it was his job, so it was the job of his father and his father before him. The day's events made little sense. In fact, they made him very uneasy.

A servant approached and told him that the emissaries had arrived. He nodded and walked quickly to the entrance of the hall. The sliding doors opened, and he rushed out onto the balcony. It sat raised above an open courtyard covered in small pebbles. On either side sat scribes of the court, to write down the words of the proceedings. He dismissed them.

Behind him and out of sight were a dozen guards ready to enter at the hint of any trouble. He noticed that the emissary and an associate were sitting on straw mats in the middle of the courtyard. The emissary was a representative of the emperor of the monkeys, the allies of the giants. He had met this one several times before. He was his opposite and a diplomat. The aide he did not know. The chamberlain sat down at the desk and pulled open a scroll of business.

'Greetings emissary,' he said.

The monkey bowed his head to the straw mat. 'My deepest respect to you, your emperor, and your kingdom here by the ocean, the Palace of the Dawn. My emperor sends his profound respect, especially on this auspicious occasion.'

The chamberlain raised his eyebrows. 'By this you refer to the death of the false god, one whom some thought was a god?'

'He was a god,' replied the monkey solemnly.

'You have said,' replied the chamberlain. 'But not anymore.'

'You were very bold in his execution,' said the monkey. 'We did not believe that you would be confident enough to carry out the deed, especially with the legend surrounding him.'

'You refer,' interjected the chamberlain, 'to the myth purported in your scrolls that one day he will return to destroy his enemies, lay waste to the cities and return peace and happiness to the forest, yes I have read all the stories.'

'Of course, I refer to those stories,' said the emissary. 'Many monkeys believe that the death of the spirit will not be permanent, but that he will return and cleanse the earth.'

'Not for some time,' replied the chamberlain. 'He will need to grow a new head.'

The monkey said nothing but lowered his eyes to the ground. 'Why have you requested our presence?' asked the monkey, changing the subject.

The chamberlain cleared his throat. 'Of course, I am confident that with the death of the false god our affairs can continue unimpeded. There are, however, some loose ends. The creature allowed three of his associates to escape, three who have now become fugitives. We need your help to arrest, detain and execute them.'

'Three fugitives you say?' The monkey exclaimed. 'The ancient one is unlikely to have companions as you know if you read the old scrolls,' said the emissary. 'But there is one old story, a very ancient one, that says that the god of the ocean recruits three friends to help him, a monkey, a fox and a rabbit and they aid him in overthrowing our ancient enemy, a race of hideous monsters. But whoever his allies are today, I am sure we can find the three fugitives who defected to his cause. Are they giants?'

The chamberlain's eyes widened. He was astonished. The red-nosed creature was allied with such animals; indeed, they were his only companions. The reaction of the official did not escape the monkey. He turned to his official for the first time, and they exchanged glances.

'Chamberlain,' said the monkey. 'Surely you jest with us?' He grimaced insincerely.

The chamberlain shook his head. 'No, I do not,' he said soberly. 'The ones you are to find are a fox, rabbit and monkey.'

'This is disturbing,' said the monkey. 'All the foxes are dead. We were certain of that.'

'One must have escaped,' said the chamberlain.

'One fox is not a problem. We can deal with her. The rabbit we know. He has been killing giants along the pilgrimage routes for some time. We know his haunts and foibles. It will not be difficult to track him down. I will send the One-Eyed Dragon. He will defeat him in battle. But the funniest part of this story is that a monkey is a fugitive in this little group. That idea is preposterous!'

He laughed heartily, as did his aide.

The chamberlain only stared. 'Why so?' he asked.

'No monkey would betray its clan. It is the worst offence, and all the clans belong to our beloved emperor. It is out of character for animals to consort with creatures outside their clan. It is highly offensive to most of us.'

For the first time, the aide to the emissary spoke up. It was clear to the chamberlain that the aide was none other than a leading member of the imperial court and far from being the aide. He may have even been the emperor of the monkeys, incognito.

'We do not presume to question your version of accounts lord chamberlain,' began the aide. 'But what you have told us gives us reason to question at least part of the story. As the emissary told you, there is at least one fox who remains alive. We fully apologize for her. I ordered the execution of the imperial house myself and, to the best of my knowledge, we were successful.

'As for rabbits, as my emissary has explained to you, they do not concern themselves with the affairs of other creatures except perhaps for the one terrorizing the pilgrimage routes along the coast, and we will redouble our efforts to catch him. He is known as Old Grey-Ears and is an outcast among his own kind. But, with the greatest respect, the notion that a monkey, one of our own kind, is working against you and therefore against us is, in our culture, a very deep insult and though we know you do not intend in the slightest to bring our reputation into any disrepute, we must insist that you stop referring to this creature as one of us.'

'I have never sought to cause offense of any kind,' replied the chamberlain. 'Nor is that likely to change, but he was most certainly a monkey, for he resided in our prison for several days. We were told that the red-nosed creature travelled with three companions: a fox, a rabbit, and the monkey, and so our plan was to kidnap one of them with the hope of luring him to our city to kill him. We chose the monkey, because our spies told us that he would be the least able to resist. This we did. We simply waited for the creature to appear, and he was easily caught by my soldiers, and he has been executed.'

The aide looked irritated. 'The creature of whom you spoke must have been a raccoon-dog in disguise pretending to be one of us, but whatever the case, we will see to it that three of them are promptly dealt with.'

The emissary and his aide arose to leave, but the chamberlain interrupted them. 'Do you believe the ancient scroll and its prophecy about the end of all things?' he asked.

The aide turned and looked up at him. 'What do you mean giant?' he asked rudely.

'I mean, have we done the wrong thing? Is the ancient story of the monkey, the fox, and the rabbit true?' asked the chamberlain.

'You are asking a monkey the difference between right and wrong?' inquired the aide. 'You know the difference and you know when you cross the line between good and evil. You don't need to ask me to tell you!' With that, the aide and the emissary left.

'I cannot believe they executed the one whose name cannot be mentioned,' said the aide outside the castle. 'They don't know what they have done.'

'What of the fugitives?' asked the emissary.

'Forget the fox, she is of no importance. She is always with Old-Grey Ears, so they will be easy to find. We can lay a trap for them. As for the monkey, if he exists, the One-Eyed Dragon has a most able daughter. She is the best tracker in the kingdom. She will track the monkey and kill him.'

'She is most capable,' agreed the emissary. 'No doubt the task will be easy.'

'I don't know,' replied the aide who was in fact the emperor in disguise. 'Now that our god is dead, the world will unravel. Everything will change. The end is coming. We must return to our palace in the forest at once and prepare for the future. I fear we may not get there alive.'

Back in the castle, the chamberlain walked the corridors of the castle alone, pondering the events of the day when one of the emperor's assistants came running up to him, with a frantic look on his face.

'Take hold of yourself,' said the chamberlain, 'What is the matter?'

The man was out of breath. 'Disaster!' he cried. 'Disaster!'

'What is it?' repeated the chamberlain shaking him.

'The emperor is dying, he has suddenly fallen ill and collapsed in his antechamber.'

'What are you talking about?' asked the chamberlain and threw the attendant aside.

The chamberlain went directly to the inner chambers of the emperor, violating protocols. He found, however, that he could not enter the palace directly for reason of a great commotion. Not only was the emperor ill, but also were many members of the imperial household. He received word that the empress was gravely ill and so were all their children.

He found the chief steward propped up against a wall, panting heavily, out of breath. He saw the chamberlain and called him over.

He grabbed the steward by the neck. 'There is something in the air,' the giant said, gasping.

The chamberlain pushed him aside and stormed the inner chambers to find the emperor. The emperor lay on his bed, surrounded by several physicians. Everyone was coughing. When he saw the chamberlain, his face gave it away. He was indeed gravely ill.

'My Lord, I came as soon as I heard.' The chamberlain bowed deeply to the ground.

The emperor looked up at him from his pillow. 'My lord chamberlain, at last, someone who listens,' he coughed violently.

'My lord, what ails you?' asked the chamberlain. He looked up at the physicians. They all indicated that they did not know the reason.

The emperor spoke again.

'He lives,'

'Who lives, my lord?'

'That red-nosed creature!'

'But I saw him die, as did you, this morning in the palace.' He looked at the emperor in disbelief. 'I saw to it personally, my lord,' said the chamberlain. 'We burnt the body, and the head was burnt and buried separately. It is over.'

'It is the end,' said the emperor in despair. Just as he finished speaking the room went dark.

'Why it is noonday,' blurted out the chamberlain, going over to the window and looking out over the ocean.

The sky was black with clouds, dark and ominous. He turned to the emperor and was about to speak when the entire floor beneath him shook violently. A lantern in the corner of the room fell over and the floor, made of straw mats, caught alight. The chamberlain was thrown forward onto the ground and the entire roof above him creaked and heaved. He looked up but the last thing the chamberlain saw of the emperor was the once-powerful giant calling out in pain as a thick wooden beam supporting the entire roof fell onto his chest. He died instantly as he coughed up blood.

The chamberlain crawled out of the room and could not put out the fire. It spread quickly to the adjoining rooms. Other lanterns must have fallen for there were other fires. The castle shook again and part of the wall on the ocean fell inside the sea, taking with it, entire sections of the enormous stone wall. He could hear the screams of the dead and the dying. By the time the chamberlain reached the courtyard, the castle was in chaos and there were fires everywhere. He looked at the town beyond and that too was on fire.

It was then that the human came running up to him.

'Lord chamberlain,' he said fearfully. 'See the ocean, it has gone, completely gone!'

He grabbed the old man and took him to a part of the castle wall that was still intact. The chamberlain looked out to sea, but it wasn't there. The ocean had retreated as far as the eye could see and there were fish and shellfish exposed everywhere. Some fishing vessels were stranded, with their fishermen amazed at the sight around them.

The chamberlain turned to the man and grabbed him. 'Take as many men as you can and ride by horseback to the edge of the city as fast as you can, and you must go now! A tsunami is coming that will destroy this city and everyone in it.'

The man did not understand so the chamberlain took the man by force down some stairs and out into the courtyard. He found a horse and brought it quickly. 'You have a purpose. Ride to the mountains. Take as many as you can but get away from here now!'

The man climbed up on the horse, called out his goodbye to the chamberlain and rode away. The chamberlain sighed with relief and then looked back. He walked to the wall and then climbed down to the beach and began to walk out across the muddy sand. He wept, looking back to the ruins of the Castle by the Sea.

'Build, build, build,' he murmured to himself. 'Build the castle wall.' He continued to weep, as his feet sank further and further into the mud.

The man tried to get some of the soldiers in the barracks to follow him out of the city, but they all laughed at him and so he rode on. They were too busy trying to put out the fires. He never saw any of them again. With great speed, he rode to the end of the city, but he was still on the plains. To get to high ground, he needed to take a road through some grasslands towards the closest hill that could easily be climbed.

The Castle by the Sea had taken up most of the arable and usable land from the coast inward, but the surrounding area quickly became difficult to work and that's why the giants avoided it. A long river that flowed from the forest ended up in the sea via an estuary that was redirected by the giants through their great system of moats that surrounded the city. It was this river the man was following as he rode through the grasslands for it was the only way to the hills.

The man eventually reached the lower foothills, jumped off his horse and climbed to the peak. From there, he could still see the edge of the city in detail and the castle tower in the distance. To his horror, it was about this time that the tsunami crashed through the outer wall of the castle and the tower toppled outwards into the sea. He knew he didn't have long and so he ran as fast as he could down the hill, leapt on his horse and galloped through the grasslands towards the mountains.

He dared not look behind, for he feared the ocean might be upon him. His horse strained and stretched as fast as she could, but she felt the fear of the rapidly approaching water. The man spied to the left a tall cedar tree that must have stood there for many years and an easily reachable branch hung outwards. He pulled the horse towards it and jumped as soon as he was within reach. His hands grasped the branch.

At that moment, the waters enveloped the horse, and she was washed away. The man hung there, breathing heavily and then lifted himself up. The waters pushed against the base of the cedar tree, and it began to creak. The man noticed the upper branches reached the edge of the cliff, so he climbed up as quickly as possible. He reached out to the cliff and found a foothold and began to stretch higher when there was a great crack and the tree fell into the water. His muscles strained as he clung onto the wall with his last remaining strength.

He looked up and he could see that he was almost at the summit. He gathered all his remaining strength and pulled himself up. The man felt himself slipping on the rock, so he reached up with all his energy to the top of the cliff. His fingers dug into the soil and tried to find solid ground. He pushed himself up further until both arms were clawing the soil, his right leg dangling and his left leg supporting his weight. He cried out and lifted himself up further. His muscles strained and his left leg felt weaker. He could feel his fingers and nails failing him, his joints at the point of breaking when he decided to give himself one more chance. With his last strength, he lifted himself over the edge and collapsed on the top of the cliff.

It was dusk when the man finally woke, his bones aching and sore. He struggled to his feet and looked back towards the Castle by the Sea. It was gone. The Palace of the Dawn had vanished. The deluge of the tsunami had advanced well up the valley, consuming everything in its path. He could see the remains of buildings, trees, houses, and bodies of giants young and old. He turned his face away and looked towards the forest. It was only then he realized the full extent of the destruction. The wave had swept up the valley, along the path of the river and the sea had extended inland for as far as he could see. This meant that the tsunami did not stop at the Castle by the Sea but could have gone deep inland, into the outer forests, even beyond. As far as he could see, it went as far as the forest palace of the monkeys and their emperor and to the territory of the rabbits and the racoon-dogs. It was quite likely that the entire world had been drowned. The man fell to his knees and wept.

15.

The kite carried Monkey, Fox, and Rabbit far from the coast, away from the Castle by the Sea, over the deep forests to the east, the vast rivers, and plains, to the mountains. The kite creaked and swayed, pushed by the wind, and Monkey, Fox, and Rabbit held onto the thick bamboo beams as tightly as they could. None of them had ever seen the world from this perspective before. Monkey was terrified, Fox simply closed her eyes, but Rabbit was elated, until he saw where the giant kite was taking them. They would land on the mountains, the most feared place for rabbits across the kingdom. As soon as Rabbit realized their landing place, he struggled to change course, but the kite was too large, and the three friends were too small.

Suddenly, the wind stopped, and the kite fell downwards. The descent happened so quickly that none of them had any time to prepare, but fortunately it landed in snow. When it landed, the main frame of the kite cracked. Rabbit was able to release Monkey and Fox from the ropes that bound them to the kite before a new gush of wind lifted it off the ground with a roar and it continued its journey across the mountains.

'We are in great danger!' Rabbit called to the others, trying to be louder than the wind that raced across the summit.

'Why?' asked Monkey, wrapping his arms around himself and shivering.

'This is the mountain of a terrible monster,' explained Rabbit. 'This mountain has snow on it the entire year-round, even in summer. They say it is kept cold by the heart of a giant with a terrible hatred for all living things!'

'Then we must be on our guard!' urged Fox, surprised that Rabbit was actually scared of something. 'Hurry Monkey!' she cried out. They all huddled together and started to walk through the snow. The wind howled and the snow fell mercilessly. It was relentless.

'We must find shelter!' called out Fox to Rabbit.

He nodded. 'I will go ahead and see what I can find.'

Fox nodded and Rabbit walked ahead quickly. The snow fell so heavily that he could not see in front of him at all. He looked back to try and see Fox and Monkey, but he saw only white.

'Monkey!' he called out 'Fox! Where are you?' But it was to no avail. He could only hear the wind. It was roaring and the blizzard blinded his eyes. He tried to go back but the snow kept falling and he found himself without strength.

'Maybe if I rest for a moment,' he thought to himself and collapsed in the snow.

When Rabbit opened his eyes, he realized he was lying in a bed, with rugs pulled up to his neck. He felt quite warm. The first thing he noticed was Monkey sitting up at a wooden table in the middle of a small mountain hut, with a sewing needle in one hand and a straw mat in the other. He was making something and was extremely excited.

'Hi Rabbit!' he exclaimed. 'I'm making a raincoat, look!' He lifted it up to show Rabbit. Rabbit looked a little confused but said 'it looks good Monkey,' and then turned to a tall long-haired old woman who stood behind him, draped in a dirty grey coat, peering down at him with a concerned look.

'Where are we?' he asked.

'In my home, small as it is, but better than the blizzard outside,' said the woman.

'But you are the giant, aren't you?' asked Rabbit.

'She makes cakes!' shouted Monkey holding up a plate of green and pink and white cake-balls on sticks, most of which had already been eaten by Monkey.

'Aren't you going to eat us?' asked Rabbit cowering under the blanket.

'Why would I want to eat you?' replied the woman. 'I…' She stopped talking and went over to Monkey. 'Be careful Monkey, the needle is sharp. You don't do it that way. Let me show you.' She held up the straw mat and instructed Monkey how to sew on the arm-piece.

Rabbit continued. 'But all the rabbits in the forest say that the giant on the mountain eats everyone who is unfortunate enough to cross her path. We even have songs about you,' he insisted.

'Such as?' inquired the woman.

Rabbit felt embarrassed. The songs would be offensive for her to hear.

'Chew chew, munch munch, the old crone eats, all rabbits across her path she meets.'

Even Monkey stopped sewing and looked disapprovingly at Rabbit. Fox stared at Rabbit in disbelief. She was seated at the table with Monkey.

'Yes, my little white friend,' said the giant. 'But you should not believe every story you hear. This is a mountain of snow. It snows all the time...' Her voice trailed off. 'Excuse me, my little white friend,' she said, and went to the hearth where a pot of tea was boiling over the embers of coal.

'Tea anyone?' she asked 'Yes! tea please!' shouted Monkey who had just finished one arm and was working on the other. 'This is Rabbit,' said Monkey. 'He is a rabbit.'

'Nice to meet you Mr. Rabbit who is a rabbit,' said the giant. 'Welcome to my home, modest though it is, it is home to me and the rats as well as the occasional wanderer such as yourself.'

'I apologize for my rudeness,' said Rabbit, feeling rather stupid with his careless words.

'Don't worry Rabbit, why don't you help Monkey with his raincoat, you will both need one for the journey tomorrow if the storm lifts. You will need both the raincoat and some snowshoes to make the journey. It could be dangerous.'

'Oh, danger is something we are accustomed to,' said Rabbit, rubbing his ears. Getting up, he walked over to Monkey. Monkey stopped, looked at him and then introduced him to a needle and thread and what seemed to be some sheets of straw.

'Come Rabbit,' he said. 'It really is easy, and fun. She told me how while you were resting in the bed. We should look quite smart in our coats!' he said happily rubbing his hands together smiling. Rabbit sat down opposite Monkey and Fox and looked at the straw mats in front of him.

The giant also prepared some fruit for them. Monkey was a good teacher. He instructed Rabbit very well in the art of making a raincoat and with the occasional suggestion from the kind old giant and several cups of tea later, the suits were complete. He seemed to have completely forgotten the events of the past day or so. During this time, the giant was busily preparing the snowshoes, which were straw shoes with extra layers for protection and stronger ropes to tie around their little legs.

After they had finished making the coats, Monkey yawned and announced: 'Monkey tired. I sleep now.' He got up and walked over to the little bed by the wall, near the fire, and lay down pulling the covers over him and adjusting the pillow, which was shaped like a brick, made of straw. 'Thank you for saving us and for dinner...' he said his voice trailing off in a whisper before falling fast asleep.

Rabbit was curious. 'How did you find us?' he asked. 'After all, the blizzard was so strong. I couldn't see Monkey or the road ahead.'

The giant tilted her head to one side. 'Ah. That is clear. I had a vision from the one whom Monkey calls Mr. Big Nose. That such a creature would have such a name for such a being as he is quite funny. He warned me in a dream that you would be coming and asked if I could keep an eye out for you.'

'So, he is alive,' said Rabbit.

'Not quite,' replied the giant. 'He appeared to me in a dream.'

She looked at Rabbit and Fox. 'Please tell me what really happened. Dreams are only fragments of light.'

Rabbit and Fox told the giant the events of the last few days, monkey's capture, their rescue, and the battle at the castle, but they also told her how they met Monkey and where he came from.'

Fox could tell that the giant was quite unlike other giants they had met. She was kind and full of empathy. 'I think from what you are telling me is that Monkey is very fragile emotionally now. He lost his family and home and has endured some terrible experiences, albeit with two good friends and Mr. Big Nose. But he is going to need you two in the days ahead, for the winds that carried you on your kite here also brought unwelcome news.'

'What news?' asked Fox, who was still knitting.

'The giants in the Castle by the Sea have killed Mr. Big Nose.'

They were all silent. Rabbit spoke first.

'I expected so,' his face fell. 'He died for us, so we could escape.'

Fox, however, was distraught. 'It is impossible,' she stated. 'He is a god, the god of the ocean. He cannot be killed.'

'He went to the castle to die and bring life to us? So, the old stories were right about him in some way?' mused Rabbit.

'That is one way of looking at it, I suppose,' said the old giant stroking her long white hair.

'One way?' asked Rabbit puzzled.

'Mr. Big Nose went to the castle to rescue Monkey,' said the giant. 'You both told me that. He may have planned to go there eventually or not at all. He and Monkey shared a bond as friends, as you do. There is nothing that friends would not do for each other.'

'But what of the ancient prophecy that the giants would be destroyed by the god of the ocean?' asked Rabbit.

'The giants, my brothers and sisters, long ago, were arrogant and proud. They thought they were invincible, that they could not be defeated. But they were stupid. They built a castle in the forest, in a dry forest.'

'And their castle was burnt by a fire caused by Mr. Big Nose,' said Fox.

'No,' replied the giant with sadness. 'Their castle was burnt because it was made of wood, and they built it in the forest and in the middle of summer they were stupid enough to burn the forest.'

The giant could see that Fox and Rabbit were very confused.

'Mr. Big Nose is life itself,' she said. 'Sometimes life can be extinguished but it comes back. Maybe, in some way, Mr. Big Nose was protecting the Forest Citadel with his own hand every day hoping that the giants would change their ways and love the world instead of hating it.'

'Did they hate the world? Did you?' asked Rabbit.

'Of course,' said the giant. 'We despised the world. That's why we built the Castle by the Lake. That is why the giants of old burnt the forest.'

'Do you think the Castle by the Sea will perish now?' asked Rabbit.

'I don't know,' replied the giant sadly. 'I was there, you know,' said the giant. 'When our people went to war against each other. All around me, my brothers and sisters blamed each other and fought against each other, but I could only sit down and weep for the world we had destroyed.'

The giant walked back from the hearth to her rocking chair and sat down. Rabbit and Fox stayed at the table.

The giant continued. 'It was a beautiful forest, cedars as old as time itself, vines and moss and rivers and a coolness I had never experienced. But it wasn't in our image. It made us feel small and insignificant. We wanted the future to know who we were and what we had made with our own hands. The trees mocked us because they were older than us and we were not in control. How quickly we built the castle, how quickly we transformed the land and how quickly we fought against it. It was only a matter of time before the world reminded us of the terrible truth we had so long fought against.'

'What is that truth?' asked Rabbit.

'We are part of this world,' said the giant. 'We are not above it or below it. We breathe the same air, and we drink the same water, we come from the earth, and we return to it.'

'What of Mr. Big Nose?' asked Fox. 'What of the old gods of the ocean and the forest?'

'I prefer a god I can talk to as a friend,' said the giant. 'I prefer someone who knows this world and loves it as much as I do. Look at Monkey. He told me that when he saw Mr. Big Nose, he laughed his head off, but you both rebuked him and told him to bow in reverence. Mr. Big Nose might be the spirit of the ocean, but he didn't ask you to bow. Instead, he made you breakfast. He ate the fish, didn't he?'

Rabbit nodded. 'So, what do we tell Monkey?' he asked.

'We will have a conversation about that,' said the giant. 'It is about the right time. It is amazing how much that monkey eats. He has a veracious appetite. Monkey told me that it takes one cake to open the mouth, two cakes to introduce, and three cakes to feel comfortable with someone else at the table,' said the giant with a smile.

After the giant retired for the evening, Rabbit sat up in his bed and pondered. His eyes looked over the little hut, becoming dimmer as the embers burnt themselves out in the fire. There were assorted farming tools by the door, sickles and mattocks and rakes, along with some barrels and boxes for stores. It would be a hard life he thought as he remembered the giant's story. She must be lonely up here on the mountain, but she had great faith. Rabbit could not place his finger on it, but for the first time in many days, he felt a sense of hope about the future. He thought it strange that he would feel this in the humble dwelling of one of his lifelong enemies. Rabbit could hear Monkey snoring loudly in the corner. Dear Monkey, thought Rabbit. He also thought of the day ahead.

Monkey woke up in a fright. He had a dream about Mr. Big Nose. It disturbed him greatly. He shook Fox who slept next to him. 'Fox,' he asked. 'Did something terrible happen to Mr. Big Nose?' He fell asleep again.

Meanwhile Rabbit and the giant stood by the entrance of the house. Both could not sleep because they were restless. The snow had stopped but the wind continued to blow. The giant seemed to be listening to something.

'What is it?' asked Rabbit.

'Wait,' insisted the giant. She listened for a long time. When she turned around, her eyes were full of tears, and she leaned against the door. Rabbit waited for a few moments. Rabbit was joined by Fox.

'The Castle by the Sea is no more,' said the giant soberly.

Rabbit and Fox were shocked. 'What do you mean?' they asked together. The giant walked back to the table and sat down on a chair. 'A great wave from the ocean has destroyed the city and the surrounding area. Most of the giants drowned including the emperor and his people. Most of the women and children, all gone, many of the men. Only a few regiments of the army, training in the forest, survived. It seems the emperor of the monkeys is also dead, his palace is gone, and so are and many of the creatures of the forest.'

The three of them sat still for a long time as the wind began to howl again. They could hear Monkey snoring.

'How terrible,' said Fox, finally. 'Mr. Big Nose brought down the Castle by the Sea.'

'How can you attribute that to Mr. Big Nose?' asked Rabbit.

'I suppose it was only a matter of time before the castle fell. After all, it was built next to the ocean,' added Fox. 'Maybe it was just its time.'

'But there is more,' said the giant. 'It is not good news. There are two new problems. The giants that survived are heading to the Castle by the Lake to rebuild it and start a new kingdom there in the middle of the forest. The second is that the general who leads the imperial army of the monkeys is now in charge. He is called the One-eyed Dragon and his daughter is leading them. She has orders to hunt down and kill Monkey.'

'What's a dragon?' asked Rabbit. 'I have heard the name from time to time, but I have no idea what it is.'

The giant ignored Rabbit, assuming he was being silly and turned to Fox. 'You must decide what to do. Speak to the other tribes and try and convince the monkeys to work with you and stop the new castle. You don't want another castle in the forest. They will simply do what they did before and burn everything.'

'Can you help us?' asked Fox.

'I am too old now,' admitted the giant. 'But I will lead you all down the mountain to safety.'

She turned to Monkey who was still asleep. 'We also should tell Monkey about Mr. Big Nose,' she said.

'I will do it,' said Fox.

'We will do it together,' said Rabbit.

Monkey said little after he woke and heard the news of Mr. Big Nose. He didn't know what to say because he was so sad. He felt terribly guilty that he couldn't help Mr. Big Nose and he was sad because he would not see him again. He was also sad that he had lost his flute. He realized that he must have left it by the ruins of the Castle by the Lake.

The three friends put on their raincoats and snowshoes and began the long descent down the mountains. They said their farewells to the giant and Rabbit, most of all, was truly touched by the kindness of a giant who gained nothing by helping them. The weather was inclement and wet, and their new clothes were suited for the days ahead. By the end of the third day, they began to see the last of the snow, and the arrival of flowers on the slopes of the mountain. They had arrived at the edge of some cliffs that looked over a flowing river that curled around the mountains. Fox and Rabbit were quiet as well. Monkey thought that they must have been sad thinking about Mr. Big Nose as well, but Rabbit was thinking about what the future held for them.

It was only Fox who was thinking of the moment. She was increasingly worried about who they might find along the path. She was always suspicious, but she thought that maybe she was just on edge because of the events of the last few days. But she was still a fox and that always got the better of her. Fox knew her suspicions were right and drew her bow pointing an arrow at a rock just up ahead of them on the path.

'Monkey! Rabbit!' she called out and Rabbit drew his sword. From behind a rock came a beautiful female monkey, short, and wearing armor. She was supported by half a dozen other well-armed monkeys.

'Well, well, well,' she said. 'Look what we have here, a scrawny rabbit, a fox and a little monkey wandering along the forest path.'

'Stand aside!' commanded Fox. 'That is unless you want this arrow through that ugly nose of yours.'

'No need to talk to me like that!' retorted the monkey, 'especially now that you are surrounded!'

Fox looked and saw that that was indeed the case. More monkeys had appeared and blocked the path behind them.

'Just give us the monkey,' shouted the leader of the monkeys drawing her sword. 'The rest of you can crawl back to whichever hole you came from.'

'I really want to kill this one,' Rabbit muttered to himself. 'What an irritating monkey.' He looked at the leader and saw that she had another sword tucked behind her. It was unusual for monkeys to carry two swords.

'She has two swords Fox!' he called out.

The monkey seemed genuinely surprised. 'I only have one sword!' she protested. 'Now you are even suggesting that I cannot fight with one that I need two! How insulting!'

'Then what is it behind your back?' asked Rabbit.

The monkey reached to her belt and pulled out a thin bamboo flute and held it up.

'It is a flute,' she announced. 'It is a present for my father, the One-Eyed Dragon!'

'What is a dragon?' asked Rabbit, turning to Fox.

Fox shrugged. She had no idea.

'A dragon is a fierce creature that flies through the air breathing fire,' said the monkey confidently.

'I have never heard of anything so ridiculous,' said Fox. 'Where do you monkeys get such strange names for all your generals?'

'The giants know what dragons are,' said the monkey. 'They fear the dragons and adorn their temples with their images.'

'Their temples are now all gone now,' said Fox. 'Who cares what adorns their temples, they are all drowned.'

'You are lying,' protested the monkey, astonished, with her mouth open. 'You are trying to trick me, so you can overpower us. You must have other warriors hiding in the bushes.'

'I don't need warriors,' said Rabbit. 'I can defeat your entire army by myself.'

This infuriated the monkey who became extremely angry, and it looked like she was going to throw the flute to the ground when Monkey interjected.

'Don't damage the flute!' he called out. 'It might be my flute. I left it behind at the Castle by the Lake, the day the giant kidnapped me.'

The monkey lowered the flute and tucked it back behind her under her belt. 'If you want the flute then you have to come with me,' she said to Monkey.

'Monkey is not going anywhere,' insisted Rabbit. 'Stay where you are Monkey, we will kill this troublesome creature, retrieve your flute and then go and fight the remnants of the giants massing in the forests.'

'What did you say?' asked the monkey, putting her sword down. 'So, it is true, the Castle by the Sea has fallen?'

'And good riddance too!' said a voice from behind Fox. Everyone turned to see the man standing there with an arrow affixed to his bow pointed straight at Fox. 'This young woman and I have unfinished business,' he said.

'Which young woman?' asked Monkey. 'This is Fox!'

'She can change her appearance,' said Rabbit to Monkey. 'And perhaps to the giants she is always a woman.'

'You knew about that?' asked Fox.

'Of course!' replied Rabbit. 'I've always known, since we first met.'

'She changes her shape like the raccoon-dogs?' asked the female monkey.

'Can all foxes do that?' asked Monkey.

'Yes, we can,' said Fox. 'But as far as I know, I am the last fox left.'

'What are you talking about?' asked the man. 'This insanity among animals knows no bounds. There is no fox here, only monkeys a rabbit and a young woman standing in your midst, a woman I met a long time ago in the forest the day my son died.'

Fox lowered her bow. 'You remember that day?' she asked the man. 'That was you in the forest?'

'Yes,' he replied. 'It was the day my family had been killed by the monkeys.'

'That wasn't us and it wasn't me,' insisted the female monkey. 'That would have been the emperor's personal guard.'

'Well, they are dead too,' said the man. 'All of them, the tsunami has destroyed the monkey kingdom.'

'That's not possible,' insisted the female monkey, her eyes wavering.

'There is too much talking,' muttered Rabbit 'And not enough fighting!' and with that, he threw his sword at the female monkey and leapt through the air. Her sword knocked Rabbit's out of the way, but Rabbit knocked her to the ground. He reached over to her closest bodyguard, pulled his sword from his belt, and killed him with it, spinning around and cutting down two more monkeys before their leader could pull herself off the ground.

At this point, she was knocked off her feet again by Monkey who had run forward to get his flute. She threw Monkey aside and her sword met Rabbit's. The two warriors fought. Monkey tumbled down the hill towards the cliff. Fox called out to him and then dropped low, firing her arrow at the man and his left thigh.

'I hope this one kills you,' she said as he jumped to get out of the way. The arrow struck his leg armor. Fox put another arrow in her bow and killed a monkey who was running towards her and used her bow to knock back several others. The man drew his sword and killed two monkeys who were near him. He pulled the arrow out of his leggings and realized that the arrow did not penetrate the skin but was caught in his armor.

He felt relieved and jumped to his feet. He rushed the woman who turned to him at the last moment, and they fought. Rabbit had just struck down the last of the bodyguards when Fox called to him, and at that moment, the female monkey knocked him out with the bamboo flute. He fell to the ground unconscious. The female monkey ran to Monkey who was lying on the ground, seemingly dead. When she came close, Monkey struck her legs, so she fell over and dropped the flute. Monkey reached for it and soon they were wrestling.

'Give me my flute!' Monkey demanded as they wrestled.

'It does not have your name on it,' replied the other monkey in an angry but persistent voice. 'I will not give it to a complete stranger!'

Monkey grabbed the flute, but they then rolled forward, and much to their surprise, they both fell off the cliff and down into the waters below.

'Monkey!' cried Fox when she saw what happened. The man thought he had a chance to kill the woman, but Fox turned and punched him in his stomach. As he curled over, she punched him in the face and he fell back, knocking his head on a rock. She ran over to the edge of the cliff and looked down. She couldn't see anything except the raging waters below.

16.

After Monkey had fallen off the cliff, Rabbit and Fox had a terrible row and parted company, blaming each other for Monkey's death. Rabbit was furious but Fox was inconsolable and withdrew into despair. Rabbit stormed through the forest, stopping here and there for rest, making a few detours to some hot springs along the way, and eventually stopping at a small village just off the main road. He was, by his estimates, three days journey from the ruins of the Castle by the Sea, three days journey from the ruins of the monkey kingdom, and three days from the coast where he originally met Monkey. It seemed a fortuitous place to rest, for he was tired, angry, and sad.

The little village, like most along the road, were the remains of old towns deserted by the first giants when they fled the forest, the ones who had built the Castle by the Lake. A few dwellings remained and they were taken over by the raccoon-dogs, a strange race of creatures known for their voracious appetites, crude manners, and creativity. They were in vast numbers deeper inland, but there were some large communities along the coastal forests where Rabbit had found himself a nice place to stay.

The raccoon-dogs were the most maligned creatures in the forest because they could change their shape at will. The traditional story was that the raccoon-dogs had invented a drink of great power able to control the mind of those who drank it. They discovered it through the fermentation of rice, and soon entire communities were held under its sway.

The foxes suspected that the original recipe came from the giants who had only just started arriving from their home across the seas, but this opinion was derided by the raccoon-dogs as scurrilous. The monkeys were able to return the forest to its relative calm after they gave the raccoon-dogs a good thrashing. The raccoon-dogs returned to what they did best, making alcohol.

The raccoon-dogs resumed the production of their rice wine, albeit in more modest amounts, strictly controlling its sale and distribution. Only they could drink it safely, for it produced violent reactions in monkeys and made rabbits delirious.

Rabbit found himself in front of the remains of an old inn. It was the only structure left in the village. He smiled at this. Everyone except the raccoon-dogs would see this as ironic. The road for the moment was empty of travelers. While he was thinking of the past, a few monkeys had gone past, carrying their wares over their shoulders. None of them stopped. Rabbit surveyed the area. On the other side of the road were the remains of a few other houses and what seemed to be an old stone well.

A path led away from the well into the forest. It seemed that trees had been felled near the inn and alongside the road. When his eyes returned to the inn, Rabbit found himself looking at a plump little raccoon-dog standing in the entrance. He had a blue apron tied around his waist and a small wooden cup dangling from his belt. His hands were on his hips, and he had thick whiskers and large dark eyes.

'Welcome traveler,' said the raccoon dog and with that he bowed deeply. 'Are you in need of a meal or lodgings or both?' he asked with a smirk on his face.

'A popular place?' asked Rabbit, taking off his hat and slipping it under his arm.

'Well,' said the innkeeper, scratching his chin. 'Today is a little quiet, I must admit, even for these sad days, but this is an important road,' he said gesturing to the path. 'A common route for soldiers and traders of various kinds.'

'Soldiers?' asked Rabbit. The innkeeper nodded.

'There is a garrison of monkeys stationed up the road to the left, near the waterfall. Even though their empire is in chaos, they keep up the daily rituals. They patrol the road each day. You just missed them. They often stop here for a drink or two, even more often now in these uncertain times.'

Rabbit entered the inn. It was dark, as it was mid-afternoon, but there were many tables and stairs led to some of the upstairs rooms. In the middle of the room was a fireplace. 'Must be lonely here,' said Rabbit, sitting down at one of the tables.

'Oh no,' replied the innkeeper. 'The path near the well leads to my village. I admit that it's not as large as our capital in the mountains but its home for a few families.'

'I see,' replied Rabbit, putting his hat on the table. He took off his two swords and put them next to the hat. 'Do you have some water?' he asked.

'I have water, but maybe you would like to try our rice wine. It is the best quality in the entire valley. My brother makes it.'

Rabbit refused politely. 'Maybe tomorrow,' he said. The innkeeper brought some water and put it in front of him.

'If you want to stay, it's a quiet time of year. We can give you a fair price.'

'I don't have any coins,' replied Rabbit. 'But I can work for my board and lodgings.'

'That's a fair deal,' replied the innkeeper smiling.

Meanwhile Fox returned to the edge of the cliff where she and Rabbit concluded Monkey had fallen to his death. Unlike Rabbit, she did not feel that Monkey was gone. She was of course upset that she could not explain this strange set of events but, Monkey remained in her heart as strongly as he did from the moment they met.

Mr. Big Nose was dead, she reminded herself. The place he occupied in her heart felt empty and vacant. He was the first one to fully understand her properly, to comprehend her pain and to listen. He told her that light shone even in the darkness, and these were certainly dark times. She couldn't understand how Mr. Big Nose could be killed, or more importantly why?

How could the world kill such a wonderful person? Maybe the old giant was right, Mr. Big Nose was life itself and she would see him again as surely as the sun rose. In any event, thought Fox, Mr. Big Nose, noble as he was, had gone for the time being, but Monkey, dear sweet Monkey with all his strange and funny ways, still sat deep in her heart.

Rabbit, she knew, felt strongly about the situation, and blamed himself. He had come to love Monkey as his own son, a strange and wonderful thing to be sure. Fox knew the shame that Rabbit came to bear for the rumor, or rather reality, that he and Fox shared the same path. He had originally rescued her from the clutches of the giants and together they shared many adventures in the hills and forests, slaying giants and escaping them. Both knew that the life they led would have been impossible in the open. Both had broken one of the fundamental laws of the land, each to their own kind. Even to her dead brothers and sisters, allies was one thing, a treaty for convenience or mutual advantage, but the notion of friendship for the sake of friendship or even love was not part of the bargain.

When they walked together, Fox did not see Rabbit as a rabbit, only as a friend. His company was intoxicating. Maybe it was something exotic, even rebellious, the idea of walking with another tribe in the forest. But if that was part of it, the experiences they shared erased any giddiness. They felt alive. But now she was alone. First Mr. Big Nose died, then Monkey and now Rabbit was gone. She felt alone for the first time since her family were killed.

Rabbit started drinking wine the next morning. The cup seemed to call out to him. He had ordered water, or at least he thought he did but before he knew it, he was drunk. It was an interesting experience. Delirious was the right word, euphoric, like the first time he broke his obedience to his parents when he was a young rabbit. But when the guilt came, he quickly drank some more. Before he knew it, the day was a haze of moments lost. This was his pattern for the next three days.

On the fourth day, Rabbit started drinking early before sunrise. He was upset that he dreamt of Monkey the night before. Perhaps after some more wine, the pain might go away, he thought to himself. Rabbit sat crouched over the table, his head in his hands staring at the wooden cup. Noontime past and so did the troop of monkeys on their daily patrol through the forest. Voices echoed in the back of his mind and the occasional patron to the inn past in and out, almost unnoticed. It seemed like the sun had already wearied itself travelling across most of the sky, Rabbit thought. He felt much the same way, weary and tired of life.

He felt the shadow of a new creature as he entered the inn. It extended across the room like a ghost. It bore the shape of a warrior in armor, in the form of a monkey. He had a patch over one eye. The figure stood still and so did Rabbit. The innkeeper stood in the entrance still bowing deeply, unmoving. Rabbit could hear the figure breathing. Rabbit suspected the monkey was either elderly or in ill health. The innkeeper had warned him that the monkeys would eventually make an appearance to collect their taxes and to enforce their laws, but Rabbit did not heed any advice.

'Old Grey-Ears,' said the figure. 'I thought you were dead.'

Rabbit said nothing. The figure turned to the innkeeper.

'Stop bowing,' he said. 'Bring me some water.' He took off his swords and put them down on the nearest table.

'I was passing by when I heard a strange tale,' began the warrior. He thanked the innkeeper for the water and tossed a coin into his hand. 'It was a strange tale indeed.'

He turned to face the entrance of the inn. He ignored the silence and continued. 'I was told that in a little village in the middle of nowhere, a rabbit had taken up refuge and was drinking himself to oblivion with the vile drink produced in this valley.'

'It is a popular drink among our people,' said the innkeeper boldly.

'You raccoon-dogs are all the same,' said the warrior. 'You always love your traditions,' his voice trailed off as he gulped down the water tossing the cup onto the table. 'And so, you should,' he said with a grin.

He turned to the innkeeper. 'We cannot stomach it as you know, and a good thing too. Alcohol is terrible for morale among the ranks. If we drink, we will end up like old Grey-Ears here. He didn't give you his name to you, did he?'

The innkeeper shook his head.

'He probably forgot it, or he tried to forget anyway.'

The warrior placed a string of coins into the innkeeper's hands.

'If he wants to drink, let him. He has a lot to forget.' The warrior stood up, gathered his swords, and left.

Rabbit sat perfectly still. The innkeeper stood at the entrance and watched the warrior disappear down the road. He waited a while longer and then told Rabbit. Rabbit asked for more wine. After a few more glasses, he tried to stand, but his arms were heavy, and he fell onto the ground. He awoke to the smell of grass and the soft patter of raindrops on his face.

His eyes opened and he looked up. It was raining and he was outside. As he shook the water off his face, it broke a dream, but he could not remember it exactly. He sighed deeply, relieved that he might have had a good sleep. He stumbled back into the village and seemed to find himself back at the inn. The innkeeper was waiting, his face apologetic. 'I wanted you to sleep here, but you vomited for hours. My wife, well, anyway, I'm sorry.'

Rabbit shook his head, picked up a bottle of wine and a small glass and resumed his seat. He asked for some breakfast and started drinking. After his first breakfast, he decided to have a little more but then it reminded him of Monkey, and he broke down again in mournful sorrow. After a few more glasses and one more bottle, he fell asleep at the table.

A loud sound awoke him suddenly. He looked up and noticed that the warrior had returned. Their eyes met briefly but Rabbit tucked them back under his eyelids and poured another drink.

'So,' said the warrior to the innkeeper, standing in the doorway. 'I suppose you are wondering why they called him Old Grey Ears.'

'The thought had crossed my mind,' replied the innkeeper polishing some glasses.

'Well, as you know,' said the warrior. 'A while back, the rabbits had something of a dispute in their imperial family over the succession of their emperor, after all, there are so many of them.'

'Yes, we know all about the rabbits and their internal disputes,' said the innkeeper. 'They are always in their factions, fighting amongst themselves.'

The monkey and the raccoon-dog laughed. They both thought it strange that they had at least something in common, but neither said anything to the other.

'There was, as there always is, a winning and a losing side. The losing side had their supporters and chief among them was a general. He was well respected and loved by almost everyone. Many thought that the losing side might stage a rebellion of sorts, especially if the general supported it, after all, he had great integrity, and many admired him for his good qualities.'

The warrior looked over to rabbit and sighed to himself. The warrior asked for more water. He gulped down the water quickly.

'What happened to the general?' asked the innkeeper.

'He left. He vanished. Left his family and friends and went into self-imposed exile. He has been hidden for years.'

Neither said anything, but both looked over to rabbit, hunched over the table with the cup in his hand. Rabbit could feel their eyes burning into the back of his head.

The old general continued. 'The new rabbit kingdom appeared, and the new king took his place and as rabbits are forgiving to their own kind, an amnesty was given to all who fought against him, but still Old Grey Ears stayed away. He spent the next few years wandering until he started killing giants along the ocean road. I always thought that one day our paths might meet, and we could fight like the warriors of old and decide who was the strongest and most able in battle.'

His smile, which had begun when he first spoke of the general, had gone. He gestured to the crumpled mass at the table.

'This I did not expect,' said the warrior and stood up, putting on his swords. 'At some point, it would be nice to have even the briefest of conversations,' he said to Rabbit, and left.

Rabbit pretended to fall asleep at the table and waited until the innkeeper was gone. He stood up, left the inn, and walked down to the river sitting at the bank. He looked into the water as it rushed down the stream. It was clear. He could see the pebbles on the bottom with some algae. This reminded him that Monkey used to talk about the pebbles in the streams. A tear formed in his eye and dropped into the stream causing ripples to spread out even to the other side of the small river. His eyes followed the ripples until they met at the other side and his eyes looked up.

On the other side of the small stream sat the general. Their eyes met. Rabbit forced a brief smile and sat down. He stared down at the river, its waters bubbling past with faint sounds. The ever so slight noise hurt his head. The general was with his aides, but suddenly a messenger arrived. Rabbit could hear the general talking about his daughter anxiously and he soon left with his aides, leaving Rabbit alone. An hour or so later, Rabbit also left.

Rabbit waited for several hours at the entrance to the forest, his hands by his side, but his sword clearly visible. A monkey patrol arrived. It was one full regiment. One of the soldiers at the head of the column had been with the general and recognized Rabbit. He motioned for him to move aside, hoping to avoid a confrontation but also out of respect for he knew of the general's high esteem for the aged warrior. Rabbit nodded ever so slightly but remained motionless. He wore the hat given him by the innkeeper.

The soldier ordered his associate to return to the middle of the column to explain the situation. He returned his gaze to Rabbit, who stood munching the piece of straw, his hat tilted forward, obscuring his face. This stance began to disturb some of the other soldiers who started to become anxious with the standoff. Their fears were realized when the official in charge stomped past them both followed by a small contingent of warriors.

He marched right up to Rabbit and demanded that he move aside. His words spat in Rabbit's face, but he did not flinch. The official repeated his demand, and one of his associates stepped forward from behind. He knocked the hat clear off Rabbit's head, and it landed in the undergrowth a short distance away.

Well, thought Rabbit to himself, at least he did not have the guilt of unprovoked attack. Rabbit narrowed his eyes ever so slightly, and if the other soldier with whom he was briefly acquainted had noticed it, the next moments may have gone differently, but Rabbit's small stature was hidden behind the bulk of the official. Rabbit lent forward and grabbed the sword from the first soldier, cutting him down. On a return stroke, the other soldier also fell without a sound. The official staggered back astonished, but not before Rabbit took a short blade he had tucked away, stabbing the official. He fell back dead.

The remaining soldiers in the column let out a shout of alarm and anger, drawing their swords and they all rushed forward. Using the monkey's blade, Rabbit moved forward one step at a time, bringing down one or more soldiers with every stroke, until only two remained. One ran off into the wood, but Rabbit killed him quickly, while the other, the soldier who had been at the head of the column remained beside his dead comrades with his sword drawn.

'What are you scheming Old Grey Ears?' cursed the monkey.

'A new war,' replied Rabbit.

The monkey tilted his head. 'Between which armies?' he asked.

'Between the raccoon-dogs and you,' said Rabbit with a slight smile.

'The general will blame the raccoon-dogs for this day's work,' said the last remaining monkey.

'So, we must convince him it was a fair fight,' he said lunging forward, but Rabbit was too quick, and the monkey fell onto the forest floor, mortally wounded. Rabbit looked up, his ears trying to pick up the scent of any survivor. He smelt something and leapt into the undergrowth in pursuit of a wounded monkey who was trying to limp out of sight.

Meanwhile, the One-Eyed general assumed his daughter was dead and he was beside himself with grief. He had been told that his daughter had fallen off a cliff with Monkey and no one could have survived that fall. This brought a double tragedy. Monkey was the last member of the nobility that had survived the tsunami, was in his right mind, and could unite the now divided families in what was left of the monkey kingdom.

The tsunami had killed the monkey emperor, his entire royal court and most of his personal bodyguard and supporters. He was the last remaining general, and while he had a lot of support, he was unsure what his next move should be. Rabbit was a different matter, but he reasoned that he was too drunk to be any threat to anyone. The fox was also no match for his army as several thousand monkeys were still under his command. The giants had, in his mind, all been destroyed in the tsunami.

But the death of Monkey dashed his hopes for peace. He had already put a plan in motion, as he was a careful planner, which could hasten the end of the conflict. Before he heard of the death of Monkey and his daughter, he thought he had something to offer him, something that would make this Monkey stop and pause for a moment.

The One-Eyed Dragon knew exactly what he could do and where to find it. But for the general to put his plans into motion, he needed to go to the worst prison the monkeys ever created. In the depths of the darkest part of the forest the general found a gangly, emaciated prison warden and followed him down a forest path. On either side, thorn bushes stood silently, their branches thick and dark.

'This way, this way,' said the warden, the keys dangling at his belt. He was stunted and hunched over, very unbecoming thought the general. He had the stench of death about him.

'How long have you been in charge down here?' the general asked.

The warden laughed and spat on the path. 'All my life,' he said.

'How is that possible?' asked the soldier.

'I come from a family of wardens,' he replied. 'Born in the prison, lived in the prison, died in the prison,' he said.

'So, your parents were also wardens?' asked the general.

The stunted monkey laughed aloud. 'No, no!' he said. 'They

were prisoners, enemies of the emperor, yes, they were. Enemies of the emperor they were. The late emperor and his family had so many of us down here.'

'What became of them?'

'Died in prison they did, executed by the soldiers.'

He looked up at the general with a cold gaze. 'They were enemies of the emperor, deserved punishment, yes, both of them.'

He nodded to himself quickly and kept moving, not before his foul odor filled the general's nostrils. He moved the lantern around to brush away the smell but to no avail.

Suddenly the wizened monkey announced. 'We are here, here we are, here are the worst of the worst, the traitors.'

'Where is the gate?' asked the general.

'No gate,' replied the warden. 'Escape is punished by death, so no one escapes.'

The general stood, it seemed at the top of some steps which seemed to descend into what looked like an arena. It was dark and there was no movement. He lifted the lantern but could see little. He looked down at the warden. 'Where is everyone?' he asked.

'In the depths,' replied the monkey, his face disappearing into the shadows. The stench of the creature lingered for a moment and then it was gone. The general had seen battle and times of peace, endured endless council meetings and the cut and thrust of political life in the court, but nothing prepared him for this feeling. With all that he had done, this secret pit made him feel that he himself was responsible. He held onto the lamp tightly and descended the stairs. Aside from the light of the lantern, he could see nothing. There was also no sound at all.

'Is there anyone here?' he called out.

There was silence.

He repeated his question. A murmur echoed from a corner in the dark. So, there were prisoners here, thought the general.

'I have come with news. A huge tidal wave has destroyed the Castle by the Sea and most of the giants are dead and our emperor, his family and most of our clans who lived at the edge of the forest are also dead.'

There was no response.

'There is one more piece of news. The one you call Monkey, still lives.'

There was silence. The general turned to leave. It had been a fruitless journey, but a faint voice stopped him.

Is it true?' the voice asked.

The general shone the lantern in the direction of the voice. A pale, gaunt monkey appeared, emaciated, with scars over his face, as if he had been in a fire or a large explosion. His eyes were hollow and dark, and he had greyish fur.

'Monkey? Is he alive?' asked the creature with a coarse voice.

The general nodded.

The emaciated monkey grinned from ear to ear. He turned to the others lurking in the dark. 'My brother is alive, my friends, yes, he is alive.'

17

Monkey opened his eyes and looked up. He could see clouds far above him, swirling around tall cliffs. He heard the sound of water, and realized his fur was soaking wet. He tried to remember what had happened and it all came back to him, the fight on the edge of the cliffs above, the wrestling for his flute and their precipitous fall to the river below. He remembered the splash and how he seemed to float to the top, but the female monkey sunk like a stone to the bottom. He turned his head and saw her lying on the edge of the river next to him, without her armor. She was asleep.

Monkey was used to the water and could easily swim, and he had fallen out of the sky once before, that time landing on the Fisher, but this other monkey could not swim because her armor weighed her down. He was angry that she tried to take his flute, but he didn't want her to drown and so he went after her and helped her remove her heavy armor. She resisted even then and this made Monkey's task more difficult but somehow, he was able to pull her up to the surface and with great effort he could drag her to shore. She was by that stage unconscious and probably exhausted or hurt from the fall. She still was holding the flute, but she had lost both of her swords in the water.

Monkey looked at her. She was extremely beautiful and peaceful, but she was shivering. He was gazing at her when she woke up with a start. She staggered to her feet and reached for her swords, but they were gone. She saw in her hand that she still held the bamboo flute and so she advanced towards Monkey swinging the flute menacingly.

'I promised my father that I would bring you to him,' she said, and with that, she fainted in Monkey's arms. He held her and realized he needed to bring her into the sun so she could dry as she, like him was soaking wet. He carried her with great difficulty to a sunny part of the riverbank and found a nice round stone for her to lay her head. He took off her outer garments and dried them on a rock and then found a fishing rod from a nearby bamboo grove, some twine from a vine, a few worms from the soil and fished in the river.

He found that if he stood a foot or so from the shore, then it was a lot easier to lure fish in. He caught a few in no time and then lit a fire by banging flint together. He made sure the sleeping monkey was close enough to the fire to be warm but not too close to be singed. He wanted to find some salt for the fish but he couldn't and so he had to be content with what he had.

He looked over to the monkey, who was fast asleep. She looked a lot more content when she was asleep. Maybe she just needed to rest more, thought Monkey. She was quite ferocious when she was awake, especially with the swords. He had never really thought much about other monkeys in quite the same way before. His closest friends were Fox and Rabbit, but even though this monkey had tried to kill him, he felt comfortable in her presence. She was only trying to gain her father's approval, he thought to himself. She was lucky to have a father. He wondered what kind of monkey he was and whether he liked to go fishing. He didn't want to leave her, but she was safe and warm and had some food and Monkey needed to find Rabbit and Fox. Monkey also thought that he needed to find some more food, perhaps some berries or nuts for the journey ahead. He picked up the flute, put it on his belt and walked off into the scrub.

Monkey walked through the forest until he came to a clearing, and he found some fruit hanging low on a branch. He sat down on a rock and ate as much as he could. This gave him strength to climb the nearest tree, scamper along the branch and leap to the next tree. He did this for some time until he had covered quite a distance. During his climb he had resolved to find his way back to the Castle by the Lake, as that was where he heard the giants were going to rebuild and start anew. Monkey reasoned that if this was truly the case, then the birds might know something about it, so he took some fruit from the tree and put them in a little knapsack and tied them to his waist. Some of them were bruised on his voyage through the trees, but he needed them all the same.

The first bird he came across was a crow, sitting on a tall branch. He simply ignored Monkey until he produced a piece of fruit and gave it to him. Then, to Monkey's surprise, he flew off into distance. This Monkey found disappointing but continued his journey through the treetops. He was approaching dusk when the crow returned and rested on a nearby branch. It spoke with a very ancient dialect, as crows and other birds rarely speak at all, but when they do, it is always in a distinguished way.

He agreed to lead Monkey to within eyesight of the old ruins but refused to go any further. He told Monkey that crows had considered the area taboo ever since the great castle of the forest burnt down in the past. Monkey explained to him the reasons for going to the old castle ruins and the dangers facing the forest, now that the castle by the sea had fallen. The crow seemed intensely interested in what Monkey had to say. He had heard rumors to this effect from other birds. Monkey asked him, if the crow felt so inclined, to tell any animal from any of the kingdoms who wanted to fight against the giants to gather at the old ruins by sunset the following day. The crow said that he eschewed violence and Monkey agreed, but something had to be done and if all the animals gathered tomorrow then everyone would have a chance to voice their opinion and they could take the proper action. While Monkey was talking with the crow, some of his friends arrived. Monkey had some fruit for all of them, which they greatly appreciated.

The crows all decided to spread the word to all the kingdoms, of the danger of the giants gathering once again in the forest and the proposed meeting, to be convened by Monkey. They also said that they would be on the lookout for a grumpy old rabbit with long ears and a fox, which they thought quite unlikely because all the foxes had been culled from the forest, though they had heard rumors of a fox wandering around with a rabbit. The crows bid their farewell except for one who took Monkey through the night to the edge of the old ruins. Once here, he flew off into the night. He never saw the crow again, but he always felt that this was the most important night of his life and one of the most significant conversations he ever had.

Monkey scampered across the ruins until he came to the exact place he stood before, the day he had been kidnapped by the man and taken to the Castle by the Sea. It was only a short time ago when he stood there with Mr. Big Nose, Fox and Rabbit and the old priest. He wondered what had happened to the priest. He had forgotten about him. There was evidence of a campfire but there had been no one there for at least a day. Monkey put extra wood on the fire, lit it and sat by the warmth until late at night, when he fell fast asleep.

When Monkey awoke, he saw two bright eyes beaming at him. It was Fox. Monkey jumped to his feet and the two of them embraced warmly.

'I just saw you lying there,' cried Fox. 'You were asleep, and I was so happy to see you. I didn't believe you died, I told Rabbit, but he didn't believe me, and he was so upset.'

She kept hugging him and kissing him on his forehead. Fox told Monkey about the huge argument she had with Rabbit and how they parted company. Monkey told her about the crows and that if anyone could find Rabbit again it would be them.

Fox then said that she brought some disturbing news. Apparently, the monkeys and the raccoon-dogs were at war again. According to her sources in the forest, a raccoon-dog wiped out an entire regiment of monkeys. The details were unclear, but it had something to do with the wretched drink they consume as it all happened near a famous inn deep in the forest. This led the leader of the remnant of the monkey kingdom, the One-Eyed Dragon, to launch an attack against the raccoon-dogs. The fighting by all accounts had been fierce and there were many casualties on both sides. Monkey didn't say anything. He could not stop thinking about what happened to the young female monkey he left by the side of the river.

As he was thinking this, the man who had tried to kill Fox and who kidnapped Monkey stepped into the clearing. Monkey jumped back onto a nearby rock and tried to warn Fox.

'Monkey, it's all right,' she said. 'We have put aside our differences.'

'I don't believe you,' said Monkey. 'He tried to kill you Fox, and he kidnapped me.'

'For both things, I am deeply sorry Monkey,' said the man, walking up to Monkey, getting on his knees, and bowing before him. 'Please forgive me, if you can, and my sword and my life are yours.'

Monkey looked down at the man and then up at Fox. 'I don't understand,' he said confused.

Fox tried to reassure him of the man's fidelity, but Monkey was very unsure. How could Fox change her mind about this creature who had caused so much misery for them both.

Suddenly it was Fox's turn to be astonished, for on the other side of the rock where Monkey was taking refuge, appeared the young female monkey who had tried to kill her and with whom Monkey fell off the cliff. She called to Monkey and ran over to him. He had barely turned around when she hugged him intimately. Fox and the man looked at each other in amazement. Monkey was also surprised and not a little embarrassed. She let go of him and smiled. He looked down and she wasn't holding any swords.

'I have good news for you Monkey,' she said.

'What is it?' he asked her. She smiled at him and stepped aside. Monkey looked, and there was another monkey standing there next to her nervously and cautiously. He could not see him because of the sun's rays, and so he had to go closer. As he did, he realized he was standing in front of his brother, the traitor. He was emaciated and pale, but alive. He had tears running down his face and he fell to his knees weeping uncontrollably.

'Monkey, I am sorry, please forgive me,' he said, bowing to him in deep respect.

Monkey was full of deep emotions. He looked at the young female monkey. She, or her father probably had returned to him his last remaining relative. He assumed they had all died in the explosion at the Hall of Masks. Monkey was full of compassion, and went to him, knelt, and embraced him.

'I forgive you brother!' he said firmly and held him.

They both wept for a long time. Fox walked over to the man and held his hand. They both looked at each other lovingly. Monkey was overjoyed to see his brother and even though he had done terrible things in the past, he had no desire to hold the past against him. The female monkey sat down next to the two monkeys and whispered to him how her father found the traitor in the last prison of the monkeys not to be destroyed by the tsunami. He told his daughter to tell Monkey that he had nothing to do with the invasion of the island, or the capture of Monkey's family. Those orders came from the emperor and his imperial guard carried them out. Those who survived the tsunami were already punished for leading the kingdom to complete ruin. Monkey thanked her for her explanation.

There was still much weeping to be had, for Monkey learned from his brother that he was the only survivor from the explosion and the storm that terrible night. Monkey had long suspected that something terrible had happened and had assumed that he would not see his grandfather or anyone from his old life again, but he was happy to see his brother. When he looked at his brother, he knew that something was wrong. His mind was gone, and he didn't know where he was. While he recognized Monkey and remembered bits and pieces, his brother must have been caught in the explosion in the Hall of Masks. Suddenly, Monkey felt older, and he rubbed his chin. There was a lot more hair there than he remembered.

'It looks like this is a reunion!' shouted a voice from across the clearing. Everyone turned and saw the priest standing there smiling. Fox ran up to him and hugged him.

'I have a surprise for you all, but I don't want you to be alarmed, so please don't be,' said the priest. Monkey said that they were able to accept any surprise. The priest said he was glad about that because then seven giants appeared with him. Fox at once drew her bow and the female monkey stood in front of Monkey to protect him.

The priest threw up his arms. 'No, no friends! Please do not hurt them! They are allies!'

He stood between Fox and the giants and outstretched his arms. 'If you must kill anyone, kill me,' he pleaded.

The tense atmosphere changed when one of the new giants spoke. 'We bring good news to you,' he blurted out. 'The one you call Mr. Big Nose is alive, we saw him yesterday.'

Monkey and Fox were shocked. The man said, 'that's impossible!'

'I don't understand,' said Monkey. 'We heard that he was dead.'

Another giant spoke up. 'That is what we heard, but he is alive. We saw him yesterday.'

'At the shrine by the ocean,' said a third.

'We are pilgrims, we travel the ancient roads because we believe in him,' added the fourth.

'We were there to apologize for the terrible things our people have done to the forest, and he found him there on the beach cooking fish,' said the fifth.

'Imagine our joy when he greeted us,' said the sixth.

'It was the most amazing experience,' said the seventh.

The first spoke again. He appeared to be the leader of the group. 'Mr. Big Nose told us that he is the life of the forest, and he wants us to have a happy, simple life. He told us about the tsunami, and we wept for our friends but then he told us about you Monkey and we are here to help you stop the giants from returning to the past, whatever happens.'

'We are all that remains of those who believe in him, in the ancient ways,' said the second.

'But we did not come alone, and we are not without friends,' said the priest beaming. 'I did what I was told. I searched and I found all who would come and fight, all who would stand with us.'

'What do you mean?' asked Monkey.

'Come and see,' said the priest and with that Fox, the man, Monkey, his new friend, and his brother all walked to the other end of the clearing. They followed the giant up a small hill where various stones had fallen from the old citadel. The priest smiled and said to Monkey, 'we are all here for you Monkey and we are eager to hear what you have to say.'

Monkey looked and far as the eye could see, there were rabbits. It was a sea of white and some grey and black. Alongside the forest, he could see deer and a few bears, and boar and the trees were full of birds. Fox began to cry with joy. She had walked alone for far too long. Now, others would stand with her. The man was amazed beyond words. He had never seen so many animals in one place before. He held Fox's hand tightly. Monkey scoured the rabbits for any sign of his old friend Rabbit, but he could not see him.

'I must speak with them,' he said to Fox. 'We will make our stand here,' said Monkey to everyone.

Fox thought it brave words for Monkey to say and patted him on the head. Fox, the man, and Monkeys friend gathered all the leaders of the various kingdoms together. The priest and the pilgrims prepared for them some baked fish over a fire, as they discussed the upcoming battle. As they talked and debated, Monkey was astounded that he was in a minority. Everyone, including the priest, the pilgrims and Fox wanted the giants dead, while Monkey wanted simply to convince them to change their ways. Monkey told the core group of leaders that he did not support violence and would not take up the sword against anyone, even a giant. Monkey's new friend didn't say anything but listened to him intently. Fox pulled Monkey aside and told Monkey privately that this course of action was impossible, that some violence was necessary, however horrible. She strongly recommended that he not announce his position of non-violence to the others, or a new leader would emerge, and Monkey's authority would evaporate. This made Monkey angry, and so he called the meeting to an adjournment for the sake of getting further opinions from the other animals present.

He decided to explore the ruins of the castle to take his mind off things. He walked down the stone steps to an old courtyard when he saw a bear. It was black and furry with a huge bottom and hind legs, little ears, and a long snout. It was trying to dig for something under a log that had fallen in the forest. Monkey walked up to the bear and introduced himself.

'Hello,' he said.

The bear stopped foraging and looked up at him. Monkey was happy he had found a new friend to talk to, someone who didn't know him at all.

'Hello little monkey,' said the bear. 'I've heard about you.'

Monkey was completely surprised. 'How is that possible?' he asked, 'I've only just arrived here!'

'The birds told me about you, and the rabbit and the fox,' said the bear. 'They came yesterday and told me all about it.'

Monkey tried to change the subject. 'What are you doing?'

'I'm digging for roots for my family. I'm sorry Monkey, but I'm running a little late. Let's talk next time.'

With that the bear tore out the root with its teeth and wandered off. Monkey sat on the log and sighed. He lay back on the log and tried to fall asleep. After a few minutes had past, he found he could not go to sleep, so he let his eyes wander. It was a beautiful day and the sun shone brightly above. He could smell the sweet incense of flowers, the rough smell of the undergrowth, and the wooden wafts from the forest. As his eyes wandered, he noticed something in the corner of his eye. It was a small thing that seemed to glitter in the sun, between a tree branch and its trunk.

'This is interesting,' he said to himself and walked over to the tree. When he reached the small glittering object, he discovered a small wasp stuck in the web of a spider who sat perched on the edge of his magnificent creation. 'It was indeed a beautiful web,' said Monkey to himself, admitting that he had not seen such a wonderful thing for quite some time. The wasp seemed to be quite asleep, and the spider sat motionless. Monkey stood perfectly still and waited so his whole body stopped moving and all he could hear was the beating of his own heart, feeling the cool breeze on his fur and across the edges of his ear. In the moments between breaths, he heard it. It was faint and momentary, but he waited and soon the sounds echoed again, vibrating across the tiny strings of the web and through the air. He stood and waited until the sounds disappeared as softly as it began.

'So, that's a curious thing,' he said to himself.

He looked at the wasp. It was still asleep, curled up in the web, not entangled but sitting precariously, between life and death, seemingly oblivious to the peril that lay before it. Monkey waited. He did not have to wait long. His long ears heard the sound, soft at first, but alluring, enticing and full of promise. It was too faint to hear clearly, but he had heard all he needed to and gently, ever so gently, he breathed across the path of the sounds, his breath warm and long. The spider at once halted, and his little eyes turned upwards. The music had stopped. The spider looked at Monkey, then back at the wasp and then to his web. It moved ever so slightly, pulling at each of the lines of his fabric, making them taut.

He assumed his original position, and Monkey could hear the soft sounds once more. He blew again quickly this time, his warm breath enveloping the wasp. Suddenly, as if from a dream the wasp opened her eyes, looked around in alarm, flying into the air. The spider looked up to Monkey. Monkey closed his eyes and bowed slightly. The spider adjusted the web once more and moved away from sight until he was covered by the leaves. The wasp, however, was free. Monkey knew the path ahead. The wasp and the spider had shown him the way.

'I will give them their war,' said Monkey to himself. 'They are so blinded by the giants, and caught in their song, they are asleep to who they really are. They have forgotten. I will give them their war, but it will be the last one. After this, they will all return to the way things were before the giants came.'

He looked at the wasp flying around him. 'We have all been caught in the web of the giants but no more. We have our own ways, and we will not follow them anymore.'

He got up and went back to the others. When he arrived, Fox was surprised at his determined face.

'This is what is going to happen,' said Monkey. 'The priest and his pilgrims and any giant who wants to join the forest receives an amnesty. The rest, we will kill on the field of battle. We will wipe the giants from the face of the earth and save the forest and ourselves.'

'How are we to do that?' asked Fox. 'Up to now, we have killed giants one by one. We don't have enough to attack an entire army.'

'You forget,' said Monkey. 'What the giants have done has affected everyone and everything in the forest and everything and everyone is against them.'

He reached out his hand and the little wasp landed on it. 'Let me introduce you to my new friend. This is Wasp.'

'Pleased to meet you Wasp,' said Fox. Fox put her head as close to the wasp as she could. She had a little voice, and it was almost impossible to hear.

'Monkey saved me from the spider. I am grateful to him,' said the wasp.

'That's nice of him,' said Fox softly.

'Yes,' said the wasp. 'But I'm afraid it is better to die under the present circumstances. The giants have caused us a lot of trouble recently. We heard about their calamity and yours. We are only small, but we are happy to help you in any way we can.'

'The wasps are only the beginning,' said Monkey. 'I will speak to all of you and see how you can contribute. We should have a plan worked out by the end of the day.'

The man went up to Monkey's female friend who stood nearby. 'Monkey will make a great emperor,' he said. 'I see in him the makings of a true leader. He reminds me of a giant.'

She said nothing.

'This is going to be just the beginning,' he continued softly, whispering into her ear. 'Once he starts killing, there will be nothing to stop him. He will be after the kingdom of the monkeys next.'

She looked at the man with disdain. She stared at Monkey. She looked at Fox who was clearly the closest thing to family Monkey had. She had spent most of the last few hours learning all she could about Monkey from Fox. She didn't trust the man as he looked too much like a giant. He had lived with the giants for far too long. She knew that giants could not be trusted. Monkey looked back at her and smiled. She decided to speak to him before she went back to her father, the One-Eyed Dragon.

She pulled Monkey aside.

'Monkey,' she said, holding both his hands. 'You are the last member of the royal family, the last of any of the noble families. The rest have died. You need to speak to my father. After I recovered at the bottom of the cliff, I realized what you did for me. My father arrived with your brother. He sent your brother with me to you, so that you know my father has nothing to hide, nothing to bargain with. He simply wants to talk to you.'

Monkey looked at her. 'What does he want to talk to me about?' he asked.

The female monkey looked at him and then kissed him on the cheek. 'I have to go,' she said. 'My father is waiting.'

She took a step back from Monkey. The priest and Fox saw this as a sign to start talking to him and soon more and more creatures surrounded him, all asking questions, all trying to get close to him. The female monkey was pushed further and further back until Monkey could not see her anymore.

She turned to the man who was sitting on a large rock, resting on his sword. 'You are wrong about Monkey,' she said.

'Time will tell,' he replied.

She left without saying goodbye, jumping off the ruins into the forest.

After Monkey had said all he wanted to say, he told everyone to get some rest. He asked the man to consult with the priest and the giants who were pilgrims on matters of strategy and report back to him. The man looked at Monkey a little surprised, but he bowed slightly and went off to find them. Fox pulled Monkey aside.

'What is the matter Monkey?' she asked.

Monkey moved away and sat down on a large stone. 'When we first met,' began Monkey. 'You and Rabbit were killing that giant, do you remember?' Fox nodded.

'Do you remember what he told us that day?' asked Monkey. Fox thought for a few moments.

'I am sorry Monkey,' she said. 'I do not remember.'

'The giant said that he was the last of the pilgrims, the last of his brothers, and that you and Rabbit had killed them all. No more, said he, would his brothers walk the pilgrimage to the shrine.'

'Ah yes,' smiled Fox. 'I remember that now. He said he was the last pilgrim.'

'Exactly,' said Monkey. 'Then who are these giants who have turned up to help us? They are not pilgrims. All the pilgrims are dead.'

Fox was shocked. She was speechless, her mouth open.

'If they saw Mr. Big Nose,' continued Monkey. 'Then what was he doing at the shrine by the ocean? They are simply telling us what they think we want to hear. They were in league with the emperor of the monkeys after all and must have still been on our trail that morning when we ate the breakfast with Mr. Big Nose on the beach. Monkeys are fast creatures as you know, I knew that on my island the night the whirlwind took me into the sky. They are silent and they are fast, especially when they want to be hidden.'

'So,' said Fox. 'What do they want, these giants?'

Monkey smiled. 'We will find out soon enough. In the meantime, tell the rabbits you trust to keep an eye on them, and place a guard around all their clan leaders.'

Fox nodded and left quickly to do as Monkey suggested.

Soon, the man came back with a puzzled look on his face.

'You see it too, don't you,' said Monkey.

'You are very perceptive Monkey,' said the man. 'There is something not quite right with those giants who call themselves pilgrims. They told me that Mr. Big Nose never died and that he wanted us to make peace with the giants so we could all live in the forest.'

'And you know that is not true because you had something to do with his death,' replied Monkey.

The man was astonished. 'How did you know?' he asked.

'The way you try not to look at me,' said Monkey. 'I see it in the way you avert my eyes and how you looked ashamed when the giants mentioned the name of Mr. Big Nose. I saw that expression on your face. I knew what it meant.'

The man knelt before Monkey and told him everything that had happened the day Mr. Big Nose died, the day the Castle by the Sea fell. After he had finished speaking, Monkey and the man sat for a while silent together on the edge of the ruins.

'I misjudged you,' said the man. 'I assumed you were just like the others. I was with the giants for so long that their ways became my ways, but they are not my ways. I am sorry for this and will support you and your family until the end of our days. It is my solemn oath and I swear it on the blood of my ancestors.'

'I cannot wear a mask,' replied Monkey. 'When I lived on the island, the one you visited, there was a Hall of Masks and I said to my grandfather that I could never wear one because I cannot hide my emotions. I know that you said that Mr. Big Nose forgave you for what you did, but it will take some time for me to forgive you, and that is just the way it is. I suspected you might have been the one who visited our island what seemed so long ago, but I was not sure. Maybe you were still that man up until the day you took Mr. Big Nose's life, but maybe the tsunami changed you. I think there is a different man standing here with me today, and he now has the opportunity to make a difference, not only to me, but to Fox, for whom I hold deep affection as one of my dearest friends.'

The man bowed even more deeply to the ground in respect.

'What are you doing?' asked Monkey.

'You remind me of my father,' said the man. 'He was the wisest person I ever knew, until today. I will stand with Fox, and with you, and keep an eye on the giants. I do not trust them.'

'Nor do I,' said Monkey, asking him to stand.

Later that day Fox and Monkey were walking amongst the rabbits. Monkey sat on an old tree log and Fox stood behind it. The wasp sat on Monkey's head quietly. Monkey and Wasp had agreed to say nothing during the proceedings and let Fox do the talking. Monkey had been examining a splinter he had in his hand from the time he met the bear.

Suddenly Fox spoke. She was holding a basket. It was small and light, knit together with thin strands, with a cover that could be tied to the basket with twine. She let his hands run across the surface of the basket and held it up to her eyes, squinting so she could see if there was a gap or space between the strands. Her eyes refocused on the small figures of the five rabbits responsible. The leader was plump, with big drooping ears and a mouthful of straw. His apprentice was a thin rabbit, who held the tools in both hands, and some tucked into his cloak, which was dusty, drenched in the smell of arduous work. His associates were all holding other baskets, some in their hands, others draped over their shoulders, while still others with small piles of baskets at their feet.

They all munched on straw, quietly. Fox, still holding the basket in front of his face peered past it towards the smallest of the three. 'You have some of that?' he asked. Without hesitation, the rabbit thrust forward his hand with a clump of straw and Fox took a nice long piece and started to munch it. The six rabbits stood for a few moments, quietly munching, not saying a word. Fox put the basket under her arm.

'You know what they're for?' she asked. The plump rabbit nodded. 'Yep!'

'Others will do the collecting. Your job is baskets,' said Fox.

'How many do you want?' asked the apprentice.

'How many do you have?' asked Fox.

'Thirty-three,' said one of the associates, 'unused of course, best quality. Five are almost done. We could finish them today,' he said, looking for approval from his brethren.

Fox followed their nods.

'Standard fee,' said Fox. 'Plus, a commission if all goes well,' she added.

The five basket-weavers all nodded in approval, loudly munching their straw. Fox held out her hand and tapped the cheek of the leader. The leader followed suit and they both smiled, happy that a deal had been struck, with terms and conditions settled and no grievances aired.

'Been weaving long?' asked Fox.

'Yep!' said the apprentice.

'Is it good work?' asked Fox.

'Yep!' said the apprentice.

Fox sighed and turned to Monkey. 'Let's get to work Monkey. These rabbits talk so much I need a break.'

18.

The giants and the kingdoms of the forest met in battle on a large field by the edge of the ruined castle. Behind them was a hall and beyond that, the lake. Monkey, Fox, and other tribal leaders sat on top on worn and weathered blocks of stone guiding the course of the battle with flags and banners, surrounded by a guard including two rows of archers who were all rabbits. It would be known for generations as 'The Silent Field.' The giants had been alerted to the presence of the other kingdoms and were keen to wipe them out so they could build their new castle upon the ruins of the old fortress. The early reports sent to Monkey and Fox were wrong. There were in fact far more giants who survived the tsunami than had been expected. This included at least three regiments of giants training deep in the lower mountains, known to have been those who fought on the frontlines against the monkey kingdom in the days before the treaty. The battle was going to be fierce.

The first giants appeared on the field, followed by more and then still more. They held up red, blue, green, and white banners. All were in full armor. They marched silently. They numbered in the hundreds. But this was only the first regiment. They crossed the rocks of the old ruins strewn across the open grass and began to march onto the field towards the remnant of the old fortress towers where Monkey and his friends were waiting for them.

Abruptly, one of the giants called out in pain, reaching for his legs. He fell to his knees, dead. He was followed by another and then another. Within moments, a dozen of the giants had fallen. There was a state of general confusion in their forward ranks.

Fox turned to Monkey, grinning for the first time that morning. 'The white snakes have made their mark,' she announced proudly. 'They have a nasty bite. Rabbit almost died a year ago when he accidently trod on one. Fortunately, she was only young and had little venom.'

She called to a rabbit holding a red banner. The rabbit raised it high and began to wave it. By now, several dozen giants lay dead on the field, but the others walked by them and continued. The giants then saw a strange sight ahead. One of them cautioned the others and approached carefully. A long row of baskets lay in front of him. The others asked him what the problem was, but he told them to wait. He crept forward and lent towards one of the baskets. He saw that there was a little rabbit hiding behind the basket who smirked broadly, and then pushed the basket over.

A swarm of wasps enveloped the giant, and then flew towards the others. They recoiled in horror. Immediately, dozens of rabbits kicked over dozens of baskets and hundreds of thousands of wasps, bees, flies, locusts, and other insects flew out. The sky went black. The rabbits kicked away the baskets and ran back to safety. There was complete confusion.

Fox ordered another banner to be unfurled. On the edge of the field rows of rabbits took aim with their bows. Giants who were not afflicted with wasps were brought down by a wave of arrows. Those who remained fled the field.

A cheer went up among the rabbits. The first engagement had been a success. The goal had been to drive them back off the field, and then into a ravine where they could be felled by more arrows and burnt by fire. This goal was proceeding as planned. Fox was about to direct the rabbits to light their torches, but it suddenly began to rain. It fell first in little drops on their faces and then the heavens opened.

'We did not anticipate rain,' said Fox in despair.

'It was not expected,' said the man in agreement. 'But, my love, we must drive them to the ravine, nonetheless. We have the high ground, and we have no other choice. I will take the giants who have come over to our side, and our priest and we will try to push them in that direction.'

Fox nodded, looking at the man and realized that it was quite likely they would never meet again. Monkey brushed aside her anxious expression and ordered the man into battle. He looked at Monkey and then bowed deeply, calling the priest and the others to his side.

'To battle my friends!' he called out. 'To glory, to friendship and death!' The man, the priest and the giants who had come over to the side of the forest ran onto the field. Monkey sighed deeply but said nothing.

The regiment of the giants regrouped and pressed onto the field once more. Fox's strategy was to continue the barrage of the arrows which slowed down their advance and allow for the man and his warriors to cut a path through the front ranks. It was slow going for the defenders of the forest that morning, because the giants began bringing shields up from the rear made of thick straw mats. They deflected the arrows and made it difficult for the priest and the others to break through.

Fox realized that the giants had no archers left, and told Monkey, but Monkey already knew this because the bear he met earlier sent him word that her family had stumbled upon the archers hiding in the forest, and with other bears, they tore them to pieces. Even so, Monkey realized that it was time to commit all his reserves to the field in one last attempt to drive them into the ravine. He had never seen so many giants in his life. He gripped his flute tightly. The rain had stopped, and a thick mist began to rise across the field.

'Monkey,' counselled Fox. 'It is time to fight.'

Monkey nodded briefly, smiled, and pulled out his bamboo flute.

'You don't have a sword?' she asked. 'I can give you one, if you like.'

'I will not take a life,' insisted Monkey. 'Not even in battle.'

Fox looked at him and hugged him. 'My life began when I met Rabbit and then you,' she said. 'In one lifetime we are fortunate to have one friend. I have had two.'

They hugged and then Fox called to the rabbits who were with her, and she jumped over the stones and into the mist. Monkey was about to follow when a rabbit called out for him to stop.

'We have another problem,' said the rabbit hopping up to him exhausted. 'Our spies have told us terrible news. The monkeys are marching towards our position. They will arrive the day after tomorrow. They think that you are going to set yourself up as emperor and they will not allow that.'

'I don't want to be emperor,' insisted Monkey. 'We must defeat the giants today then.'

'There are simply too many of them,' protested the rabbit, rubbing his ears anxiously, but Monkey dismissed his criticism.

'More will come to help us,' he said, 'including Rabbit.'

The other rabbit seemed unconvinced. 'Old Grey Ears will stay away,' he lamented, 'like he always does.'

Monkey gripped the flute and wiped his brow. He sighed and for some reason thought of the first time he saw the female monkey at the top of the cliff. But it was time to fight. He wanted the giants gone and decided not to negotiate. It was a gamble, and he lost. Monkey was about to enter the fray when he heard a shout to his right at the edge of the forest. It was not a normal shout and it echoed through the mist. It was in a strange language. Monkey had never heard that language before. It was an old dialect, like the language of the crows and the birds but it was not them. It was deeper, and there were many voices.

He left the despairing rabbit and climbed to the highest rock of the old fortress peering out across the mist. Suddenly, in the distance, he saw them emerge from the forest, dozens then hundreds, then thousands of raccoon-dogs, all marching in union, all shouting, all wielding sticks, spears, banners, and swords and at the front of the army, marched Rabbit.

He saw Monkey and ran up to him, and Monkey scampered down the rocks to Rabbit and they hugged and laughed. Monkey felt that all his problems had been solved and hope returned to his heart.

'Who are these creatures?' he asked with curiosity.

'These are my drinking companions,' said Rabbit proudly. 'They all decided to come out of hiding and help us today. They are raccoon-dogs.'

Monkey admitted that he had never seen one before. He thought they might have been larger.

'They know how to drink, and how to fight,' said Rabbit, pointing down to a jug of wine hanging from his belt.

'Are you drunk?' asked Monkey, greatly surprised.

'Absolutely,' said Rabbit.

'We have just routed two regiments of the giants who were coming up behind you to cut you off. Before that we fought them with our allies in the Valley of Tears. It was a horrible battle, a terrible slaughter, full of tragedy and triumph and many surprises that will change our world forever, but I will tell you about it all tomorrow. Now, I need a good drink.'

Monkey bowed to the raccoon-dogs who passed him, and they

all entered the battle cheering and screaming and raising their banners high.

'Where's Fox?' asked Rabbit drinking from his bottle. 'Is she still alive?'

Fox had worked her way across the battlefield and had felled many giants with her bow. Fewer and fewer rabbits followed her because they too had fallen in battle. She passed many bodies lying on the field. As she went forward a mist rose and enveloped her in swirling dust and fog. It appeared from nowhere, spouting up in little funnels from holes in the ground where swords, spears and arrows had made their mark. Gone were all the sounds of battle replaced by only a swirling wind which seemed to whisper as it brushed past her. Fox reached out into the mist. It was thick to touch, and it felt alive. It also seemed to have a faint perfume, a mysterious scent.

The mist had also risen around the man, the priest, and the giants who soon were separated. 'Where are we?' asked the priest. No sooner had the words left his mouth than the ground shook and a warrior burst out of the mist. The priest knelt on one knee, drew his sword and swinging forward in an upward motion caught the warrior off guard. As soon as he fell in the dust, another replaced him. Standing up, the priest at once swung his sword back and brought it down on the second. To his right, a third appeared. The priest stepped back on his left foot and brought his sword across horizontally. The third fell at his feet.

A few minutes later the priest heard a loud wailing which seemed to come from deep inside the mist. Deciding to follow the sound, he soon found two of the pilgrims lying in the dust, with a third sitting cross-legged in front of them. His eyes were full of tears.

'Where are the others?' asked the priest.

'All dead,' replied the pilgrim. 'We have shame even in death. We lied to Monkey, but we just wanted to make amends for all the terrible things our people had done in the past. It was an honor to fight alongside Monkey, Fox, and you, dear priest.'

'Your reasons for fighting do not matter. What matters is that you fought. Come with me,' urged the priest but the giant refused to leave his friend. The priest left him. They never met again. The priest continued to walk through the mist, though he could not see anything.

Fox had not gone far when she heard a sound. Turning, she drew her sword, only to have it knocked from her hand. She reached for her bow, but it was torn from her shoulder and broken in half. She was thrown to the ground. When she looked up, giants surrounded her.

'It is a fox,' said one of them to the others.

'How can you be sure it is not one of us?' said another.

'It was a fox a moment ago and then it suddenly changed into a giant,' said a third.

Fox looked at her hands. She had changed into human form once again. There was something strange about this mist, she thought. She used to have control over her ability to change, but ever since she had met the man, she seemed to be turning more into a woman and she found it more difficult to change back again. In fact, the man could only see a woman, which meant that her days as a fox were coming to an end.

'We should kill her,' said one of the giants. The others disagreed.

'The curse will fall to us. No, the monkeys must kill her,' said another.

'But they are not here,' said a third.

'We should draw lots,' said a fourth. He reached down to the ground and began collecting sticks and twigs. He walked to the edge of the clearing in the mist and found several small, thin twigs lying in the dirt. As his eyes searched the ground, they gazed upon two sandaled feet standing still. He looked up and saw the man standing in front of him. He recoiled in horror, fleeing back to his companions. They all stared at him, some drawing their swords.

'Wait,' said one of them. 'He is the outsider.'

The others squinted and relaxed their grip on their swords.

'Ah yes,' said another. 'The general's pet.'

'The dog,' said a third.

'I know!' exclaimed a fourth gleefully. 'The outsider can kill the fox, so we won't have her blood on our hands.'

The others snarled. They grabbed Fox and threw her at the man's feet. Fox lay in the dust silent. She looked up at the man. She did not know what to say. The man spoke only three words.

'Stand behind me,' he said quietly. Fox got to her feet and moved to the other side of the man. Now, he stood between her and the giants. They all seem a little bemused by the affair. They laughed. The man did and said nothing, staring at them with determination. The one who had collected the sticks dropped them from his hand and slowly reached for his sword.

'The pet no longer speaks for his master,' murmured the giant. 'How dare you challenge us!' he shouted in rage. 'You are a foreigner, an outsider, a guest in our land, you exist by our mercy, you breathe by our benevolence! The pet needs to be taught a lesson, brothers!'

The man said nothing but dug his feet into the ground and raised his sword. His blade flashed through the mist. They had no chance. He killed them all in moments, their bodies falling like flowers in spring. He then reached down and pulled Fox to her feet. She held onto him and cried.

The priest searched the fog and dust clouds for life, but all around him lay bodies of the dead. The sounds of battle could still be heard through the fog, the shrieks and calling of various creatures, their words lost in the depths. Truly, he thought, the age of the giants has passed into memory. He found himself stepping over so many bodies that it became difficult to walk. Some faces he recognized. He realized that he had not released his grip on his sword the entire day. He tried to pull it free, but his fingers refused to be released.

He let the sword fall by his side and continued to walk through the mist. Soon, the bodies became fewer and fewer, and the air became cooler. It seemed that he had moved close to a river, though he could not recall seeing it before. In his lament, he must have strayed far from the field of battle. The priest thought it strange that the temperature was much colder when a giant emerged from behind and struck him across his back with his sword. The priest cried out in pain and fell, but as he did, he swung around and impaled the warrior with his blade, who came closer for a final blow. The warrior fell back into the mist, taking the priest's sword with him.

Another giant appeared, and seeing him without his weapon, struck him again and the priest fell headlong into the dust. Rolling over onto his back, the priest reached into his cloak, pulled out his dagger and flung it into the warrior as he raised his sword. The giant disappeared into the fog. The priest tried to push himself up onto one knee but fell again, this time with a splash, and he found himself by a stream.

His hands grasped deep into the pebbles that lay on the floor of the river and tried to rise again, but his energy was leaving him, and he felt a heavy weight as if gravity itself was pushing him to the ground. The waters seemed to envelop him, and he sank into the river, his clothes drenched, mixed with his sweat.

He was the last of the priests, the last keeper of the traditions, the one who brought the ancient wooden relic to the Castle by the Sea, the last idol of his people. All would die with him. All the memories, all the stories, all their dreams and ideas, even their faith. How could it all come to this? He remembered that he had never said goodbye to Monkey or Fox or Rabbit, determined Rabbit, young Monkey, childish but strong, and mysterious yet sad Fox, how he sought to counsel them all. At last, he thought of the one whom Monkey called Mr. Big Nose.

Then, in the blink of an eye he fell asleep. When he awoke, the priest found himself at the edge of a river. He was lying on his back and the sun blinded his eyes. It must have been mid-morning, he thought to himself for the sun was warm but not too hot and the ground still felt cool. The water of the stream ran past him and all around him was a thick forest. He raised himself up and found to his surprise that his strength had returned.

He immediately thought of the battle and felt for his wounds, but they were gone. This greatly puzzled him, and he breathed deeply. After he drank from the cool stream, the priest felt refreshed. He had no sooner washed his face when he noticed on a small rock just in front of the forest, a new set of clothes, neatly wrapped. He did not think to ask why or how, but he tore off his ragged and torn cloak and belt and leapt into the stream. He felt the water rush over him, tickling his side, and dug his toes deep into the pebbles on the bottom of the stream. He tried to float on the river but found that he was too heavy and from time-to-time little fish swam past, brushing his side.

After a while, he left the river and sat on the rock to dry. He put on the clothes, pulling the belt tightly around his waist. Walking to the river he bent down and found a nice round smooth pebble, putting it in his sleeve pocket. He bowed deeply in the direction of the forest and prayed. After he prayed, he looked and saw in the forest what seemed to be an opening, the beginning of a trail. Looking behind him, he remembered the past, smiled, and entered the forest.

The next morning, the result of the battle was clear. The giants had been completely exterminated. Rabbit, Fox, and Monkey saw the extent of the horror. No one said anything for a long time. The field was covered with thousands of dead giants, rabbits, snakes, wasps, and other creatures. When Rabbit saw the desolation, his sword fell from his hand in disgust. He looked down at his feet. The sword lay in the dust.

'I will never touch a sword again,' he said. 'From the Valley of Tears to this silent field I fought, but I am not full of joy. Joy has left me, it is no longer my companion, for I am ashamed.'

He turned to the other rabbits. 'We will find a different path,' he said to them. They also put down their swords.

Rabbit fell to his knees and wept bitterly.

Ever practical and sensible while sober, the raccoon-dogs wanted to give the giants a proper burial. They were discussing the planning of this when Monkey and Rabbit joined them. One of the raccoon-dogs proposed that the tradition of the giants themselves be respected and their remains be burnt. It seemed to Monkey an appropriate way to make a final farewell to the giants and so throughout the morning until noon, everyone prepared the pyres.

When the pyres were completed, the raccoon-dogs sung laments to the giants. Fox and the man stood nearby, hand in hand. Fox was now fully a woman with long, flowing black hair, visible to all. She would not return to her Fox form again, as long as Monkey knew her. The raccoon-dogs explained to Monkey that foxes also had the ability to change into human form, but they also had the choice to stay in that form permanently, unlike the raccoon-dogs who found it difficult to sustain the illusion. Monkey was glad that Fox had found the man for she seemed to be happy for the first time he had known her.

That night, Rabbit and Monkey looked up at the stars. They were both exhausted from the day's events.

'It is a big sky isn't it Monkey,' said Rabbit.

Monkey saw a shooting star dart across the heavens. 'It is beautiful.'

Rabbit looked up at the moon. 'You know, Mr. Big Nose said that the raccoon-dogs see a rabbit on the moon making rice cakes.'

'Yes,' said Monkey.

'I do see a rabbit,' said Rabbit. 'A fat rabbit, eating something tasty.'

Monkey smiled.

The next morning, Rabbit, Fox, Monkey, and the man convened a council to discuss the situation with the monkeys. The raccoon-dogs and the rabbit clans were weary of war, and decided they did not want to fight again. They were happy to flee to the other side of the forest. If the remnants of the once great kingdoms could lose the monkeys on the way, then the anger of the monkeys might evaporate as well. Throughout the discussion, Monkey could see the man looking intently at him.

'We must organize our forces to strike them before they reach the deeper forests,' he said earnestly. Fox agreed. 'We have everyone here, and we have just fought a battle. One more will not be difficult, especially against monkeys.'

'No,' countered Rabbit. 'I will not fight again, I have laid down my sword, and so have my tribe. We have spent too long behaving like the giants. It is time to go back to the old ways.'

Monkey stood up. He was glad that Rabbit had finally agreed with him. He sighed with relief.

'I will go and speak with them,' he announced.

Everyone was silent.

'They must understand that the time for fighting is over,' he concluded.

'They will kill you Monkey,' said the man. Fox agreed, and so did Rabbit. 'I agree with you that we should not fight,' said Rabbit. 'But I too agree that the monkeys are now full of anger after losing their emperor, and who knows how long we will need to endure their wrath. I counsel you, as your friend not to confront them.'

'Then we shall flee,' said Monkey. 'We shall take our chances in the forest.' He looked at all of them carefully. The man and Fox, though eager to fight, seemed overwhelmed by the recent battle. He could see it in their eyes. They had barely escaped death. The death of the priest weighed heavily on the man who felt responsible, and he would carry this burden throughout his life. Rabbit and his tribe had made their decision, and Monkey knew that rabbits rarely changed their minds. He had no choice.

Monkey led the various clans away from the ruins of the old castle among the trees, away from the lake and deep into the woods. He made sure all the wounded were able to be carried and that they went first, and the more able-bodied warriors took up the rear. That is where he left Rabbit, Fox, and the man. For Monkey had another plan which he kept to himself. He had no intention of fleeing. He had no intention of prolonging the situation by waiting, for that was what happened last time. The animal kingdoms who saw the castle in the forest burn waited too long, and argued for too long, and then the new giants came, and the circle of death began again. He knew it had to stop.

The last time he saw them all together, they were laughing. Monkey bowed to them politely and ran to the front of the column. He found his brother talking to himself, mumbling, and staring into space, and pulled him aside.

'I have an extremely important job for you,' he said to his brother. 'You are to lead your army into the depths of the forest. You are the new leader of our army.'

'I am?' asked the brother, smiling.

'Yes,' said Monkey.

Monkey looked at his brother. His eyes were red and sunken, and his smile drooped on his face. Monkey reached out and touched his cheek.

'My dear brother,' he said. 'I remember the days we used to run together on the island. They were good days!' he smiled.

His brother didn't reply but stared at him without emotion.

The column moved off into the forest. Those at the back of the column could not see those at the front for the sun was already setting, but if they could see, they would see a monkey about the size of Monkey leading them. Everyone was all too weary anyway to notice that Monkey had gone. The procession walked long into the night. They left the grassy plains far behind and entered the deeper forests, unknown to most except a few rabbits. The trees were taller and stronger, and the smells of the forest were more pungent and richer. The trees were full of fireflies, and they gave light to the animals as they walked. His brother did not know it, but he was following the ancient paths back to the Great Mountain.

At some point during the night, Rabbit wondered why Monkey had not stopped for a rest. They had certainly put a fair distance between themselves and the approaching army of the monkeys, so there was no real immediate cause for concern. He told Fox that he would go to the head of the column and ask Monkey to stop for a while for everyone to rest. Rabbit ran up to him and pulled him aside.

'Monkey,' he said with a smile. 'When will we have a rest?'

What he saw shook him to his feet. Rabbit was speechless. He was looking at Monkey's brother.

'Where is Monkey?' he demanded. His brother just looked at him with a blank expression. He shook him again, and as he did, he knew the awful truth. Monkey had planned this from the beginning.

Fox and the human were walking together next to a group of rabbits, hand in hand when Rabbit rushed up to them. He was out of breath.

'What is it?' asked Fox.

'Monkey has gone to stop the army by himself,' he blurted out. 'We must stop him!'

The man was astonished. 'He will be killed,' he said emphatically.

Fox agreed. 'We must stop him!' she said turning to the man and looking up at him. 'We must reach him before he finds the army, or we will be too late.'

The man agreed. 'I was wrong about him, he is the greatest of us, but his way of thinking will not be enough! I know monkeys. They killed my son and can never be trusted.'

The three of them agreed, and headed off into the forest quickly, retracting their steps.

Meanwhile, Monkey had returned to the Castle by the Lake. Monkey tied his belt firmly around his waist, took off the bamboo flute and laid it on a small rock by the path. He found a sword of the giants and put it over his shoulder. He was going to walk into the forest when he heard it. Before he reached the edge of the trees, he could hear a loud thumping on the ground which seemed to lift the soil. It was the sound of marching feet. He followed the edge of the forest until he was able to look down across the plain where the battle had occurred. The mist had gone. He could see the army of the monkeys marching forward. Monkey smiled to himself, picked up a piece of grass and put it in his mouth. He tightened his belt and walked towards them.

Rabbit, Fox, and the man ran through the undergrowth with great speed. They didn't speak to each other, but they knew what was about to happen and they feared the worst. By dusk they had arrived at the lake and ascended the hill where Fox and Monkey ordered the rabbits into battle. Fox noticed the bamboo flute on a rock. She pointed to it, and they looked down at the field below.

What they saw astonished them.

Rabbit smiled and sat down.

Fox laughed out aloud but said nothing.

The man exclaimed, 'This is impossible!'

19.

The sun shone directly onto his face as he turned over in his bed. Monkey pulled the covers over his eyes. The blanket exposed his feet and he lay there for a few moments and sighed deeply. 'I must remember to get a longer blanket,' he thought to himself. As he stirred in the bed preparing to get up, he remembered that this thought was one that often occupied him in the waking hours, only to be forgotten by the time he could smell the soup from the kitchen, prepared by one of his great granddaughters.

He stretched himself painfully toward the sliding door but groaned in disappointment as he was only a few inches away from his goal. He pulled himself along the floor slowly and with effort pushed the sliding door closed. The slap of wood echoed through the house. Monkey's ear pricked up. Maybe they were also asleep he thought to himself, but his nose told him differently.

'Get out of bed grandfather!' came a voice from down the long wooden corridor. 'Soups ready!'

Monkey sighed again, sat up and threw off the blanket. A sharp pain echoed in his chest which surprised him. He clutched his heart and breathed in deeply. It soon passed but it woke him up completely and he coughed. He looked around for his cane which he found on top of a pile of parchments and scrolls. This reminded him of the unfinished work that occupied him the night before. He needed to write the last words about Fox. 'Must do this straight after breakfast,' he murmured to himself.

Struggling to his feet, he made his way down the dimly lit corridor. He could see the light from the large open hall where most of his family had already gathered, but he made a sharp left and went instead into a small room. It was dark except for two candles shining bright and the smell of incense. He closed the sliding doors behind him and walked forward and sat down. He prayed.

'For another night and day, thank you. For strength in these bones and a beating heart, thank you. For my family and their families thank you. For all that is past thank you.'

He sighed and leaned towards the altar. He picked up a small black tablet and held it in his hands. Today, for some reason, the memories were stronger and more vivid. He squeezed the tablet hard. 'I've almost finished my book on Fox. You would be happy. She was such a good friend of ours.'

He was silent for a few minutes.

'I saw Rabbit yesterday. He was in good spirits. His wife passed on her respects to us. She said, 'I am always thankful that you found such a nice husband, even though he is a little fat."

Monkey laughed aloud. His eyes filled with tears.

'I do miss you, my love,' he said. 'I do miss our conversations and I miss your cooking. Your granddaughter is such a good monkey, but she wouldn't know the difference between soup and porridge. Your brother says that the reason I pray in the morning is my hope that all the soup will be gone by the time I join them.'

He chuckled again to himself. He put the tablet back in its place and hobbled out of the room. He glanced back one more time. By the time he had joined the rest of the family, he discovered the soup had all gone. He smiled to himself. Sitting himself down, he passed on the morning greetings. The hall was full of monkeys eating and drinking, and small monkeys running around. There was his wife's brother and his wife, three children and their families, their children and families and a few other assorted relatives. At this time in the morning, he could not remember all their names. He also noticed a few rabbits probably relatives of Rabbit or one of his cousins.

'Grandfather,' spoke up one of the monkeys from across the room, his mouth full of rice. 'Please finish the story of the Great Battle. It is such a wonderful tale.'

Some of the other monkeys nodded with interest. The rabbits were more respectful, keeping their eyes on their writing tablets in case Monkey said something interesting to record. Monkey put down his bowl and cleared his throat. All the monkeys moved forward in anticipation. Monkey looked at all of them in the eyes before beginning.

'The giants had been defeated but the monkeys, our clans, still wanted to fight, as monkeys do you know. We had no strength or inclination for further bloodshed. We had all experienced the terrors of battling the giants. My plan was to convince them not to fight.'

One of the rabbits interrupted with a question. 'Please excuse me Monkey, but how did you manage to persuade them?'

'He is coming to that rabbit,' said a small monkey. 'Stop interrupting!'

'Thank you for the good question rabbit,' said Monkey. 'I approached the army as it came towards me. I was alone.'

'That is incredibly brave of you,' agreed the rabbits, all nodding their heads and writing down notes on their tablets.

'Perhaps incredibly foolish as well,' added Monkey. 'But I did not want to kill anyone, in fact, I have never killed anyone in my entire life. I believe in life and so should all of you. We used to have a tradition in our culture, the ritual of the truce, where one party places a sword in the ground as an act of faith to discuss terms of surrender. So, I placed my sword deep in the ground and went to meet the general of the monkey army, a fierce warrior, a monkey of great strength, wisdom, and courage. I reasoned with him the case for peace, and he listened to me. He put his sword in the ground and so did the entire army, thousands of them. It became known as the 'Field of a Thousand Swords,' and from that day forward, no monkey, or rabbit has lifted a sword again.'

There was silence at the table.

One of the monkeys cleared his throat. 'I heard a different version of your story,' he said disrespectfully. 'In this version, the monkeys invited you to talk to them and the peace plan was their idea, and they were the ones who defeated the giants.'

'I've heard that version, but it's just nonsense,' countered one of the rabbits. 'Mr. Big Nose turned up and all the monkeys saw him and fell in fear before him.'

Monkey had no time for another argument over the trivial matters of what happened. All he could think of was Fox. His mind wandered and he put down his bowl.

'Is the rice also awful grandfather?' asked one of the young monkeys. Monkey looked up puzzled. 'No, no, it's good, really tasty,' he said.

'You looked unhappy,' she insisted. Some of the other monkeys looked over. He could hear them whispering 'Old

Grandpa Monkey doesn't like the rice, maybe his teeth have all fallen out,' but he ignored them.

'I was thinking of something entirely different,' he said, taking another mouthful of rice. Slightly irritated, he added, 'unlike the soup, which tastes like porridge, the rice actually tastes like rice.' This produced some laughter from the older monkeys who agreed with him. They were all interrupted by a large and fat monkey who thumped the table.

'No!' he shouted, 'it is time for a new view. We need to respect new ways of looking at the old stories.'

This reaction produced an uproar from some of the rabbits who protested as did some of the monkeys. Monkey was completely ignored, and he continued to eat his rice in silence. The argument persisted over the fish and the pickles and more soup, this time made by his wife's sister-in-law.

As Monkey took a sip, he realized that the recipe had for some reason changed, and he smiled. His sister-in-law seemed happy. Monkey hadn't smiled so much at breakfast for a long time. The argument about the Great Battle continued well past the time the plates were all cleared and most of the family had left for the day. Only the rabbits remained. They all sat at Monkey's feet. His sister-in-law came in with some tea and joined them.

Monkey sipped the tea and smiled. He looked at the bowl. 'This is a nice bowl,' he said, placing it down on the table.

The rabbits all sat quietly.

'Let me tell you about the day I met Mr. Big Nose,' said Monkey. 'My life began when I met him.'

After the lesson, Monkey returned to his room. One of his relatives had put away the bed and laid out his clothes for the day. He put them on slowly and then sat beside his writing table. The scrolls that were strewn around his floor from the night before were all in a neat stack. Behind him on the floor was another pile of scrolls all neatly tied up. He glanced over to them.

'Nearly done,' he sighed to himself. He picked up the stick and ground it into the ink-stone, dampening it with some water from the vase. Into the black soup he dipped his writing brush. It was a present from Rabbit on his last birthday. He noticed the flower in the vase had also been changed in the morning. Its petals were rigid and bright. Monkey smiled and was distracted for a moment. He looked at the bamboo flute that sat beside it. He reached for it and held it to his lips for a moment, but he closed his mouth and decided that he would play it after his walk, as he did not have enough strength.

'The last words to say about Fox,' he thought to himself and brought his mind back to his work. He dipped the brush into the ink again and began to write. The memories returned faster than he thought, and he laughed to himself as the image of Fox dwelt in his mind as if she stood in the room beside him. He felt as though she was reflected in the rays of the sun as it shone through the small holes in the paper screen.

His last memory of Fox was one year before, when the autumn hues began to appear on the hills and the wind ceased its merry dance through the grass and sang a colder tune. On this day, he and Rabbit were having an argument about food. Looking back, Monkey could not remember the reason, but Monkey remembers throwing some food at Rabbit and then a few insults later, both were pushing and shoving and causing havoc.

It was a few months after his wife's passing but this was no excuse. It was a spectacle for many to see and both were ashamed. Rabbit was chastised by his wife for many days afterwards and Monkey could not look his children in the eye for a few weeks. But it was Fox who broke up the fight. After tearing them apart she scolded them firmly but lovingly.

'You should have the closest bond. Why do you so readily turn to anger?'

Monkey and Rabbit could say nothing. They both looked at their feet.

'I will not always be there to help you.'

'How is your husband?' asked Rabbit rudely.

Fox turned to him with her eyes full of anger.

'He will not put down his sword, as you know, as he promised me when we married. He wants to be emperor and all he thinks about is war and rebuilding the wretched castle.'

She looked at Monkey her eyes full of tears and walked off into the forest. Monkey recalls that this was the last he or Rabbit ever saw her again. They searched for Fox together, first in the forest and then in the ruins of the old city and then finally at the old shrine by the ocean, but they did not find her. At the shrine, they remembered all the good times they enjoyed with Fox, cried together, and left with good spirits. To overcome the memories of losing Fox he began to write.

His mind drifted for he was an old monkey and not as sharp as he used to be. As he dreamed, the splinters of light faded, and Fox was gone from his mind. He woke with a start. The ink had dried on his brush, but the work was done. The last characters were etched in ink and the last words had been spoken. The last chapter closed.

'Rabbit will take care of all of these, I think,' he thought, glancing at the scrolls. 'His family will copy them all, no doubt, like they did the rest.' He thought it a pity that none of the monkeys were interested in his writings, despite all that had happened.

The man who refused to give up his sword lived in a small fort near the ruins of the old castle, the site of the battle with the giants, the Silent Field. He rode his horse around the forest with his sword on his waist. Monkey had heard rumors from the birds that new people had arrived from across the sea and the man, who had proclaimed himself emperor, was hoping to elicit their support to build another castle by the sea, probably on the ruins of the old one. His children took the side of the emperor and all of them knew the way of the sword. None seemed particularly concerned that their mother had gone.

The emperor had built Monkey a small hut on the edge of the ruins of the Castle by the Lake shortly after the events of the Great Battle. Rabbit was given a small house in the forest, as he asked, so he could be closer to his family. Most of the monkeys and rabbits had since then returned to the forests and few animals walked openly among the human and his family.

Monkey thought back to that day of the thousand swords. The only desire he really had that day was to see the young female monkey again. He didn't even know her name. Her father came forward when Monkey had thrust the sword of the giant into the soil. The first thing her father said surprised him.

'My daughter is in love with you,' he said. 'She explained to me what you did for her the day you both washed up on the riverbank, how you took care of her, dried her clothes, and made her some food. She has lost all interest in fighting now. But she is extremely concerned about you. She told me about what you said to your war council, that you truly reject violence and that you believe that we should stop following the giants and their way.'

Monkey didn't know what to say, so he explained to the general what had happened the last few days, how they fought the giants and how terrible the battle was and how he refused to take up a sword, the progress of the battle and its consequences. He also told him how the rabbits had given up the sword and had decided to forsake the ways of the giants.

'What do you propose then?' asked the general.

'When I was young,' began Monkey, 'my grandfather told me that in the early days we never used swords, only words to resolve disputes, but sometimes we used our fists against the raccoon-dogs. If they cause trouble in the future, we will do that again. We don't need to resort to swords. They are not our traditions. They belong to the giants. It is not our way, it is theirs. Why do we have to copy them? One giant is enough for a world of trouble. All they have ever done is destroy the world, and they want us to be complicit in their actions by forcing us to behave like them and live like them. I believe it is time we put it all behind us and be who we are meant to be.'

'I completely agree,' said the general. 'That is what I had come to tell you. We have no interest in fighting anymore. Now that the giants are finally gone, fear has left the forest and many of our soldiers long for the trees and the forests and the simple things of life. Hearing how you went fishing made me remember my youth and how my grandfather took me fishing along the river. Maybe we could go fishing so I can get to know you more. Monkey, I think you misunderstood my question. I was asking you about my daughter, what were you proposing?'

Monkey felt embarrassed. 'She has to decide for herself what she wants to do,' he said. 'My only request is that she puts down the sword.'

'She put down her sword the day she woke up on the edge of the river Monkey. Who do you think convinced me?' said the general and with that, thrust his sword into the earth as a sign of truce that the war was over. 'Let's go fishing Monkey,' he said.

Monkey looked in the distance and he could see all the monkeys putting their swords into the ground, laughing, and walking off into the forest. Monkey could count at least a thousand.

Monkey laughed to himself as he remembered that day. 'How unlike giants we are,' he thought to himself. He stood up and grabbed his cane. Looking back across his room, he went to the window and pulled back the sliding doors. The sunlight gushed in like a waterfall and he felt its warmth on his fur.

'It's as it should be,' he said and left.

Monkey walked out on the balcony to stretch his legs. He hobbled along the wood and surveyed the garden. The azaleas were blooming. Beyond the garden was the beginning of a rice field. The air was crisp. The sun was shining. The pain in his chest returned suddenly and he leaned on the railing to catch his breath. The sound of running feet alerted him.

'Grandfather! grandfather!'

A voice came from across the field. He peered out into the sun and saw the little figure of a small monkey running towards him. As the figure came closer, he saw that it was one of his grandchildren, a young and curious monkey, always collecting things and dreaming. His name eluded him as there were so many grandchildren. He ran up to the balcony and he had something in his hand.

'Do you have something in your hand?' asked Monkey. 'Do you have a present for your grandfather? How kind of you.'

The young monkey nodded.

'What is it?' He held out his hand. The young monkey had a small, grey, round pebble. 'Here, I found this in the stream. Isn't it a nice pebble, so smooth and round?'

'It is so beautiful!' said Monkey. 'It is a wonderful gift.'

He held it in his hand and felt its texture. He hadn't held such a nice pebble in his hand for a long time. As the memories of the past filled his mind, he looked down at his young relative.

'Why don't we go and look for some more of these fine pebbles together!'

The young monkey squealed with joy and grabbed his grandfather's hand. Monkey put on his sandals, and they walked off together across the rice field, into the sun.

They had not gone far when a familiar voice called to him. He turned around and saw the man who now called himself the emperor.

'Run along little one,' he told his grandson, and he did as he was told.

'Your Majesty,' said Monkey bowing as far down as he could. The emperor waved his hand in protest.

'No, please don't Monkey, you do not need to bow to me.' Monkey smiled at him but winced when he straightened his back.

The emperor was also much older now, leaning on his own walking stick. His hair was grey, and his face riddled with many lines of anxiety and deep anguish. Monkey realized that they had not met for about a year, when he and Rabbit went to visit the castle, when the foundations stones were laid.

'It is a nice morning,' said Monkey.

'Yes, it is,' replied the emperor.

Monkey looked out across the grassy plains. In the distance his grandson played in the river and beyond that the forest began. He could see the wind blowing across the tops of the trees like a painter brushing his canvass. The hills beyond were colored in various shades of green and yellow, as the vivid summer pastels gave reluctantly way to the red and orange of autumn. In the distance, clouds swirled over the mountain peaks and on the other side were many memories tucked deep in his heart, which he only brought out in the morning, standing on the grassy field.

The emperor was silent. They both stood on the grassy plains together, the monkey and the human, both waiting for the wind. Monkey was about to speak when far behind him he could hear the rustling of the grass, which fluttered gently, until the hair on his legs began to stir and then the gust lifted him slightly off his feet. He turned to the emperor who smiled briefly.

'Is your family well?' asked Monkey, staring at the mountains.

'Well as can be expected,' replied the emperor. 'As you know, we have laid the foundations for the castle in the ruins of the castle of the giants. We are making great progress. It will soon be finished.'

'For what purpose?' Monkey asked.

'For the defense of my domain,' replied the emperor.

Monkey leaned on his walking stick and stared at the emperor standing above him. 'Where is your domain? Where are the hordes of warriors pressing against your borders? Who are the enemies that seek to meet you on the field of battle? I do not hear their cries for war. I do not see their banners raised high across the plains. I cannot feel the tread of their feet in the forest. How can you expect your domain to follow you if even your wife has deserted you?'

'I do not know why she left,' protested the emperor. 'I have searched my heart day and night, whether sleeping or waking, whether riding or walking as far as the old shrine to the tallest mountain, this mystery has remained unanswered and there is a deep emptiness in the very heart of my being.'

'The answer has been obvious from the very beginning,' replied Monkey. 'You never put away your sword. The day I made peace with the monkeys and a thousand swords were stuck in the earth, Fox threw her swords away, but you kept yours. Fox thought that it was just a matter of time before you did likewise but, you kept yours close, even closer than she was.'

'But I must protect these lands from our enemies Monkey. You more than anyone know the dangers we face,' retorted the emperor.

'Then we face them together as we did before,' replied Monkey.

'You do not understand the realities of the world Monkey. I came from an ancient empire, a land of war and travail. It is only a matter of time before others come to this land and take up arms against me,' said the emperor.

'We are not human,' said Monkey. 'Fox was tired of war and fighting, having lost all her family to the giants. She thought that by marrying you, she could escape the nightmares of the past. She thought, as we all did, that you would be different.'

'Are you saying that I pushed her away because of my interest in defending my home?' asked the emperor angrily.

'The only difference between you and the giants is that you are slightly smaller and have smoother skin, without the thick hair and the large eyes. We all thought you would be one who would cut a different path, lead the forest instead of destroying it, but looking at you now, I admit that we were all wrong, even Rabbit and Fox. You are all the same my dear emperor, just like the giants, cut in the same mold. Men are broken, what is wrong with them?'

He looked up at the frail man beside him. 'We both are no longer young,' said Monkey, 'Near here is where so many laid down their swords. Why don't you add yours?'

The emperor laughed. 'I am an emperor,' he said. 'What emperor puts down his sword?'

'Then,' said Monkey looking with deep sadness to the distant mountains. 'Your wife will never return to you and all that you built will turn to dust.' Monkey could not look upon the man again. He turned, his heart heavy and weak and full of pain walked into the field. They were the last words spoken between Monkey and the man who became the husband to Monkey's friend Fox.

The river was cold, but he felt so young again. His little grandson was pointing out some nice pebbles and collecting them at the same time. There was a small pile of them by the stream. The air was cooler at the river than back at his home, and there was a pleasant breeze.

'The wind is so nice today,' he said to himself as the breeze seemed to curl around him, between his toes and across his fur.

He and his grandson talked for a while, about rocks and their shapes and sizes, the nature of fish and the types of birds in the area. After a while, Monkey felt in his heart a strange sensation. He was suddenly out of breath and had to sit down on the grass.

'What shall we do now?' asked his grandson.

'Well,' said Monkey. 'I want you to go back home, take some of these fine pebbles and bring your father and my sister-in-law. Can you do that for me?' He nodded and was about to run off, but Monkey stopped him.

'I enjoyed collecting pebbles with you young Monkey,' he said 'You can learn a lot from pebbles in the stream. It has been a fine day.'

The little monkey smiled and ran off into the grass. Soon he was gone.

Monkey stood up and hobbled along the river. The sun was shining brightly. He continued to walk along the river until he came to an unusual sight which startled him.

It was a wooden bridge.

He didn't think there was a bridge in this part of the forest, but maybe his memory was fading. He decided to walk closer towards it. It was real enough. He ran his hands along the railing. It was smooth and strong, the wooden pillars running deep into the ground of the river. He stood on the bridge and decided to see what was on the other side.

He could not see clearly because there was a mist obscuring the path. He did not notice it before. He walked a few steps before he stopped. He thought he saw something in the mist. Monkey looked intently ahead. He saw the nose first, protruding out of obscurity, then the bright eyes and then the smile. Soon, the whole being was in front of him.

'What's your name?' he asked.

'I'm Monkey,' said Monkey, 'Who are you?'

'Someone once called me Mr. Big Nose,' he said.

'I don't even have any energy to greet you properly as old friends should,' complained Monkey. 'My old hand seems stuck on this stick and the other has no strength at all.'

Mr. Big Nose stepped forward and embraced him.

Monkey looked at Mr. Big Nose and laughed.

'Let me tell you my Name,' he said softly and spoke it gently. Monkey smiled.

'What a beautiful name!' he exclaimed. 'I should tell the others! They should know!'

Monkey heard voices in the distance. He turned around and saw his relatives by the edge of the river. They were all looking for him. He heard his name being called.

'They must know where I am,' he said to Mr. Big Nose. 'They would be so happy to see you!'

Back at the river, his relatives searched and searched but to no avail. His body was never found. The young grandson who was with Monkey that day told his family later that he saw Monkey on a bridge with Mr. Big Nose, but no one believed him. Rabbit is said to have just smiled.

The family took the writings of Monkey and his letters and entrusted them to Rabbit who was responsible for copying and distributing them to the ordinary folk. Rabbit outlived all the characters who were involved in the life of Monkey. He and the next generation put all Monkey's important writings together in one volume which soon became widely accepted as the definite historical account of the period.

Each generation however saw fewer and fewer monkeys or rabbits showing any interest, but the few who did, read about the importance of life, the value of friendship, being true to yourself, accepting others for who they are, loving and caring for the forest and every creature in it, and respect for all, even with those with whom we disagree. Most left his book unread and in time all the animals returned to the way things were during the ancient order of things before the giants came.

Rabbit was last seen walking in the forest smiling and laughing on a day in the middle of spring.

NOTE FROM THE AUTHOR

Monkey and the Castle by the Sea began in 2003 when I was living and working in Tokyo, Japan. It was originally to be a children's text, a series of allegorical morality plays for teenagers, based on a short story about a plush toy I bought in Tokyo, whom I named not surprisingly, 'Monkey.' He had adventures with me in Tokyo, but along the way, the story evolved and went through different versions, one involving a sheep, not surprisingly named 'Sheep.' Sheep went by the wayside, as did many other characters.

In 2005 I was reacquainted with the classic Chinese novel 'Journey to the West.' This saga involved a powerful immortal called Monkey who fought monsters and demons on his way to eternal happiness. I wanted to approach the question of life distanced from eternity, immortality, and power. Life is more fragile, and love more beautiful, if it is transitory. It is easy to overcome all problems if you cannot die. Thus, Monkey moved towards an earth-based, non-magical saga due my time in Japan and my interest in the novels of J. R.R. Tolkien and Japanese and Chinese classics.

In those early drafts, written between 2003-10, there were some important scenes that were not included in the final version, such as an encounter Monkey had along a mountain path, a much longer version of Rabbit's adventures after Monkey fell off the precipice, and a backstory to the man's life before he arrived on the island.

Most of the pivotal scenes in the book have been there since the early days, such as the story of the fisher, the female monster in the mountain, who was originally going to be in the final battle, the scene of Mr. Big Nose and Monkey at the ocean shrine and the flight from the castle on the kite, as well as the last battle, the whirlwind, and the strange creature Monkey found under the bushes. In Japan, there are amazing kite festivals, with some kites weighing over a ton, needing one hundred people to lift it, and these kites gave me confidence to include the kite scene in the novel. The fox, raccoon-dog and other animals can also change their shape in East Asian folklore, and the fox is famously connected to many important myths and legends.

The omission of names assigned to the characters was deliberate as I wanted to broaden the appeal of the book as much as possible. This became clearer to me as I researched these myths and legends only to discover than many Japanese myths and legends did not originate in Japan, but have earlier versions in China, and India. I didn't think it was fair to talk about Monkey and his friends set in some imaginary ancient Japan because that would exclude Chinese, Korean, and Indian traditions.

It would also be a problem because ancient Japan did not exist, and did not begin with the claims of Shinto, in a cave with the goddess Amaterasu. It was formed by successive ways of migration across the islands. Before the arrival of the Yamato, there was the Emishi, and the Ainu, among others, some who came from South Korea.

Of course, Monkey is not real, so I could place him wherever I wanted, but at the same time I did not want to fall victim as many do to the romanticization of Japanese culture as a unique, closed canon of experience and tradition. That deeply concerns me. Since the war, a cadre of academics in the West have cultivated, crafted, and defended a myth about Japanese culture, a homogenous society, a society of peace of harmony, of Zen and gardens, of enigma and mystery. Their fictional Japan is not only patronizing but deeply xenophobic.

All societies evolve and change, and while traditions remain and can be both a blessing and a curse, there is much more to Japan than the Western myth about a Japan that never existed. The Tengu for example had earlier versions as the Heavenly Dog in ancient Chinese mythology, and before that Garuda in Indian mythology. I found that I could not identify Mr. Big Nose as a Tengu without diminishing the other traditions.

The early versions of the novel had Monkey being the only one without a name and the other characters more clearly identified from Japanese folklore. Readers familiar with Japan will know the inspiration for Mr. Big Nose is the Tengu, a yokai or Japanese non-human monster, a Japanese Loki, a trickster, and duplicitous. The giants were originally Oni, who are Japanese monsters that live in the dark places, I suppose like goblins or elves. They tend to be larger than humans, incredibly strong, and difficult to overpower.

I decided to locate Monkey and this ancient world in a land that predates China, Japan, and India, but could be, in some way, within any of these ancient places. It is set on an ancient island, unnamed, and rich in life. In fact, the abundance of life gives rise to the problem of animals living like humans. As a result, I deliberately chose not to give any of the characters actual names. I think this broadens the identification of the reader with Monkey, Rabbit, or Fox, and it avoids the politics of origin or ownership of these animals and their legends with a particular nation.

Monkey is also an accidental retelling, in a way of the ancient Chinese classic of 'Journey to the West,' where Monkey, and a few friends travelled with a Buddhist priest from China to India to retrieve the sutras from Buddha. Perhaps it is a reimagining of the classic for a new generation, not versed or comfortable with the 'supernatural' or tired of the rut of Asia stories that all say the same thing, with bamboo forest fights, huge battles, complex love stories, monsters, secret assassins, and the like.

The Monkey of this classical Chinese epic is the opposite to my Monkey. He was a lover of war and conflict, disobedient to his elders, and an immortal. In many ways, King Monkey is not a monkey at all, but a kind of deity, or minor deity, in a complicated pantheon of demons, spirits, and gods, making it difficult for the reader to identify with him or any of the characters in that exceptionally long epic. I wrote Monkey and the Castle by the Sea as a character people could identify with, especially kids who do not fit the 'norm' or what is considered 'normal.'

I wanted to write a story about how the world is, what people are like, and how each generation can make a difference. In some ways, the world is a circle, a cycle, and each new generation confronts the same tensions, and problems the previous generation faced. I wanted to write about the horrors of environmental destruction, and the rapacious violence of humanity on the natural world, but in a way from the point of view of the animals.

In some ways, the final battle has animal kingdoms wiping out humanity. I suppose this is a dark story, but there are a few giants who fight for what is right, and their story is not forgotten. We always have a choice, and we are never alone if we have friends who walk with us through life. A true friend loves us for who we are, and they often are closer than our relatives, and this is fine too. The search for true friendship is one of the great journeys in life, and if Monkey and the Castle by the Sea teaches us anything, it is that this is indeed a worthwhile journey.

ABOUT THE AUTHOR

Michael J. Sutton was born, raised, and educated in Sydney, Australia, before embarking on a decade of work in Japan, and America, followed by another decade training for and working in Christian ministry in Australia. Michael has a First-Class Honours in Economics (Social Sciences) and PhD from the University of Sydney, a Master of Divinity from the Australian College of Theology and a Diploma of Bible and Ministry from Moore Theological College, Sydney. He is currently the founder and CEO of Freedom Matters Today that looks at freedom from a Christian perspective. He is the author of *Freedom from Fascism, A Christian Response to Mass Formation Psychosis, Is Russia Our Enemy? Is God on America's Side?* and *Following Jesus when the Church has lost its way.* He is also the author of two novels, *The Third Tsunami* and *The Curse of Crooked River.* All books are published by Hidden Road Publishing.

www.ingramcontent.com/pod-product-compliance
Lightning Source LLC
Chambersburg PA
CBHW031950240626
47153CB00003B/929